I0770868

Cargill Falls

The Mill Conspiracy

R. F. Mineo

Acknowledgments

The journey to self-publishing is often a collaborative effort, as I found in the creation of "Fatal Conspiracies". The dedication and support from friends and family are invaluable, providing not just moral support but also critical feedback that enhances the quality of the work. **Power Readers** play a crucial role in this process, offering fresh perspectives and identifying areas for improvement, from spelling and grammar to character development to storyline consistency. Their insights help refine the narrative, ensuring that the final product resonates with readers and maintains a high standard of storytelling. This collective endeavor not only strengthens the manuscript but also reinforces my resolve and passion for writing.

Thank You

Carmine Angeloni	Nicole Audet
Vanessa Mineo Bonevich	Dr. Debra Campbell
Steve Kempain	Claire Minio
Diana O'Connor	Geri Salerno
Rick Sellano	Laura Steinke

The inclusion of expert knowledge in the crafting of a novel is indeed crucial for maintaining the integrity of the story. It lends authenticity to the narrative, allowing readers to immerse themselves in a believable world, even within the realm of fiction. This meticulous approach to research and fact-checking can enrich the story, providing depth and credibility. Authors often collaborate with specialists in various fields to ensure that their depiction of complex subjects is accurate and plausible. Such diligence not only respects the reader's intelligence but also honors the subject matter, resulting in a more engaging and trustworthy reading experience.

Having a dedicated support team is invaluable in the process of authoring a novel, especially a team that includes a knowledgeable and experienced physician, a skilled editor, and a mentor that knows and understands the complexities of writing and publishing. This trio significantly enhances the accuracy, readability, and depth of my work.

Dr. Debra Campbell, Emergency Department Physician, ensured that any and all health-related details in 'Cargill Falls' are described with precision, contributing to the story's authenticity.

Micheal Rahab, College Valedictorian and High School English Teacher, Editor polished the manuscript, refining the language and the storyline to better resonate with readers. In the process he added humor to my day.

Rick Sellano, owner of My Ink Shines, my mentor extraordinaire and my cousin, provided the overarching guidance and encouragement to navigate the complex process of novel creation, from conceptualization to publication. Rick's advice proved invaluable.

The creation of a book cover is a significant task that requires not only artistic skill but also patience and adaptability. **Vincent Bourgeois, my grandson**, has demonstrated these qualities admirably, managing to produce an exceptional book cover despite the challenges of ongoing revisions.

My wife Wanda's dedication to promoting 'Fatal Conspiracies' is a testament to her unwavering support and belief in my work. Her tireless efforts at events and signings, and her keen ability to seize every promotional opportunity, have undoubtedly contributed to the success of "Fatal Conspiracies." It's clear that such a long-standing partnership as ours is built on mutual respect and shared goals, making **Wanda** not just a spouse, but a true pillar of support in both life and work.

Together, they formed a formidable team that elevated 'Cargill Falls' to new heights.

Cover Image provided by: newenglandwaterfalls.com.

Cargill Falls

The Mill Conspiracy

Conspiracy – Murder – Civil War Treasure

In the middle of an old mill's renovation, a tale of greed and betrayal unfolds. The discovery of hidden Civil War treasure ignites a deadly game of power, where trust is a liability, and every handshake hides a betrayal. As the body count rises, the Connecticut State Police find themselves outmaneuvered at every turn. The killer, a ghost in the night, remains elusive, her motives as hidden as the treasure itself.

When an unexpected alliance forms between the assassin and one of the investor groups, it seems the tide may turn. But in this high-stakes treasure hunt, alliances are fragile, and the assassin, ever the master of deception, has plans of her own. She kills again and disappears. Her disappearance, facilitated by a new identity and substantial financial resources, leaves a trail of unanswered questions.

With the immediate threat seemingly neutralized, the investors' hunt for the hidden treasure continues with renewed vigor. Still, cautiousness remains paramount, and they cleverly devise a contingency plan to ensure their safety. This foresight proves to be well-founded as their trap ensnares not one, but two would-be assailants, confirming suspicions that the danger they face is far from over. The discovery of the trapped culprits brings a heightened awareness that their quest is fraught with unforeseen dangers, and that they must identify the mastermind before they fall victim. All the while, they relentlessly search for the treasure.

Prolog

The Purity Pharmaceutical Company's story is a complicated story of corporate intrigue, ethical breaches, and criminal activity. The crisis that unfolded was not just a corporate scandal but a human drama, involving the lives and careers of many individuals. The FDA ordered Purity to stop the sale of an exceptionally lucrative proprietary drug. Then the DOJ arrested a number of executives, and the company implemented a major downsizing.

The crisis was set in motion years earlier when Purity's extraordinarily successful pain killer, Relieve®, failed normal testing and a group of employees created an imaginative, but illegal work around. When other employees found evidence of the covert testing, they attempted to use the information to their advantage. When an assassin murdered two Purity Pharmaceutical Company executives while they worked late in their offices, a major investigation began.

The Nassau County Police brass assigned their top homicide detective, Lieutenant Jim Hines, to lead the investigation. The investigation proceeded slowly in the preliminary stages as Purity executives stonewalled Lieutenant Hines. Frustrated, Hines needed an insider and recruited Phil Messina. Working together, along with the assistance of Detective Karen Parisi, they uncovered the illegal testing scheme. They identified the assassin and co-conspirators.

Many of the employees arrested or downsized blamed their situation on Hines, Messina, and Parisi.

In recognition of his efforts and success in solving the Purity murders, Lieutenant Jim Hines became Commander Jim Hines. Phil Messina remained with Purity for three years to help guide the company back to profitability and become again a respected company and an excellent place to work. Phil left the company with a golden parachute and moved to Cargill Falls Connecticut. Detective Karen Parisi became Homicide Detective Karen Parisi and assigned to the Homicide Squad full time.

Chapter 1

"Phenomenal, absolutely phenomenal. When you told me you lived in an old New England mill town, I expected a dead or dying town. Instead, I see activity everywhere," Jim exclaimed, his surprise clear. "There are, what, five restaurants with outside dining and specialty shops, as well as antiques stores. And street performers. *And* you recommended our wives go shopping. Are you crazy?"

"If you're worried about our wives spending too much money, stop. You're a retired police commander with a big pension. Just relax and enjoy it. This is a pretty cool town, and the weather on this fine August day couldn't be better," Phil reassured him.

"Easy for you to say. I still live on Long Island with its excessive cost of living and high taxes," Jim replied.

"Actually, I feel for you. Living here costs a lot less, but I understand that you have to stay near your extended family."

"It is. But Cargill Falls is only three hours away, a short drive," Jim responded.

Jim and Phil had stayed friends since solving the Purity Pharmaceutical murders, despite their different political views. Physically they were more similar than different. Both were close to six feet tall, and a layer of fat covered both of their large, heavily muscled bodies. Five years ago, they had exposed several conspiracies involving current and former Purity Pharmaceutical Company employees. Those conspiracies had set off events that caused employee deaths and almost led the company to go out of business. Phil had continued to work for Purity for three of the five years, then had retired with a golden parachute and moved to Cargill Falls. Commander Jim Hines had recently retired from the Nassau County police department, the promotion to commander in recognition for his success in solving the Purity case.

With some emotion in his voice, Phil said, "Jim, I have thought a lot about working with you and helping solve the Purity murders. It was the right thing to do and made me feel like I was contributing to society more than I did as a cog in the pharmaceutical business. Even though another opportunity will probably never present itself again, I would go out on a limb to solve another crime."

"I know how you feel because I feel the same. It was satisfying, in a way I think it's probably the same feeling a mathematician has when the solution to a complex problem is uncovered."

"Jim, if you're serious about moving to Cargill Falls, let's take a walk and look at the falls."

"I am serious. Let's go," Jim replied, nodding affirmatively.

After a quick walk they stood on the bridge overlooking the falls where the river dropped about thirty feet and spread out as it plunged over huge boulders. It was beautiful, even in August when the water's flow was at its lowest. The town had recently constructed a linear park that ran along the river for three miles, with the falls at its center.

The park boasted paved walking trails, a bandstand, numerous trees, and open lawns.

"It's a marvelous sight, isn't it? And it's right in the middle of town," Phil said.

"It certainly is."

"The old Mill across the street used the river to power its equipment. A raceway runs under the street and through the Mill. I understand that after the renovation, the river will again supply most of the electricity for the Mill. Environmentally friendly."

"I like the idea of having a view of the falls," said Jim. "When it's finished, will it be commercial space, living quarters, or both?"

"I've heard both. I'll look into it for you. Let's drag our wives out of the shops and grab some dinner." They walked toward the town center, leaving the rush and crash of the waterfalls behind.

While Jim and Phil stood on the bridge discussing their future plans, Larry Davidson and his co-conspirator, who was an old friend, were strategizing their next moves to purchase the Mill. Larry was currently working for the Mill owners as the renovation manager, and his friend was head of a recently formed investor's group. Larry had shared his find with him.

"Larry, I really appreciate you coming to me for advice on how to manage your discovery. Our offer to buy the Mill was at least a million dollars above its market value, even at the most generous valuation. And the owners turned it down, even though they're in financial trouble. If we sweeten the price, I'm afraid the Mill owners will get suspicious, wonder if we have an ulterior motive, and investigate."

"But a hired killer? That's a major step, and I am uncomfortable with killing Martineau," Larry pleaded.

"Tina is the best money can buy, and the organization that runs her is first-class. They won't share our identity with Tina let alone the authorities. The police will never connect us to the murder."

"If something goes wrong, we will spend the rest of our lives in prison."

Larry's co-conspirator smiled.

"Don't focus on what can go wrong. Visualize your life with all that money. Think about living in the lap of luxury. Trust me to do everything possible to protect our little conspiracy. I believe we will baffle the police. Now tell me again… what are Martineau's plans for tonight?"

Tina had forged her career as a hired killer over the past sixteen years, and it had proven to be a lucrative profession. She marveled at the sheer number of individuals someone believed worthy of elimination. Clients often chose her because of her gender, believing that women, especially those who appeared plain, could move through the world nearly unnoticed. Tina embraced this belief and worked diligently at maintaining a nondescript appearance.

Her current assignment involved the owner of an old mill in a small town in northeast Connecticut. Tina had secured an Airbnb unit approximately ten miles outside of town to start her surveillance. However, luck was on her side. The Instigator, her handler for this contract, had informed her that the target would be alone in the Mill from eight o'clock tonight until eleven. Tina was prepared to fulfill the contract tonight.

The Hines and Messina families opted to have dinner at the historic Cargill Falls train station, eager to relish the beautiful weather. Seated in the outdoor dining area near the tracks for the Worcester–Providence Railroad, which still saw reduced but active traffic, they hoped to experience a passing train. The prospect of moving to Cargill Falls appealed to Mary Ann, who appreciated the idea of a place that would consume less of their income. However, she expressed concern about the lack of diversity in the area, a sentiment shared to a lesser extent by her husband, Jim.

"Spend some time here, get to know the people. They won't complete the Mill for at least six months. That's the earliest you can move in," Phil suggested.

"Okay, I'll make a final decision after I spend some time here. I'd like to try out all the restaurants in town," Mary Ann replied.

Just then, a train approached. The tracks were only ten feet from their table, separated by a knee-high concrete wall. As the train slowly passed, the engineer leaned out of his window, greeted them, and asked if they were enjoying their meal. The gesture left a lasting impression on Jim and Mary Ann.

Jim made a sound, a kind of satisfied snort, and said, "Let's start on the appetizers so we can get our meals. It's late, and I'm tired." The four shifted their focus to their meals, and the conversation took on a lighthearted tone.

Phil shared anecdotes about life in a small town, while Rose talked about biking. Jim humorously recounted his struggle to adapt to retirement, and Mary Ann regaled them with stories about her customers at the diner. After dinner, they strolled a few blocks to the Messina home.

In the living room, the men enjoyed limoncello, while the women savored their wine.

Tina toned down her sex appeal in an oversized white blouse and baggy jeans, deliberately styling her hair to look unkempt, and strategically applying makeup to give her face an entirely altered appearance. Despite her inherent beauty, Tina, a trained makeup artist, possessed the skill to transform herself into a remarkably different woman for the night.

As she worked to change her look, Tina mentally reviewed her conversation with the Instigator. He had supplied crucial details: the best place to park, the entrance to use, and the specific route through the Mill to access and leave the Mill owner's office. Tina had opted for a silenced Glock 9 as the perfect weapon, expecting that she might need it if she could not get up close and personal.

Tina's thoughts wandered to her idyllic childhood while she flipped the takedown lever on her Glock, deconstructed it, and reconstructed it mechanically. Born as the first and last child to older parents, she was a cherished miracle. Her parents, while older, had provided her with an intellectually stimulating environment and all the material comforts a young girl could want. Only her mother's untimely death before her college graduation had clouded those rose-colored days.

Post-college, Tina had embarked on a successful career with a major corporation in Boston. She met Bryce, a wonderful man from a wealthy Boston family, and they became engaged. Tragedy struck again when her father suddenly passed away before their marriage, leaving Tina alone in the world with no family. Thankfully, she had Bryce, a kind and caring companion, and then they were married.

Now, dressed and ready for the task at hand, Tina looked at herself in the mirror and thought, "Let's get this party started." With her appearance transformed and her resolve firm, Tina prepared to execute the mission laid out by the Instigator.

The Instigator's directions proved flawless. Tina parked in the vacant lot across Route 44 where it passed the Mill. As planned, she entered a door on the lower level, then easily navigated the dimly lit hallways, which were tainted with the scents of mold, mildew, and oil. Despite the unpleasant odors, Tina found the route easy to follow, stopping just ten feet from the Mill owner's office.

Moving silently, Tina approached the door and checked the knob, finding it unlocked despite the Mill owner supposedly being alone in the building. It seemed that the people of Cargill Falls harbored a false sense of security. Gun in hand, Tina slowly pushed the door open, revealing a small office. The target sat at a table behind his desk, engrossed in paperwork, oblivious to the slight creak as the door opened and to Tina's presence.

Pointing her silenced Glock at the back of his head, Tina took careful aim and squeezed the trigger. In an instant, the mill owner's head literally exploded, bringing an abrupt end to his days on this earth at 18,143.

Tina found the bullet that had exited Martineau's head, picked up the shell casing and conducted a visual sweep of the office to ensure no evidence remained. Tina then retraced her steps, exiting the building via the same route. Making her way to her small SUV, she started the engine and drove east on Route 44, then turned right on Kennedy Drive to access I-395 north. Tina planned to stay on the interstate system until reaching exit 4 of the Maine Turnpike. A short drive would then take her to her oceanfront home in Ogunquit, Maine. The job done, Tina left behind a lifeless office and a silent witness to her deadly efficiency.

Chapter 2

Bob Martineau's wife woke up around three in the morning and, for the first time, realized Bob was not in bed. Tired from a long day, she went to sleep early last night. When she did not find Bob at home, she called both his cell and his office at the Mill. Unable to reach her husband, Mrs. Martineau panicked and called the Cargill Falls police and asked for a wellness check at the Mill.

Officer Jim Parry knew the Mill well, his parents worked in the Mill their entire adult life and he had been in the Mill many times since childhood, and he played Pitch with Bob Martineau. Officer Parry drove to the Mill and quickly made his way to Martineau's office and found his friend's body. After regaining his composure Officer Parry called his findings into headquarters, who in turn called for an ambulance and the Medical Examiner.

After assessing the scene, the EMT called the Emergency Department at Day Kimball Hospital and asked to speak with the ER doctor assigned as medical control. Once on the phone the EMT informed the doctor that the victim had a gunshot wound to the head, brain matter was present on the wall, and rigor and lividity have set in, and he needed a time of death. He also informed the doctor that the medical examiner arrived on scene and thinks it happened last night, so they did not attempt CPR. The doctor gave the EMT the current time to use as time of death for their paperwork.

Jim Hines and Phil Messina sat in the kitchen drinking coffee and popping aspirin, trying to relieve the pounding in their heads. They had clearly had too much to drink last night, as had their wives, who were still sound asleep. Phil was casually dressed in a pair of khaki cargo shorts, a t-shirt advertising the Hog's Breath Saloon in Key West, and tennis shoes with no socks. Jim, on the other hand, wore a pair of casual pants, a dress shirt, and a pair of leather loafers and socks.

Phil said, "Jim let's walk into town and grab some bagels and pastries at the bakery. Don't expect a New York bagel, but they're pretty damn good. And the walk will do us good, maybe even clear our heads. I'll leave a note in case they wake up. And don't be surprised if people stare at you. You're dressed for New York not Cargill Falls."

Jim replied. "We won't see them until this afternoon. Our wives drank themselves unconscious last night." He grinned while poking some fun at Phil. "I enjoy looking good and wearing good clothes, unlike you. People will gawk because they will think I am walking with a homeless person."

"Okay, let's go." Phil said after he finished scrawling the note. "Homeless my ass."

As they walked, Phil told Jim about the Monday night bowling league. "A couple of days ago, I signed up for the

Monday Night Men's Social League. I met the guys on my team and a lot of the guys in the league at the meeting. Overall, they seem like good guys, and they should be fun, although the league has some high-average bowlers. I'm just not sure I can compete."

When Phil and Jim rounded the street corner, blazing lights and commotion took them by surprise. Some twenty or twenty-five police vehicles, lights flashing, were on the Route 44 bridge in front of the old Mill. The gathered townspeople stood and stared. Uniformed officers and detectives in suits walked or stood and talked.

"It looks like the scene around the Endo building after the pharma execs were murdered," said Jim. "I wonder what's going on. Was anyone working in the building last night? Nothing happened when we were in town."

Phil saw Matt, an auxiliary police officer, whom he had met about a year ago, ducking under a row of caution tape. He was clothed in full uniform. Phil called out, "Matt, hey, what's happening? Do you know?"

Matt turned and called back, "Let me see if I can find someone to ask. All I know is that there was a shooting, and they transported someone to the Gilman and Valade Funeral Home, I'm sure Bob will handle things, he is a good man. I have to go."

After talking with several other people, Phil received little added information. He and Jim decided to buy the bagels and pastries and head back home. They would get the latest news on WINY, the local community radio station. WINY sat in a squat building directly opposite the Mill and across Route 44. Phil hoped that Harry O, WINY's owner, had the information and was broadcasting. The station's location made that possibility more than likely.

After arriving back at the house and tuning in to the radio station on WINY's website, Phil and Jim leaned over Phil's smartphone and listened keenly. Harry O's smooth voice emitted from the speaker, describing several key details: someone had shot the owner of the Mill, Bob Martineau, in the back of the head while in his office last night. Martineau's wife called the Cargill Falls police when he failed to arrive home last night. They also learned he was a stockholder of the investor group that owned the Mill. He was also the CEO and was alone in the Mill last night working on some financial issues.

This was the first murder in Cargill Falls since 1983 and the most significant crime in the Northeast corner of Connecticut.

Jim folded his arms, his expression grave. "I plan to follow this murder investigation. Maybe it's because solving the Purity case was extremely rewarding, or maybe it's because I'm seriously considering moving into that building. I want to be involved until the police, or you and I, find the motive and the killer. Since you have a few connections here, Phil, I want you to get as much information on the building and its ownership as possible. You never know. It might come in handy."

"Handy for what?"

"Handy, because I was an outstanding homicide detective most of my life, and maybe those skills will help solve the case. I know that when trying to solve a homicide, you can never have too much information. The smallest fact can break the case wide open."

Phil again returned to his unique sense of gratification and accomplishment after solving the Purity murders with Jim. The idea of another case was compelling. He responded, "I am also retired and have lots of time on my hands. I want to be on the team."

The Instigator sat in his office, and the scene played much the same as his conversation with Larry: dim light, the shadow of a bookcase. Yet now, sitting before him were two other moneymen who were "in" on the deal.

"Last night was a success. Tina's work was pure perfection. She got into the Mill, did her job, and got out unnoticed, and therefore isn't on the authorities' radar. As of now, she is safely out of state. I will wait for one of the Mill owners to reopen negotiations. It will take time, maybe even a couple of months for them to realize that we are their best alternative. Questions?"

One of the two moneymen leaned forward in his seat. "What if they still don't accept our offer or don't want to reopen negotiations?"

"Tina is available to us until we conclude her contract."

The other moneyman raised an eyebrow, clearly thinking the idea was ridiculous. "Killing another owner will raise suspicion."

"Our plan is simple. We started negotiations before we killed Bob, and we won't reopen. They will. We can wait."

The first moneyman leaned back again; his lips drawn tight with worry. "A lot of money is riding on this deal. I don't want it to fail."

The Instigator extended his arms with his palms out and defiantly said. "We will succeed. We might make Tina a wealthy woman in the process, but we will succeed."

Chapter 3

Phil's first night of league bowling didn't meet his expectations, highlighting his need for knowledge and practice. Luckily, he found a valuable resource in Mike Robertson, a skilled bowler on his team who shared both his love for the sport and for biking. Inspired to improve his game, Phil turned to YouTube for tips on bowling techniques and equipment.

Armed with newfound knowledge about reactive resin balls, proper approaches, and ball release techniques, Phil invested in four reactive resin bowling balls. Committed to honing his skills, he set a goal of bowling at least ten games a week, applying the techniques he learned from online tutorials.

Simultaneously, Phil embarked on his research into the history of the old Mill. Discovering that its original purpose was converting raw cotton into cloth, he realized that there was much more to uncover. When Phil had first retired, he had wondered how he would fill his days after retiring. Now he had too much to do.

On his return to Long Island, Jim began following the case by enlisting Karen Parisi in the effort. Karen had played an essential role in the Purity Pharma case. Since she was still on the Nassau County police force, Jim hoped she could access information from the Connecticut State Police, who took over the investigation from the Cargill Falls Police, about the murder. She and Jim had stayed in touch after Jim retired, and now and then, Karen would call him for advice on challenging cases.

Jim called Karen at home. "Karen, it's Jim."

"Jim, you still don't seem to remember that there's a thing called caller ID on our phones. I knew it was you before I answered."

"Yeah, I know. Look, when I was visiting Phil, there was a murder. The mill owner, Bob Martineau, was alone in his office in an old mill he was having renovated. Someone shot him in the back of his head. No one even heard the shot. So far, there are no witnesses. My question is: can you access the Connecticut State Police files on the case?"

"I should be able to. Give me thirty minutes, and I'll find out."

"You can find out from home?"

"There is a thing called the internet. I will call you."

As soon as she hung up, Jim dialed Phil's number to update him. "Phil, it's Jim. And don't say it. I know there is this thing called caller ID."

"Okay. What's up?"

"I asked Parisi to get the police files on the murder investigation from Connecticut so we can track it. How are you doing with gathering info about the building?"

"There is a ton of info on the internet. I have to read it all and figure out which websites are dependable. It will take a while because of the sheer volume. I should be able to get more than we need."

"Good. I'd like to have regular meetings, say once a month, to see what we have and to plan our next steps. Are you okay with that?"

"No problem."

"How about we meet in a month?"

"Let's meet in Oyster Bay at Piccolo Sicilia. I miss their food."

"Done. I will set up the first meeting." Just as Jim's mouth started to form another word his phone beeped. "Hold on, Phil, Parisi is calling. I'll connect the three of us."

As soon as the calls merged Karen started speaking, she said, "When the lead investigator learned I wanted the info for the retired Nassau County Commander and the retired Purity Pharma exec who uncovered a major conspiracy and found the killer, he cooperated. Especially when he realized Phil lived in Connecticut and paid state taxes."

Jim replied, "Karen, Phil and I discussed meeting in a month if the case is still open by then. Do you want to join us?"

"Yes, but it depends on my work schedule. Unlike you two old farts, I'm not retired."

Jim smiled. Her lighthearted sarcasm made him feel like he was on the force again. "I'll keep you involved," Jim replied. "Goodbye for now."

Phil said goodbye to Karen and Jim and hung up. He looked forward to the meeting, and happily, he looked forward to the food at Piccolo Sicilia. Phil found it interesting to look at the murder investigation using police files without putting himself in danger.

Chapter 4

It was a beautiful late September day, and Phil wanted to get his BMW 635csi out on the highway. The first song he played was 'Born to be Wild' as he emerged onto I-395 south. Traffic was light, and he accelerated to 85 MPH and held it there until he was about a mile from merging on to I-95 South. Traffic was heavier on I-95, slowing him down a bit but offering the opportunity for more fun. Phil drove his BMW hard but safely, changing lanes and shifting between 4th and 5th gears to take advantage of every opportunity to pass a car or two.

Phil arrived at the Bridgeport ferry terminal early for his reservation. Being one of the first in line meant he would be one of the first off in Port Jefferson, New York. He chose to take Route 25A instead of the Long Island Expressway and drove through the small towns on Long Island's north shore, rolling down a window to enjoy the warm salt breeze coming off Long Island Sound. He had plenty of time to get to Piccolo Sicilia. Having arrived a half an hour before Hines and Parisi would, he ordered a drink, and salivated over the lunch menu. The smell of fried calamari wafted over from another table and his stomach growled.

Jim's arrival narrowly prevented Phil's stomach from forcing him to order early. He slid onto a stool at the bar.

"How was the drive here? Traffic must have been light unless you left early this morning."

"Great. I got to exercise the old BMW on the interstate and ferried across the sound, then drove to Oyster Bay via route 25A. Smooth as silk."

"Before Parisi gets here, would you agree she shouldn't have to pay? After all, she is helping us with what is our pet project, not hers."

"Absolutely,"

"Good, glad you agree. Now let me see the menu. I've been looking forward to eating here for a month."

When Parisi arrived, she ordered a diet soda and they all proceeded to their table. Comically jabbing him with an elbow, Karen said to Phil, "Long time no see, paesano."

Jim sat bolt upright and immediately chimed in, "You're starting that Italian shit already. Jesus Christ, give me a break."

"Phil, I believe Jim is feeling outnumbered." Karen remarked, laughing, and shaking her head.

"I believe you're right," agreed Phil, grinning deviously. "Jim's still sensitive."

Jim scowled. "Being black is difficult when you're alone with two self-righteous Italians. Oops, I almost said goombahs."

They all chuckled, remembering Jim's embarrassment when he called a suspect a goombah in front of them, and then became all apologetic.

The waiter appeared at their table and asked, "Drinks?"

Phil ordered a Proper12 neat, and Jim ordered a godfather. Karen said she was good.

Jim ordered two servings of Calamari Nuovo for the table, much to Phil's pleasure.

When the drinks and appetizers arrived, they ordered their meals. Jim settled on the Brasato, Phil, the Gnocchi Alforno, and Karen the Tagliatelle Alla Bolognese. They sampled their drinks and ate some calamari before getting down to the business at hand.

Jim wiped a crumb from his lips and spoke. "We must find the motive to find the killer. Remember Purity Pharma? Once we figured out the motive, we found the killer and the co-conspirators. The police in Connecticut have been trying to figure out the motive for the murder for a month and have failed so far. When they've figured it out, Karen will know. For now, we'll just gather information. Phil, what did you learn about the building?"

"The Putnam Group, LLC owns the Mill. Bob Martineau was the CEO and had a 40% share in the LLC. They split the rest between Janet Howell, who owns 30%, and Greg Adams, who also owns 30%. Ms. Howell's husband bought the Mill originally, then set up the LLC and sold some of his shares. When the renovation began sucking money, it forced them to restructure and get equity partners. The Putnam Group is currently $17 Million in debt and struggling to make the minimum payments on the loans. Janet Howell's husband, Harrison, died from aggressive prostate cancer a year ago. Rumor has it a group of investors made a confidential offer at a very fair price for the Mill a little while back."

Karen tapped the back of her fork on the table a few times, thinking. "We need to look into the offer. The police aren't even aware of it, maybe the investor group wants it kept confidential. It's likely meaningless," she noted.

"Karen, why don't you fill us in on the investigation status," Jim said.

"Overall, the Connecticut State Police haven't made any real progress. Their first theory was that despite not finding a gun at the scene they speculated that Martineau committed suicide. They theorized that between the time Martineau died and his wife called the police she removed the gun and any shell casings. Insurance money motivated her actions. They spent time working on the theory before the Connecticut coroner laughed at them. He said it was impossible for a human being to hold a gun in that position, let alone pull the trigger. So, they scrapped that theory. Now they are looking at Janet Howell and Greg Adams, but they have nothing solid yet. I believe they really want to shut the investigation down."

"Okay so there's little progress so far. Looks like a long investigation," Jim confirmed, nodding to himself. "When do you have to get back to work?"

Karen said she was okay for another hour give or take.

The waiter showed up with the meals. Which glistened with fresh olive oil and smelled like heaven. The food both smelled and looked fantastic. The conversation stopped abruptly, forks and knives were brandished, and eating began.

When the three had finally slowed down, Phil inquired "What do we do next?"

Jim took a quick sip of water. "We keep track of the Connecticut police work. Phil, you keep looking for info on the Mill and keep your ears open around town. If that offer was real, it might lead us to someone interested enough in the Mill to commit murder. I'll set up our next meeting."

After Karen had returned to work, Jim and Phil each ordered another drink and caught up on personal matters. They had developed a convivial relationship over the last five years. Despite initially disliking each other, they had each realized that the other was a good man and a good friend.

"How's the bowling league going? Are you able to compete?" Jim asked, leaning back in his chair.

Phil smiled sheepishly. "I am not a good bowler yet, but I get better each week. I made a new friend, though. We have been on two long bike rides and have had lunch, burgers, and beer each time. And we have had some long talks. So far, our friendship is based on the four B's– Bowling, Burgers, Beer, and Bullshit or Biking, Burgers, Beer, and Bullshit. Judging by our conversations so far, he is a good man, and I'd like you to meet him. On an unrelated note,

Rose met a woman whose brain is like a filing cabinet for northeast Connecticut history, her name is Noelle Lefevre. If you still think we need all the information we can get on the Mill, does that include its history?"

"I start an investigation without knowing what is important and what isn't. I don't assume. Back on the job, if I could get information about an element of a case, I'd get it. I was successful throughout my career because I never ruled anything out early in the case. See what you can get out of Noelle."

"Okay."

Jim paused for a second, calculating, and asked. "Am I correct in thinking that the guy you want me to meet is white?"

"I thought you didn't assume." Replied Phil good-humoredly, patting his belly and standing up from the table. He tucked his payment and tip under his whiskey glass, and continued, "I'm heading back to Cargill Falls. See you in a month."

Chapter 5

The weather in Ogunquit, Maine was beautiful, and Tina had decided to walk to town for breakfast. As she strolled along the Marginal Way, she enjoyed the view of Maine's rocky coastline and the morning sun glittering on the Atlantic Ocean. In addition to breakfast, Tina wanted an opportunity to seduce a gorgeous young server she had in her sights. Kathryn was in the last weeks of her work visa and would have to return to Ireland if she could not secure another job. The thought of having Kathryn as her live-in housekeeper and keeping her warm during the cold Maine winter nights brought a smile to Tina's face.

Memories of Tina's wedding day streamed into her brain, as they always did when she was contemplating a new relationship. Before marrying Bryce, she had been physically attracted to women too, but had never acted on her feelings. She repressed them.

I remember being happy and sad at the same time on my wedding day. I was pleased that I had someone to love me, cherish me, and supply a life free of monetary worries. I was sad because my parents were not alive to enjoy my adulthood, let alone any other blood relatives to share my happiness.

My wedding day was a fairytale. I loved everything about it, the church service, the food, the dancing at the reception, and even meeting Bryce's haughty family and friends. I happily awaited but was a little worried about the wedding night. Bryce and I had been seeing each other for nine months and had agreed we would 'save ourselves for the wedding night.' It was hard, but we did it. That night everything would change.

When we got to the penthouse suite, we lay on the king-sized bed, relaxed, had a drink, and discussed the day. I was awestruck by the opulence of the penthouse and wedding venue. Bryce was not. I excused myself to slip into something more comfortable.

I shimmied into the sensual lingerie I bought for my wedding night. Before returning to the room, I gazed at my image in the full-length bathroom mirror and thought, "damn, I look fabulous. I am a very sexy young woman who will rock his world." Acting as sexy as I knew how, I walked out of the bathroom, hoping that I would arouse Bryce.

As I sauntered toward the bed, Bryce stood in front of me and, seemingly for no reason, punched me hard in the stomach so hard that the blow knocked the wind out of me. The pain was overwhelming. I doubled over, crippled and terrified because I couldn't draw a breath. He pushed me onto the bed, wrapped his hands around my neck, and choked me while violently raping me, twice. After he finished the second time, I lay flat on my back on the king-sized bed in the opulent penthouse suite, stunned and terrified, and in unbearable pain. Bryce had always treated me as if I was breakable. I was confused. He had always been kind and caring. Had it all been a lie?

Bryce ordered, "Sit up! Now!"

When I hesitated, he slapped me hard across the face and said, "Now!"

I obeyed. The sting from the slap intensified my pain.

"Let me spell out the rules for you. You will never leave me or even consider a divorce. If you do, I will kill you. You will be available for sex whenever I want it, the way I want it, as rough as I want it. I will frequent prostitutes. You will look beautiful whenever you are with me. I will date other women. You will exercise, stay in shape, and never get fat, or I will kill you. I will do as I please. You will stay home and wait for me; when I am home, you will serve my every need. Understood."

I whimpered, "Yes."

"I'm out of here and don't know when I'll be back. Enjoy the suite."

I lay on the bed and cried for hours. Sobbed because I was in horrific physical pain. Wept because my husband violently raped me twice. He had humiliated me and for the first time in my life, I cried: cried because I had no family to save me, and finally, because I had no hope of getting out of my marriage alive.

Tina found herself almost on the restaurant's doorstep when she returned to the present. She got herself together and entered, looking for Kathryn.

Phil and Mike Robertson had lunch at The Fix Burger Bar in Worcester. The burgers were fabulous, the beer was cold, and the atmosphere was very relaxed. Mike had spent the morning giving Phil bowling lessons at Auburn Lanes, which is, as the name implies, in Auburn, Massachusetts.

Neither man spoke until their burger was almost gone.

"Thanks for the lessons. Soon my league average will be higher than yours," Phil said, mostly in jest.

"You should live so long," Mike replied. "But in all seriousness, you are improving rather fast. I'll have to keep practicing in order to compete with you."

Mike was being self-deprecating. Phil was nowhere near as good as him; an outstanding league bowler would have an average of 200 or higher and Mike's average was 211. An excellent bowler would have rolled at least one perfect game. A perfect game is all twelve strikes in one game for a score of 300. A genuinely outstanding bowler would have at least one three-game series over 800. Mike owned five 300-game rings and two 800 series rings; all league sanctioned. Phil had none.

"Thanks for taking the time to work with me. I have learned a lot from you," Phil said. "My league average is improving, and I even had a 207-game last Monday."

"Keep it up."

"Mike, I told you about Jim Hines, the Long Island cop I worked with on The Purity murders." Mike nodded. "I would like us to get together next time he and his wife are in town," Phil concluded.

"Sure, I think Tess would enjoy that."

Despite his affection for Jim, Phil felt compelled to say something about Hines' attitude. "Hines is a great guy, but he wears the fact he's black as a badge of honor. He feels that he is accountable to solve the problems of every Black person in America and defend them against any perceived slur." Phil said. "Just be aware of that in advance.

Mike nodded seriously, but the expression on his face seemed sympathetic. "Phil, I can understand exactly why he feels that way. I had a lot of issues when I was a young man. Most of the issues were with white guys, name-calling, supposedly in jest, and not involving me in activities. Ignoring me. I learned how to manage things and project an attitude that white people would respond to positively. Because I changed and because of the changes that have happened in America, my life is much better."

"Fill me in. What did you do?"

"We'll have the opportunity to discuss it when Hines is with us. I'll fill you both in, but I have to get back to my business for now. See you Monday night," said Mike.

"Take care. Maybe I'll beat you Monday."

"In your dreams."

Tina lingered around the Ogunquit streets until Kathryn finished her shift. She had given her a little snippet of why she wanted to talk to her. Kathryn had seemed excited and agreed to have a home-cooked dinner with Tina and would maybe even stay overnight.

When Kathryn finally stepped gingerly out of the restaurant door and onto the sidewalk, Tina smiled. She took the lead, guiding Kathryn to her house via the Marginal Way. Kathryn enjoyed the view of the Atlantic and the sound of the foamy waves caressing the shore while she listened with great interest to Tina's job offer. She imagined living in an ocean front house for the winter, doing light housework, and getting her server job back in the spring. It did not hurt that she thought Tina was beautiful.

When they got to the old lighthouse just off the walkway, Tina said, "My house is just around the bend. We're almost there."

As she stood on the Marginal Way, Kathryn struggled to find words to describe the house before her. Tina's house was big by usual standards but small when compared to the enormous homes that loomed over the Marginal Way. The house's façade was Mediterranean, totally unlike the classical and neoclassical architecture of the surrounding mansions. Set on Maine's rocky coast, forty feet above the Atlantic, the house maximized its seaside view with windows of assorted sizes and shapes that dominated its east-facing front. Fretwork decorated the windows with unique appealing geometric patterns. A beautifully finished mahogany double door entry opened onto a large front terrace surrounded by a knee wall. Large fieldstones sided the house and the wall.

A doorway led from the house to a small, architecturally concealed, enclosed porch, which also opened onto a large front terrace.

Realizing that Kathryn was overwhelmed, Tina said gently, "Let's go in and start dinner. If we just walk back to the old lighthouse, go up Israel Head Road, and then take a left again on Lighthouse View Way, we're home."

Kathryn was blown away by the makings of a lovely evening: the most beautiful house she had ever seen and a gorgeous woman. Kathryn had had sexual feelings for women since she was ten years old, and, being here with Tina, her feelings for women reemerged.

Chapter 6

Phil and Rose arrived at Grill 44 a little early and found Noelle Lefevre seated with a glass of red wine in her hand. She stood and greeted Rose first, and Rose then introduced her to Phil. Noelle wore what looked like an extremely expensive form-fitting dress and, ankle-high boots, and she positively glittered with jewelry. Noelle made her living as a genealogist and finder of missing relatives. She was also a local historian and a blogger about all things in the northeast corner of Connecticut. They sat and ordered drinks.

Over a Jameson on the rocks, Phil explained his interest in the history of the Pomfret Cotton Mill. "Noelle, I love living in Cargill Falls, and I think the people are great. However, recent events have disturbed me. I'm not one to sit by, so, I'm looking into the murder in the Mill with an old friend, a retired Long Island police commander. We're certain that knowing all we can about the Mill may shed light on the killer's motive. I know it's a long shot, but five years ago, some information we uncovered helped solve a series of murders."

Noelle's blank expression remained unfazed. She responded promptly. "The police are working on the case. Why get involved?"

"My friend and I know that half of the murders in this country go unsolved, and if someone unknown to the victim commits the murder, the unsolved percentage is higher still. We hope to help the police if they run out of leads."

Noelle nodded, content with his response, and replied, "I have a lot of info on the old Mill, but I have unanswered questions as well. I'll tell you what I know and dig into the rest. It sounds like a challenge, and I like a challenge."

After taking another sip of wine, she set her glass down and started relaying the Mill's basic history to Phil. "In 1720, David Howe established Cargill Falls' first industry on the site, a small gristmill. In 1730, a Scotsman named Captain Benjamin Cargill bought Howe's property and built a new mill. His gristmill could grind out 500 bushels of corn daily using three large millstones which Howe had installed. In the 1760's a distillery, malt house, fulling mill, trip-hammer shop, sawmill, blacksmith shop, churning mill, and Pomfret's first creamery were all added to the site."

Noelle took a minute to refer to her notes, flipping through a well-worn legal pad, before resuming.

"The Pomfret Manufacturing Company bought the site in 1807 and started the Pomfret Cotton Mills to produce textile products. It is the oldest site of its kind in the nation. Samual Slater of Rhode Island is often referred to as the 'Father of the American Industrial Revolution' because he introduced the idea of mass production into the United States. He founded Samual Slater and Company in 1798. Later, in 1812, he started a textile plant in Pawtucket Rhode Island. A group of stockholders in the Rhode Island plant, which included Samuel Slater's father-in-law, Oziel Wilkinson, had established the Pomfret Manufacturing Company. They built a four-story wood-frame mill building on this site and used the foundation for one of the later 19th-century buildings. That mill directly emulated Slater's mill in Pawtucket, Rhode Island, and produced cotton thread. The town's growth around this mill complex was instrumental in the eventual incorporation in 1855 of the town of Cargill Falls, which included portions of Pomfret, Killingly, and Thompson."

Noelle continued, "The Mill occupies a prominent location across the Quinebaug River from downtown Cargill Falls, set partially on a point projecting eastward on the south side of Pomfret Street, US Route 44. A roughly 30-foot drop in the Quinebaug River at the point saw early industrial use in the 18th century, with grist, saw, and fulling mills operating along the river. Sitting on 10 acres, the complex includes seventeen interconnected structures. All the structures were used in the textile manufacturing process. The buildings vary in size and height, with the largest reaching five stories tall. The most recent buildings began operation around 1950, although there have been subsequent alterations."

Again, she stopped, shuffled a few papers, and looked at her notes before resuming. She added,

"I'm going to back up a bit. The Pomfret Cotton Mills produced textile products as early as 1800, the oldest such site in the nation. The four-story square stone mill west of the detached hip-roofed office building is the oldest standing factory building, circa 1823, in the valley. They added a three-story stone mill in the mid-1840s."

Phil chuckled, impressed by Noelle's extensive knowledge of the Mill's history. "Yes, that is helpful. The operations and intricate processes involved in these early industries are fascinating. Please, continue."

Noelle took another sip of her drink before delving back into the historical narrative. "During the mid-19th century, the mill complex expanded significantly. By 1850, they had added a machine shop, a weave shop, a second carding room, and a boiler house. The machine shop still stands but is largely unaltered from its original construction. I found records regarding a later expansion of the boiler house, in order to house more boilers, as demand increased. The expansion was necessary because of the increase in machinery."

She glanced at her notes again, ensuring accuracy in her account. Then she said, "The post-Civil War period saw further growth with the construction of a large weave shop in 1876 and a picker house in 1883. The picker house contained machinery used to clean and separate cotton fibers, a crucial step in the textile production process."

Noelle leaned back, taking a moment before continuing. "In the second half of the 19th century, a substantial fire damaged several buildings, leading to extensive rebuilding. The reconstruction included a new weave shop, a picker house, and the addition of a dye house. The dye house still stands, a testament to the Mill's resilience despite setbacks."

Phil interjected, "The fire must have been a major setback for them."

Noelle nodded. "Indeed, but they bounced back. The dye house allowed them to expand their capabilities and move toward producing a wider range of textile products.

In the early 20th century, the Mill continued to evolve, adapting to changes in technology and market demands."

She concluded, "This brings us closer to the present, and I'll continue to gather more information on the Mill's recent history and ownership. If you have any specific areas, you want me to focus on, feel free to let me know."

"Close enough," Phil replied.

He appreciated Noelle's dedication to the research and added, "This is fantastic, Noelle. You're providing us with a comprehensive understanding of the Mill's journey through time. As we dig deeper, I'll keep you posted on specific areas we'd like to explore further. Together, we'll uncover the secrets hidden within these old walls."

Noelle smiled.

"There is a lot of information on the families that owned the Mill, but I haven't dug into it. In the late 1800s Isaac Putnam, a Civil war veteran, ran the Mill for his family, and there are still descendants of the Putnam's living in the area. I hope they'll speak with me," said Noelle.

"We expect to pay you."

"No need. I always wanted to do the research, and now I am very motivated." Noelle responded.

They stayed awhile, engaging in small talk, then parted.

Chapter 7

Since the police investigation into the shooting was going nowhere, it had been put on hold. According to Parisi, the Connecticut State Police sought a reason to pull resources from the investigation and declare it a cold case. Their current theory of the case was that one of the creditors hired a hitman via the Russian mob in Providence. According to the theory, the hitman flew to the States, killed Martineau, and immediately returned to Russia. Seventeen million dollars was a lot of money; killing the CEO would send a powerful message. The State Police believed that they were investigating a perfect crime and simply wanted to move on.

Yet the police hadn't moved on because the owners of WINY, the local radio station, kept up the pressure on them to find the killer. WINY was a small, locally owned community station, and the State Police typically would not give WINY's on-air opinions an afterthought. However, WINY's owners, Harry O, and Joyce Oliver, were active in the community, advocates for the area's citizens, and well-respected people. And the citizens wanted the killer found.

Karen, Phil, and Jim were on a three-way call discussing options. "We sure as hell won't be able to make progress on our own if the State Police are getting nowhere," said Jim.

"I feel like there is nowhere to go to get information or leads on the case," Phil continued supplementing Jim's thought.

Karen replied, "The State Police aren't going to shut down the case in its entirety, not with Harry O and Joyce around. We can still follow what the police are doing and maybe sweep up some crumbs, then try to make sense of them. I know it's a long shot, but it's all we have. I'll stay in touch with Connecticut and hope to get something. Now I must get back to work. Bye." Karen hung up.

"I guess that's all we can do. Jesus, I wanted to solve this case… or at least help," groaned Jim.

Phil refused to give up. "I think Noelle is the best hope for a lead," he told Jim, "and that's a long shot. I've talked to her, and she's still digging into the family that owned the Mill in the late 1800s. She said it's going slow but apparently, she has uncovered some interesting facts."

Jim's exasperated sigh sounded through Phil's speaker. "I will be pleasantly surprised if it leads anywhere."

"Okay, Mr. Positive. If Noelle comes up with something, I will certainly remind you of how wrong you were. Now on another subject. I still want you to meet my friend, Mike. In fact, Rose wants you and Mary Ann to spend the weekend the week after next, and if you can, she will invite Tess and Mike. The girls can do their thing, and the boys can have fun," Phil said.

"Mary Ann has wanted to visit for a while, so I am sure she'll agree." replied Jim, sounding somewhat more relieved.

"Great. We'll have an enjoyable time, and you'll like Mike."

"As long as I don't have to bowl, and Mike is likable."

Chapter 8

"I can't believe the holidays are almost upon us, and I'm just not ready," Rose said.

Mary Ann chimed in, "You're not the only one. I have more things to do than I have time. It's time for me to retire. We don't need the money. I work because I have worked as a server most of my life, and I genuinely like it. Even more so, I like the people I work with; they're the salt of the earth." She turned toward Jim, who was speaking with Phil as the two relaxed on the living room's leather sectional. "If I got a little help from that big lug relaxing on your couch, I'd be able to get it all done and wouldn't have to quit work. But I can't wait for hell to freeze over."

"I completely understand," Rose replied. Phil only lifts a finger around here when I start yelling because I'm completely frazzled. And that only lasts one day, then it's back to his do-nothing routine. That is until I blow up again."

Phil and Jim listened with one ear while mostly ignoring Rose and Mary Ann's comments. They had been discussing how to save the world, a world quite different from the world they lived in as kids. Neither of them realized that they were rapidly becoming stereotypical old men.

The four of them were killing time while waiting for Mike and Tess Robertson. Then the women would go shopping, and the men would figure out what to do…, or maybe they'd just sit around.

Calling out to the living room, Rose hoped to catch Jim's ear. "I think you will like Mike and Tess. They're both very nice. Their son Mike Jr., their only child, is starting medical school next year." The doorbell chimed their arrival as soon as she spoke."

"Here they are now. I'll show them in and introduce everyone," Phil said, slowly hoisting himself up from the sectional and trotting over to the front door.

Phil returned to the living room with his visitors and looked at Jim immediately, wanting to see his reaction. Jim's eyes widened and his lips parted slightly with either surprise or shock. Phil couldn't tell the difference. Both Mike and Tess were quite tall, Tess was about an inch short of six feet, and Mike was three inches over six feet. Tess had fine facial features and porcelain white skin. She wore black pants and a blue turtleneck sweater, loosely fitting and flowing freely over her body. Mike, on the other hand, weighed 230 pounds and had a wide receiver's body, large muscular arms, and a small waist. He wore a brown leather jacket, jeans, and a Tom Brady jersey all topped off with a Patriots Super Bowl hat. Mike was the archetype for a handsome black man.

"Jim, Mary Ann, I'd like you to meet Mike and Tess Robertson. Mike and Tess, this lovely couple is Jim and Mary Ann Hines. After the women do a little shopping, we'll head into town for dinner. As for the boys, a little football is on the agenda," Phil said.

Tess scowled darkly at Phil, stopping him in his tracks and exclaiming, "Look, macho man, I like football as much as the next guy. But I also want to see the shops in this town, so never think only guys like football."

Phil realized he sounded like his father and winced. "Sorry."

It became painfully evident to Jim that Mary Ann couldn't take her eyes off Mike. Gazing sadly at her mouth, which was slightly open, and wondering whether she was drooling a little, Jim felt inferior. He knew that Mary Ann loved him, and that Mike was married and the shock of seeing Mike for the first time would surely hold Mary Ann's attention. None-the-less Jim was a little jealous.

"Come, ladies, let's get going; times a-wasting!" Rose chided. Soon the women were on the move.

Flopping onto the couch, Phil tuned the television to the Penn State game against Rutgers, and the three men watched in silence until halftime. The silence was broken sporadically by their commentary on the excellent plays. Phil went to the kitchen to fetch a few beers, and Jim asked Mike, "Phil tells me you're teaching him how to bowl?"

"Phil is rather good already. I'm helping him improve his game," Mike replied. "He bowled when he was a teen, but equipment and the lane conditions have changed since then. He's improving every week."

"You guys also go on long bike rides?"

"Yes, I finally found someone who likes riding."

Having returned with three Sam Adams, Phil said, "I like our lunches, burgers, beer, and BS more than the bike ride. I tolerate the ride."

Just then, his cell chirped. Looking at the number flashing on the screen, Phil turned pale for a moment. "It's my mother. I should get it." He sped out of the room to answer, and returned a few moments later, saying anxiously, "It sounds serious! My father passed out, and my mother is worried. He's breathing, thank God, and an ambulance is on the way. I'll stay on the phone with my mother and keep talking to her until we know what is going on." Phil hastened to another room.

"I hope his father is okay," Mike said. "He has had heart issues and is on medication."

"You seem to like Phil and spend a lot of time with him. Don't his conservative views bother you?"

"No, not in the slightest. Phil's a good guy that doesn't have a racist bone in his body. You've known him for over five years and still hang around him, so you must already be aware of that. And I think his opinions on individual responsibility versus looking at others to solve your problems are right. I hope you understand that Phil's opinions apply to everyone, regardless of race. Do they bother you?"

"I like Phil," replied Jim, a bit puzzled with Mike's nonchalant attitude toward race relations. "He has a good heart, but I'd like him more if he understood how badly mistreated black people are. But enough about Phil. Tell me a little about Mike."

Mike smiled, leaned forward, and netted his hands. "I will start with a tale about ants. I can't find out who first told this story… some people attribute it to David

Attenborough, others to Kurt Vonnegut. Some people attribute it to Mark Twain. I just don't know.

"If you store 100 black and 100 red fire ants in a glass jar, nothing will happen. They will go about their business. But if you take the jar, violently shake it, and leave it on the table, the ants will start killing each other. The attacks will be based on color. Reds believe that black is the enemy, while blacks believe that red is the enemy, and the real enemy is the person who shook the jar." Mike paused.

"You are trying to say this applies to race relations? We are not ants."

"The world I live in is more like the unshaken jar. My company employs people of all colors from diverse cultures, and the squabbles are about work, not skin color. Now think about who does the shaking: white supremacists, black leaders, and the government. They all have something to gain when there's unrest, power, and money."

At first, Jim did not accept Mike's theory, but every time he tried to dispute it, he could not find the right words. He frowned then said to Mike, "You've given me something to think about. I'm not sure I buy your theory, but I will think about it."

Phil walked into the room abruptly and reported, "My father was unconscious for half an hour before he woke up. No loss of memory or function. He's in the hospital. They'll hold him overnight to make sure he's alright. I'm going to stay on the phone with my mother until her sister gets to the hospital. Are you getting along?"

Jim waved him off and replied, "We're fine. Take care of your family."

Settling back on the couch, Mike and Jim watched the rest of the game. They talked about football and other lighthearted subjects. They enjoyed each other's company and concluded they liked each other.

Not long before the end of the game, their wives returned. Rose stayed close to Phil, and the others got ready for dinner.

"Looks like my father is okay," Phil told her, seeming relieved. "My aunt Rena will spend the night, so all is well in Scranton. Let's go to dinner."

They headed to the Courthouse Bar and Grill on foot, a short walk from Grove Street. A popular place where locals gather for fun and tasty food.

Chapter 9

Straight from bed after a good night's sleep and still dressed in men's boxers and a loose-fitting top, Kathryn stood in front of the large living room window that looked out on the enclosed porch, the Marginal Way, Maine's rocky coast, and the Atlantic Ocean. She could only see the back of Tina's head. Tina sat in a chair on the porch and looked out at the rise and fall of the waves. Kathryn believed she was crying, and in fact, she was. Overcoming her fear, Kathryn ventured out to the porch and sat next to Tina.

"What's wrong?"

Tina looked up, tears in her red-rimmed eyes. "I was just thinking of my parents. They died too young. I'll be alright."

Tina wasn't being honest with Kathryn. She was upset because the instigator had called and said he would need her for another hit, maybe two. When she had started to balk at the idea, he had reminded her that their contract would remain in force until he no longer needed anyone else killed and that the organization, she worked for would enforce the agreement. That could be deadly. Tina desperately wanted out of the business so she could concentrate on building a relationship with Kathryn and living a quiet, peaceful life in Maine.

The other thought that jumped into Tina's mind was about whether she should tell Kathryn about her husband's death? She dismissed it and locked it in that special compartment in her mind for later analysis. She turned toward Kathryn and saw her sorrowful eyes.

"Kathryn, I'm okay. I'm over it for today."

Kathryn returned a sympathetic frown with pursed lips. "I worry about you. Sometimes you become so distant I start thinking you feel you made a mistake taking me in and want me to leave."

Tina winced. "That's the last thing I want. What I want is you in my life forever. I have been afraid to say it, but I am falling in love with you."

Kathryn didn't know how to respond or what to say. She had strong feelings for Tina too, and felt something that was probably love, but she also believed that she was too young and immature to keep Tina's interest. She knew that she was attractive, but that was impermanent. Kathryn was confused by her emotions; especially because many of her desires were deep and sexual. She turned to Tina and kissed her on the lips passionately and deeply.

Tina returned the kiss with equal passion. They continued for a while until Tina pushed Kathryn away and asked, "Are you sure this is what you want? Maybe we should take it slow, be sure we are right for each other. I'm a lot older than you and carry a lot of baggage I haven't shared with you."

Kathryn placed her hand on Tina's breast, gently squeezed, and said, "Let's adjourn to my room, the bed is still unmade."

Afterward, they sat on the enclosed porch and looked at the Atlantic Ocean. Tina was content to have her arm around Kathryn.

She gently stroked Kathryn's hair and asked, "Have you always been attracted to women?"

Kathryn stared out over the water for a moment, then said. "No matter what was happening in my life, I knew from an early age that I would be happiest if I spent the rest of my life with a woman I loved and who loved me. How about you?"

"As I said, I am older and have a lot more baggage. I knew I preferred women at an early age, but I fought it. Maybe it was the times, maybe my conservative parents. I went through stages; I focused on men, then after my husband died, I tried both, men and women and was never satisfied. I know now that my original feelings when I was young are right for me. Let's enjoy the rest of the day."

Chapter 10

The second day of the 'getting to know each other' weekend at the Messina household started with a morning meal at The Painted Bakers Café. Another good eatery a short walk from Grove Street, the café featured traditional breakfast favorites along with excellent baked goods. It was truly a terrific way to start a Sunday.

When the three couples were loitering outside after their meal, Phil called his mother to get an update on his father's condition. After the call ended, Mike asked, "Phil, how's your father doing? Will he get out of the hospital today?"

"Seems he is fine now that they got his Thinadin balanced. The doctors believe that he forgot to take his medication, and his heart issue returned. My mother will check his medication in the future, but I think we should hire a nurse to stop by every day and check. My mother herself is getting forgetful and may need help with her own meds. I'll work it out."

Jim asked, "What's the plan for today?"

Phil replied, "I think we should take a walk in the park and check out the falls and the building that will be home to Jim and Mary Ann."

"Great idea, and then we can watch the Patriots beat the crap out of Tennessee." Mike said.

Rose grimaced at the thought. "I can still get three tickets to the play at the Bradley Playhouse." she offered. "We won't get great seats, but anything will be better than football. You can watch grown men beat the snot out of one another. We girls will absorb some culture."

Tess chimed in, "You know, I like football as much as the men, but I also like absorbing some culture. My choice is the girls and enjoying a play."

Mike smiled. He decided to bait Tess and teased, "Perfect. Now we can enjoy the game in peace and quiet." Then he quickly added. "Just kidding. I know you like football, and I know you'll enjoy the local playhouse."

With their plans in place, they headed toward the park, the falls, and to take a look at the old Mill that Jim and Mary Ann planned to call home.

As they strolled down the sidewalk, Mike said, "I'd love to get the maintenance contract on that building. The pace of the renovations looks to be slowing down. Is that because of the murder last summer? And where does the investigation stand?"

"Yes, the renovation has slowed down, and the investigation is stalled, to answer your questions," replied Phil. "Also, rumor has it the Mill owners are behind on their loan payments, and the bank may foreclose. As for the investigation, the State Police are trying to shut it down, but there's pressure to keep working on it. A real mess."

"Jim, your dream of moving to Connecticut and my dream of picking up some new business opportunities are on hold for a while," Mike added with a fake moan.

"Let's keep walking," Rose ordered.

They returned to the house an hour later, had lunch, and the theatergoers left. The football game entertained the men until halftime. At halftime, the Patriots were up twenty-four points over the Titans, and the game had become boring. As the second half was about to begin, Phil's mother called and asked him to please talk some sense into his father. Phil left, and Jim was alone with Mike.

Jim took the opportunity to speak. "Mike, I am curious. How did you get the knowledge and the ability to handle the responsibility of owning a business? Especially a business as complicated as providing services for commercial property owners. I think that once they farm out the work, they are never satisfied with its quality or cost."

"Pretty insightful. What prepared me was listening to and understanding Doctor Martin Luther King's message."

Jim looked confused. "I'm afraid you will have to give me more context. I respect what he did for black people, but I'm unsure how his speeches would have prepared you."

"It's hard for me to put into words, but I'll try. When I was young, I was angry at the world and at white people in general. Right out of high school, I went to work in a foundry. It was hot, miserable, and dirty work. It took advantage of my strong back and supposedly weak mind. The Worcester public schools didn't have high standards, and I played more than I studied. I saw myself as a victim, and believed the world was against me and all black people, for that matter. I felt the suffering of discrimination and the pain of being a second-class citizen."

"You weren't wrong. It still happens to us."

"That may be true, but I don't think that way anymore. After listening to Dr. King, I began thinking that being angry and seeing myself as a victim was self-destructive. The world reflected my anger back at me, and the whole victim mentality held me back. I hadn't even tried to get ahead, to learn or try new things. Why bother? It would do me no good. I was the wrong color."

After a moment's thought, Mike continued. "Dr. King's speeches were realistic and positive. He gave me hope instead of despair, and I literally felt lighter. I was upbeat instead of dragging my chin on the ground. I left the job at the foundry to find a new job where I could learn something."

"Weren't you afraid to fail, to become more bitter and disappointed?"

"Failure is always a possible outcome. Another is success, and you can't experience either outcome if you don't try. Companies turned me down for jobs and told me I didn't have the right skills when what they really meant was that I didn't have the right skin color. Then things changed, the Bickford Company interviewed me for a maintenance position. Bickford is a Worcester firm that owns and manages property all over central Massachusetts. They were looking for someone to paint, fix plumbing issues, fix crumbling concrete, snowplow, and other duties as needed. I didn't know how to do any of it. But before I could admit I didn't have the skills, the boss asked if I could learn? He said I looked like I was smart enough. Was I willing to give the job a try?"

"Why would he do that? Was there no one else applying for the job?

"There were other applicants. All white guys. I asked him later, when I got to know him, why did he hire me? He said he liked my attitude, and believed I would learn everything else. My first job was painting, then plumbing, and I learned to do both. Next thing I knew, I was supervising the entire crew."

"Quite a story. How did you get to own a company?"

"Also, quite a story. I was on the job for over ten years and loved it. I wasn't only supervising. I also worked with the guys when needed. Then one day, the owner called me into his office. He told me he was considering creating a separate company to take over the property maintenance work. I said to myself, 'Oh shit,' I'm out! What he said next changed my life. He said he wanted to keep things the same for his renters and offered to set me up in business if I wanted. I jumped at the opportunity, and we set it up so my ownership in the company would get to 100% in a few years. He also encouraged me to grow the business by acquiring new clients.

"I don't believe any of that would have happened if I saw myself as a victim or was still an angry black man."

"Wow, I'm impressed and a little shocked." Before Jim could continue speaking Phil's return interrupted him.

"What are you guys talking about?" Phil asked.

Mike replied. "Just some black guy talk."

"Then, I don't want to know. I have enough problems. I think I got my father straightened out with his meds for now, but it won't last. I'll have to hire a nurse. Now let's get back to this boring game. I'd suggest switching to the Giants game, but Mike will blow a gasket."

"Screw Mike, I like the Giants," Jim said.

Chapter 11

Phil's bowling team was in the middle of the third game. The Monday Night Men's League competed, as the name implied, on thirty-three Monday nights in the Fall through Spring of a season. It was a few weeks after the Christmas holidays, and it was cold in Auburn, Massachusetts. Mike and Phil along with two other men named Craig Lathrop and Tim Brookings, were members of the Tuttle Post team.

The owners renovated Auburn Lanes last year, and it now sported a state-of-the-art computerized scoring system and a lane oiling robot. The once wooden lanes were now synthetic. The changes turned it into a modern bowling center.

Mike was in teaching mode, and Phil was listening intently. Phil's first two games were a 183 and 191. Tuttle Post won the first two games, and winning the third would move the team into first place. Phil had the lowest average on the team and therefore had the highest handicap. If he had a great third game, they could sweep. Mike could hardly restrain his disappointment when Phil missed a 6-10 spare in the first frame and missed a ten pin in the second frame. Phil rebounded with five strikes in a row. Mike took him aside to make sure Phil understood the movement of the lane oil and how to change his shot to correct for the oil.

Phil said he understood and threw a strike in the 8th frame. Mike was ecstatic. Phil repeated with a strike in the

9th and three strikes in the 10th frame for a 257 game and a 631 series. With Phil's handicap, Tuttle Post won all three games and total pins and moved to first place. The team considered Phil the night's hero and said he could buy the first round at the bar. The team moved its celebration to the Chester P. Tuttle Post 279 bar. The team's sponsor. After the celebration calmed down, everyone settled into some drinking and not so serious talking.

Mike, more interested in the investigation then engaging in not so serious talk, asked Phil. "How's the investigation going?"

"It's not. The State Police claim they're working the case hard, but Parisi's source told her they've completely stopped any effort on the case. I can't blame them. They don't have a lead, and they don't even know where to find one."

"I'll bet Jim isn't happy. He wants it solved. It's almost like since he is going to live at the old Mill, he's afraid it'll curse the building if the killer gets away with it," Mike responded.

"You're getting to know Jim. Do you like him?"

"I think he's a good man but a little tightly wound. He needs to relax and enjoy life more."

"What do you think of his views on race?" Phil asked.

"Same as you. Trying to defend all black people is wearing him out. The error in his thinking is that he believes all black people need defending. Black people are the same as everyone else. Some good, some bad. He needs to get past that."

Phil's phone rang, and after seeing who was calling, he told Mike he had to get it. It was Noelle. He hoped that she had found something. He stepped away from the table for a moment, and Mike saw him return soon later with a bounce in his step and a smile on his face.

"Noelle has been meeting with the Putnam Family, and she gathered a lot of information… which she wants to share with all of us at the same time. She wants me to arrange a meeting in three weeks. The family gave her all the documents they had on the Mill from 1860 to the early 1950s. Luckily, they are all digitized."

"Why wait three weeks?"

"She wants to go through all her notes and reread the documents and organize a presentation. Do you want in?"

"Yeah, I'd like that, if I have the time."

"I'll let you know when and where."

"What's Noelle's story?"

"I don't know much about her. I know she's local and was an outstanding athlete in high school. She married young and has a couple of kids. A drunk driver killed her husband in an accident with a FedEx truck, and she wound up with a good settlement. She and her husband had planned well for the future and had a sizable insurance policy and decent savings. Now she's a genealogist and blogger and knows everything there is to know about the history of northeast Connecticut."

"Good thing you didn't know much."

"What can I say? People in small towns talk."

"Good bowling tonight. I'm looking over my shoulder and shaking in my boots, afraid you'll replace me as the team stud."

Noelle took detailed and voluminous notes at her meetings with the Putnam's. The family was incredibly open and willingly shared their family history. They also agreed to set up a meeting with Elijah Putnam, the 92-year-old family patriarch. They assured her that it would be worth her time. As Noelle was getting ready to leave, a junior family member handed her a 500-gigabyte drive. She told Noelle that it held all the family's history pertaining to their ownership of the Mill. It was hers to keep and use for her research.

Noelle organized her notes into categories and had topics in each category. She planned to handout an outline of her presentation for the group to use while she was talking. Then she would supply a handout detailing each topic after the meeting. It would mean a lot of reading. Noelle's takeaway after listening to the family is Isaac Putnam was the key. When this was over, she would have a treasure trove of historical information about the Pomfret Cotton Mill.

Noelle got to work.

The Mid-1800s

Both Isaac Putnam and Adam Beck were born in 1840. Isaac in Connecticut and Adam in Virginia. Both were born into families that farmed a small plot of land for subsistence. Both boys grew into strong men forged by long hours of hard physical work. Both Isaac and Adam benefitted from an innate intelligence that was far above average.

Life on a subsistence farm in the mid-1800s was a testament to the rhythms of nature and the unwavering spirit of those who tilled the soil. The days began at dawn, the rooster's crow signaling the start of another round of labor. The Putnam's and the Beck's, like many other families of their time, relied on the land for their sustenance.

The farmstead was a patchwork of crops, carefully rotated to ensure the fertility of the soil. Rows of corn rustled in the breeze, standing tall and resilient. In the garden, the women tended to vegetables with care, their hands calloused from years of nurturing the earth. The bounty of the land provided a modest but essential variety to their meals.

Their livestock, maybe a cow named Bessie, and a few clucking hens, roamed freely in the yard. Bessie, a docile creature, provided milk for the family and occasionally pulled a plow through the fields. The chickens offered eggs, a valuable source of protein.

Each season brought its own demands. Spring was a flurry of activity, plowing, planting, and hoping for favorable weather. Summer brought the daily ritual of weeding and watering, while fall ushered in the harvest. The entire family worked side by side, hands stained with the richness of the earth.

Winter was a time of rest, relatively speaking. Chores still filled the days, but the pace slowed. The family gathered around the hearth, the warmth of the fire offering solace against the biting cold outside. They spent evenings repairing tools, telling stories, and reading by the flickering light of an oil lamp.

Their connection to the land extended beyond the crops and livestock. The forest at the edge of the property provided timber for repairs and hunting grounds for sustenance beyond the farm. The man of the family and his sons, young men with dreams of their own, honed their skills in carpentry and marksmanship.

In the quiet moments, the family marveled at the simplicity of their life. The challenges were many, but so were the rewards. The sense of self-sufficiency, the reliance on family and community, and the deep connection to the changing seasons shaped their worldview.

Life on the farm was not a story of opulence, but of resilience and the quiet beauty found in the ebb and flow of rural life. As the years passed, the farm witnessed the cycles of life, the birth of calves, the growth of crops, and the changing faces of the seasons. The families, like the soil they cultivated, were deeply rooted in the land, their lives intertwined with the very essence of subsistence farming in the mid-1800s.

Despite coming of age in similar environments, Isaac Putnam and Adam Beck had vastly different views on life. Isaac Putnam possessed a rigid sense of right and wrong along with a high ethical standard of behavior. Adam Beck had a flexible sense of right and wrong and thought it right to cheat and steal to get what he needed and wanted. Adam believed that his struggles on the family farm gave him that right.

The two men would confront each other later in life.

Chapter 12

It took Noelle over a month to organize her presentation to Phil's team. She had always thought of the group as Phil's team because she knew Phil and Rose, and they lived in the area. But Phil had told her that the retired commander from New York was driving the investigation and that when he worked with Jim on a case on Long Island, he felt, uniquely, like he was contributing to society. In a brief phone call, Noelle told Phil that she would feel more comfortable and do a better job if she got to know the others on the team. In response, Phil and Rose arranged for a Saturday night 'Get to know you' party at their home before the presentation.

Mike and Tess Robertson, Jim and Mary Ann Hines, Karen Parisi, and Noelle joined the Messinas at their home on Grove Street. The out of towners would spend the night. Noelle chose to spend the night at her own home so she could relax and continue to prepare. She knew that the group would have lots of questions, and she wanted to have lots of answers.

Judging by the animated conversation early in the night, everyone was comfortable and spoke freely. As the evening wore on, a few women claimed the living room. The men, along with Tess Robertson and Karen Parisi lounged in the family room to watch a little college basketball. A BIG TEN conference game between

Michigan and Ohio State played on ESPN. Before Phil could settle into the game, he got a call from his mother, and he left the others alone. It was a brief call, and Phil returned after ten minutes.

When passing through the living room on the way back to the family room, Phil found Tess and Karen frowning and talking with the other women. They had left because Jim and Mike were in the middle of a heated argument about critical race theory. As soon as Phil returned to the family room, the two other men grew quiet. "Is your father, okay?" asked Jim.

"All good," replied Phil. He felt uncomfortable, even a little angry. He wanted to be a good host, but Jim's constant race commentary was starting to get on more nerves other than his.

Phil began, "critical race theory is simply another way of dividing people based on the color of their skin. People are either oppressors or oppressed. In this case, it is dangerous because oppressors are evil and have no redeeming virtues and the oppressed can do anything they choose to the oppressors. For example, Israel and the Israelis are the oppressors and Hamas and the people they govern are the oppressed. Did you ever ask yourself who assigns people to each group and what motivates them?"

Before Mike or Jim could respond, He added, "Maybe we should deal with the Fentanyl crisis rather than divide the country."

Jim said, "It's not that straightforward."

Before he could continue Mike spoke up. "Ah, but it is. Dividing people into groups has to happen before shaking the jar will create conflict, remember? The government, with the full support of the media has divided us into oppressor and oppressed and is shaking the jar. In my opinion we're on the way to becoming an authoritarian state, another China, with centralized control of the economy and the people. I genuinely believe that is the motivation driving the creation of conflict in our country."

Phil's compatriots suddenly realized that the three men had been left alone. Jim said, "All we accomplished tonight was driving our friends away. Let's save the discussion for another time and adjourn to the other room and party."

Chapter 13

After a hearty breakfast at Marisa's Breakfast and Lunch, they returned to the Messinas' home. They settled in the living room to hear what Noelle had learned from the Putnam Family. Noelle cleared her throat and slowly looked at each person, one at a time. When she was sure she had their attention, she began.

"I met with the family's younger generation for a full day. They were very hospitable and exceptionally open about the prior generations. The family ran the Pomfret Cotton Mill until around 1950 or 1960. They weren't sure. The family became wealthy from the profits of running the Mill and from its sale. That money still funds their lives. The family also had significantly more detailed information about the operation of the Mill in the early 1900s than they did about the operation in the late 1800s. Their information was interesting, but I didn't think it helped us. However, one bit of information caught my attention. It seems that Isaac Putnam, who ran the Mill from around 1869 to 1891, was obsessed with stories about lost Civil War treasures. I believe he was interested in one particular treasure and may have hunted for it. I also believe it could lead us to the motive." Noelle paused.

"Please go ahead," said Jim.

Everyone nodded in agreement.

Noelle had her audience's attention.

"The family seemed to remember a story about a particular treasure. A confederate Major named Adam Beck was known as 'The Ghost' because he seemed to appear out of nowhere and disappear just as fast. Major Beck of the 43rd Battalion Virginia Cavalry apparently had a lot of freedom other Majors didn't have. He and his men infiltrated enemy lines undetected and wreaked havoc. Their commanders allowed them to keep the spoils of their raids on the Union soldiers and civilians. The rumors of Beck's buried treasure started because they kept the plunder rather than turn it over to confederate army officials."

Everyone seemed to be intrigued by Beck's story and remained quiet as they contemplated what this information meant to the murder. Then Jim said, "Where do we go from here? Do you have more information, or can you get more?"

"If you believe it will help solve the Martineau murder, then there are some things we can do. I'm not sure it's worth the effort, but I guess it's possible that it may lead to the reason an assassin murdered the part owner and CEO of an old mill in his office. There are two Putnam family members I intend to talk with. One is ninety-two years old, and the other is in his late eighties. The family has agreed to set up a meeting when Elijah Putnam – that's the ninety-two-year-old – is feeling better. It should be in a few weeks. His younger brother, Nathen, will also attend."

"I have a large amount of Putnam Family information and architectural drawings for the Mill on a thumb drive. I can put the information on three thumb drives, and you can look at distinct parts. The couples will work together, or you can create another drive if you work separately. Mike, I assume you and Tess are the right couple to look at the architectural drawings."

"We'll be happy working together," Tess said.

After Noelle's presentation ended, the conversations at the Messina home no longer centered on the Putnam Family or the Mill but on the present-day town of Cargill Falls and all the events and activities available. Phil only contributed to the conversations on restaurants and food.

It added a little normalcy after the group sorted through the nuances of Bob Martineau's murder and the failed investigation.

Chapter 14

A favorite of locals and tourists alike Huckleberries Diner on Beach Street featured large pancakes chalk full of Maine huckleberries. Tina and Kathryn, seated at a large window that looked out at the Ogunquit Town beach and the Atlantic Ocean, hardly said a word to each other as they ate breakfast. It was unusual for two women who lived together and typically had much to say to one another. Kathryn knew Tina was brooding over something, but she had no idea what.

At this point, Kathryn had been living with Tina for months and had never seen her in this foul a mood. In her mind, she and Tina were always open and honest about their feelings and kept no secrets. Kathryn hoped that Tina was not hiding something, but clearly, she was upset. She would wait to confront her until the walk home.

Kathryn didn't like thinking about her life in Ireland, but in the silence, as they ate breakfast, her thoughts drifted to her family in Ireland and the abuse they had heaped upon her. Her family had lived in a very remote area and were extremely poor. Kathryn's parents and brothers had sexually abused her from the time she was eleven. Whenever she had gone to her mother to escape her father and brothers, or to have some feminine comfort, her mother would kiss and caress Kathryn. The abuse from the men in her family had never stopped, but by the time

Kathryn had turned nineteen her mother had scrounged up enough money for her to get to America.

Kathryn hated men, and it was clear. When a man tried to strike up a conversation – which happened often, because she was attractive, he would sense her hostility toward him. He would inevitably turn and walk away.

As soon as they left the restaurant, Kathryn asked, "Is something wrong? Your silence is scaring me, Tina. You've never treated me like this. I'm concerned about you… you're obviously upset. But you still love me, right?"

"There is a side of me – of my life that, you should know about, and I've been afraid to tell you. Afraid you will leave me, even hate me."

Kathryn reached for Tina's hand. "I have never been as happy in my life as I have been since you found me and invited me into your home and your life. I don't want it to end. Nothing you tell me will change that."

Tina couldn't make eye contact. "Once you discover what's happening in my life, you'll change. Not only do I think you'll leave me, but I'm also afraid you'll turn me into the police. What I've done and what I still may have to do is unforgivable. I can't live with myself, and I don't expect you to continue to live with me, to love me."

"I can't imagine what you're talking about. You're a good woman."

"We are almost home. When we're settled, I promise I will tell you everything."

"Promise."

"Yes."

After the two passed over the threshold, Tina walked into the kitchen, opened a wine bottle and brought two glasses into the living room. She served Kathryn, who sat on the couch, then she sat in a chair and began.

"I had a wonderful childhood, with great parents who supported me in everything I tried. Unfortunately, they died young before I married. My wedding reception took place in a beautiful downtown Boston venue and was extremely expensive, all paid for by the groom's wealthy family. After the reception, my life changed. We adjourned to the penthouse, and I prepared for my wedding night. When I emerged from the bathroom, Bryce choked me, beat me, and raped me twice. That night he assumed control of the marriage and me."

Tina looked at Kathryn, who had a horrified look on her face, "My god, on your wedding night! I'm so sorry."

"My wedding night set the stage for the rest of my marriage to Bryce. I was afraid for my life. He would do whatever he wanted, and we lived by his rules. After his parents died in a car accident, he inherited a literal fortune and became more of a control freak. He even spelled out the rules I would have to live by. He explained that he would have sex with me anytime he wanted, that it would be as rough as he wanted, and that it wouldn't just extend to me. He would date other women whenever he chose to…he even, made it clear that he enjoyed prostitutes and would visit them whenever he wanted. I wouldn't be allowed to complain. He told me that he would kill me if I ever left him or even thought about it. I had to stay silent and be his eye candy whenever he went somewhere. I must always look good and never get fat."

"My God, my God, my God!"

"There's more. Byce put all our money into an account only he could access. I had to ask for spending money. He essentially had me trapped in the marriage."

It was a beautiful late winter day in Maine, and they decided to get more wine, move to the enclosed porch, and open a window.

Kathryn broke the silence first, she tried to be gentle, saying, "What a horrible way to live. How did you escape?"

Tina didn't hesitate. "I killed him."

Kathryn was shocked. But as the shock of Tina's confession wore off, she realized that she was incredibly proud of Tina. Tina had taken charge of her life, and her abuser paid the ultimate price. Kathryn said firmly. "Let's go to bed."

"It's not even noon. Are you tired or upset?"

"Neither. I am horny."

Afterward, as they lay in bed, Tina asked, "What will you do with what I just told you? What are you feeling?"

"I'm feeling enormously proud of you. I wish I had your strength, your power. I have to tell you about my childhood for you to understand my reaction."

By the time Kathryn finished her story, they were both crying uncontrollably, two damaged women reliving their abuse.

When they both stopped crying, Kathryn spoke, "How did you go about killing the bastard?"

"I took advantage of all my free time when he was with other women and prostitutes and learned to shoot. I frequented a shooting range in Needham. I learned fast and soon became quite good, in fact outstanding, with both handguns and rifles. Because I hated the son-of-a-bitch and dreamed of being free of him, I started fantasizing about killing him. The fantasy soon became a desire, and I started planning. I bought a gun in Southie and hid it deep inside a junk box in the garage."

"Before you go on, I have some questions. What is Southie? What gun did you use at the range?"

"Good questions. I borrowed multiple different guns at the Shooting Range. Southie is what people in the area call South Boston."

"Thanks."

"Bryce was so rich and so absorbed with his women, and with doing drugs and drinking, he stopped caring what I did. I would steal some of his cash when I had the chance and often tell him I needed money, and he gave it to me to shut me up. Bryce never knew the money was funding his murder. He had no memory of all the times he gave me money.

"I practiced with my Southie special every chance I had until I felt comfortable. Next, I bought a professional GPS device and tracked his movements until I found a pattern. It didn't take long. He would park his Mercedes in the same area every Tuesday night at six o'clock and move it at about nine. I observed him for a couple of Tuesday nights, and he would walk to the car with the same woman and give her some money. I assumed she was a hooker, and he had a scheduled session. There was a quiet spot between where he parked and the hooker's house. Do you want to hear the rest?"

"I do"

"I dressed in shoddy clothes, made myself up so I looked totally different, I am a trained makeup artist. When I saw them walking toward his car I walked toward them. When they were close, I stepped in front of them and shot Bryce right between the eyes. His hooker hyperventilated. I calmed her down by saying I had no intension of killing her. I had her get his wallet and watch and hand them to me. I did shoot her, though, when she asked me to pay for Bryce's session. The gun and the mobile GPS unit went into Boston Harbor. It was just as easy to remove as it was to install. Since I was wearing disposable gloves, his wallet, and watch would only have the hooker's prints. I even made sure I wore a different brand of glove than I used at home. Crazy, huh?"

"No thorough. I am impressed. Were you a suspect?"

"I was the prime suspect. The police laser-focused on me. I was his heir, and I was taking shooting lessons and practicing at the gun range. They focused on me for a year and couldn't put a case together. It's still unsolved, and now it's a cold case."

"Why did you move to Ogunquit?"

"Bryce's brother, his only living relative, believed I killed him and made a pain in the ass of himself but couldn't find any evidence. When he grew tired of looking, I moved here and started a new career."

"Doing what?"

"I became a professional hitman. I had been totally subservient to Bryce. He had dominated me, and I felt weak. I decided I was better than that, that no human being would ever dominate me again, never. I chose to take control of my life. I needed to be powerful. I wanted to kill men I saw as arrogant and abusive, and that included most men. Because of what Bryce did to me, I hated men, most men. I felt powerful when I killed, and that power became addictive. I no longer felt weak and irrelevant."

"A hitman, an assassin. Will you teach me? I want to be your partner in every aspect of your life."

Tina felt a rush of pleasant surprise. "Yes."

Chapter 15

Larry Davidson relaxed in the recliner in his condominium in Webster, Massachusetts, his temporary home until the Pomfret Cotton Mill renovation was complete. He would move again and start a new project if things happened normally, but it seemed that his life was anything but normal.

Earlier, while he was checking out the next area of the Mill on the schedule his crew would renovate, Larry had stumbled on a room or hallway concealed behind a door that blended into the foundation wall. Stones and cement covered the door and the surrounding area so it would look just like the rest of the foundation. Larry noted a slight change in the foundation wall. The cement applied to the stones in front of the doorway was disintegrating and accumulating on the floor. The stones concealing the door were uniformly smaller than those in the rest of the foundation. Given the nature of the work, Larry estimated workers cut the entranceway into the foundation about fifty to seventy-five years after building the foundation, then concealed it to prevent anyone from discovering it. Larry meticulously removed the stones and cement until he managed to open the door. Behind the door Larry found a small room, about four feet wide by three feet deep, and two old wooden boxes. Larry quickly opened one of the boxes and found antique household items made of gold and silver; the box also had high-end vintage jewelry, copious quantities of diamonds, rubies, and other precious gems. After opening the other box, Larry estimated their combined value at five million dollars. Larry also found the remnants of a map, which was virtually unreadable. The items in the wooden boxes were old. As it was difficult to find the doorway, Larry believed it was possible that no one alive today knew about it.

Larry knew he didn't have the knowledge or contacts to deal with his discovery. Even his estimate of the treasure's value could have been totally inaccurate. The information would be of value to the right person, and he knew the right person but was not sure he trusted him.

After struggling with how to proceed, Larry decided to share the information but not give an exact location of the room. He wanted to have some leverage in case things fell apart.

Today, many months later, Larry was feeling extremely anxious. The only other person to know of the existence of the treasure was acting as if something was radically wrong. It appeared to Larry that his partner didn't trust him with the secret. He decided that he needed to do something more – something foolproof – to protect himself. After all, his coconspirator had already ordered the mill owner's murder.

His plan was to place some incriminating items in one of the wooden boxes and then reseal the door to the hallway. He wanted to make it as difficult as possible for anyone to find.

Cargill Falls – The Mill Conspiracy

The next day Larry returned with the items to place in the box and the materials he needed to re-conceal the door to the hallway.

The conspirators conferenced on their untraceable phones to plan their next steps. The Caregiver, the Connecticut State Senator, and the Director of a small Massachusetts manufacturing company were in attendance.

"We have a lot to discuss tonight. Some of the items are particularly bothersome. First and foremost is Larry Davidson. I'm concerned that he's panicking and will crack if things don't go as planned, or if, for some unknown reason, the police start talking to him. I believe we should act now and have Tina take care of him. He's the weak link in our group. Do you agree?"

Both confederates agreed.

"I'll call Tina and get things started. A possible advantage to taking Larry out is that the murder of another person involved in the renovation may shake up the owners and motivate them to sell. A disadvantage is that it might stir up more interest from the State Police. Currently they're not interested; in fact, they've pretty much shut down the investigation. I'll have Tina kill Larry away from the Mill; maybe that will keep the cops on the side lines.

On to the next item. I think we should make a reminder offer on the Mill at the same price and terms. It will look like we just want the Mill but aren't anxious, and it won't cast suspicion on us for the murder of Martineau."

The Senator asked, "Are you sure the information Larry gave you is solid, and correct? We're betting a lot of money on his word."

"As sure as I can be. I'm fairly certain Larry would be afraid to anger me, and I don't think he is smart enough or devious enough to leverage the knowledge."

The Director asked, "Is it possible for you to have the freedom to roam around the Mill and check out Larry's story?"

"No, but I will make sure Larry's replacement is someone I can completely depend on, someone who won't crack under pressure. As the renovation manager, he'll have free access to all areas of the Mill. He'll check out Larry's story; if Larry wasn't straight with me, he will find what we are looking for. In any case, let's talk about money. How are you doing raising your share of the down payment? Hopefully, things will happen fast after Tina kills Davidson."

The Director replied, "Already have it."

The Senator replied, "I am not independently wealthy like Mr. corporate guy here, but I've arranged loans from a couple of my campaign contributors for the full amount and will have the cash in a couple of weeks."

"The Putnam Group, LLC is deep in debt and hemorrhaging cash. They already owe close to $15 or $20 million, and they are burning through cash like a brush fire. Connecticut's governor wants to help them out with a large grant. If it passes, it'll give them some breathing room. Governments tend to move slowly. Hopefully, getting the approved grant won't happen before we buy the Mill."

The Senator said, "I should be able to slow it down or even stop the grant. I know how to put obstacles in the way, and I know how to remove obstacles. The grant will not be a problem."

"Are there any other buyers interested?"

"Larry has shared the condition of the Mill with me. There is a lot of lead paint, mold, mildew, crumbling concrete, and structural problems that will scare potential buyers away. We will have plenty of money for the remediation and repairs."

The Senator caught the Director's attention and asked, "What was it like being in prison? I heard you were in for about a year for some white-collar crime."

"I'll be happy to tell you the whole story since we're in this together and have already paid for one murder and are about to commit another. I was working for a product manager who played fast and loose with some federal regulations, and I got involved. It came to light a few years later. I had moved up in the company by then and had some money. The federal government didn't want the public to know how I beat their regulations, so they let me plead to a lesser charge and sentenced me to a year in prison. I only had to serve six months, and they agreed to expunge my record."

The Senator interrupted, "That explains how you landed your current job. I would have thought that no one would hire you if your employers knew you were in prison."

"I don't think it would have made a difference. I was Director level, and experienced executives are hard to find. You asked me what it was like being in prison. I pleaded to a white-collar crime and went to a prison built for white-collar criminals, for nonviolent criminals. I nevertheless hated it every day for six months. It'll be a lot different if we go up for murder. We will live with hardened criminals who will hate us from the day we arrive until the day we die. And we will likely die in prison."

"Enough," Said the Instigator, "We'd best stay alert and not make any mistakes. Meeting adjourned."

After the call ended, the instigator poured himself a Macallan and thought about the events in his life that turned him into a murderer.

Bobby and Amanda, always Bobby when his thoughts involved his beloved Amanda. They had first met when they were eight years old, and although it is hard to believe, they had known that they would be together for the rest of their lives. They managed to stay together throughout elementary school and even throughout high school. Their teenage years were difficult because they wanted to remain virgins, and they did. They both attended and graduated from Boston College. However, when they graduated, they were no longer virgins.

Bobby, he now preferred Robert professionally, earned an engineering degree and Amanda earned a BS in accounting. Both landed jobs at a large Massachusetts Construction Company headquartered in Worcester, Massachusetts. Their life plan was on track.

Their first year after graduation flew by. They had little downtime between working extra hours and buying items for their new life. One

Sunday, they decided to look for a new apartment in a recently renovated old mill building. Amanda, who was excited, walked about ten feet in front of Robert, who was checking out the construction details. Robert noticed a stack of drywall panels leaning against a wall next to Amanda just as the floor beneath her feet settled about six inches. The heavy sheets of drywall fell and hit Amanda on her right side, crushing both legs. Robert could only watch in horror as the love of his life lay on the floor, crushed under the weight of the fourteen sheets of drywall. She looked as if she were dead.

Robert's cell buzzed and he returned to the present. It was the Senator. "I just talked to you."

The Senator replied, "I just want to be on the record. I think Mr. Director has an agenda that is different from ours. He has something up his sleeve."

"Like what exactly?"

"I don't know. Just keep your eyes open." The Senator clicked off.

Chapter 16

Kathryn and Tina spent the beautiful Maine morning, as they did most mornings recently, at the Wells gun range. Kathryn was no longer a novice with a gun. She was a quick learner and had rapidly become more than proficient. Tina saw in Kathryn a younger version of herself. She had excellent hand-eye coordination, intense focus, and a drive to learn everything that she could to become a top hitman. Tina intended to teach her how to plan for a hit, to protect her identity, and to disguise herself so that she would not be memorable, even if several people saw her: essentially how to become invisible. They were also working on setting up their new life should events get at cross-purposes with Tina's control organization.

Should they become targets instead of hunters, they could quickly move to new locations and still leave a literal fortune in their offshore accounts. They had chosen three different areas where they could start their new lives. They set up new bank accounts, which contained enough money to live under the radar for three years. Both women preferred to stay in Ogunquit, but sometimes life does not work out as intended.

Tina's phone rang, and she knew at once who was calling. Turning to Kathryn, who was reloading a magazine, she said, "I'll talk to him later, after we have lunch in town and sit on the beach for a while. I want to enjoy our day, and he will only ruin it."

"Does it mean a job?"

"It's the instigator for the Cargill Falls contract. Remember, he told me he needed another hit. Well, it looks like he's ready to move. It'll mean another fifty grand plus expenses. I'll call him when we get home, then fill you in on the details."

"Can I go with you? I'm ready and want to help."

Tina looked down for a moment, then slowly looked up at Kathryn. Kathryn interpreted the look in Tina's eyes and the set of her lips as love mixed with lust. The longer she and Kathryn were together, the more Tina's love deepened, and as their passion grew, the more heated their lovemaking became. After a full minute of gazing at Kathryn, Tina finally responded, "Yes. You know your way around guns and are an excellent shot. When we get home, I'll show you how to protect your identity and stay off the police radar."

They walked along the Marginal Way, hand in hand, to their home. Kathryn relaxed in the living room while Tina went into their bedroom and talked to the Instigator. Thirty minutes later, Tina returned to the living room with an ear-to-ear grin and said, "Let's get to work. We have a complicated kill to plan, and I want to get to bed early because I'm horny. I want you tonight. The target is a man named Larry Davidson and the Instigator assures me he will provide us a lot of info and make our work easier. But first things first however."

"I'm excited, both for what is going to happen tonight and for my first mission. First kill."

"Before we do anything else, I want to show you how I protect our identities while we're doing the job in case we're pulled over for any reason." Tina beckoned Kathryn towards the door. "Let's go into the garage. Here's the combination to the safe. When we get there, I want you to open it."

A few moments later, Kathryn entered the combination and gently pulled open the safe door. The safe held what Kathryn thought was normal for a person of means. A pile of cash sat on one shelf, which Tina said amounted to fifty thousand dollars. The other shelves held mortgage and banking information, personal correspondence, and assorted items, all of a personal nature. Kathryn frowned and said, "I don't understand, the contents are what I would expect…, it's all normal. I don't see how any of this can protect us."

Tina closed the safe door and said, "Here's the combination; go ahead and open the safe again."

Kathryn didn't understand, but said, "Okay." As she started to enter the combination, she abruptly stopped and said, "This isn't the right combination."

Tina smiled and replied. "You have a good memory. Try it and see what happens. Then we'll talk."

When Kathryn pulled the door open, what she saw was entirely different. The shelves were full of unusual items: stacks of license plates, a large amount of ammunition, a variety of pistols – both semi-automatic and full-automatic, an Uzi, and assorted long guns. When Kathryn looked more closely, she saw a stack of driver's licenses and automobile titles. She also saw several passports, and a large pile of cash, which Tina said amounted to over half a million dollars.

Tina continued. "Now let me explain. The tan mid-size SUV in the garage is special, and I use it exclusively to get to jobs, as we will for this job. It has padded compartments to carry both semi-automatic pistols and full-automatic pistols, the Uzi, and one long gun. All stored under panels covering the inside and attached to the under carriage. I have registration documents for the SUV in Vermont, New Hampshire, and Massachusetts. I have a set of license plates for each registration. I also have a driver's license with my picture and an address corresponding to each registration. The address for each state registration is legit, and I own each property, which is no more than an empty lot. Finally, suppose somehow the police trace us back to this house and get a search warrant. In that case, I'll fully cooperate and open the safe with the first combination. Are you with me so far?"

"Yes. So, we'll choose a state and make sure we put the right plates on the SUV, and you'll carry the identification. But what about me?"

"Yes, what about you. Do you remember the head shot I took of you with my Nikon SLR? I took it to my man in Boston, who created the phony documents for me and all the town mobsters and had a new ID created for you. You are my black-haired daughter. I also have IDs for you as a blond and a brunette with addresses corresponding to car registrations. So, you are all set. We will travel as mother and daughter."

"Hold on. How could you register the same car three times? The Vin number would make that impossible. Don't they check?"

"Actually, its four times. It's also registered here. Of course, I used the actual Vin to register it here. The company manufactured over one hundred thousand copies of this model SUV. It was simple to get Vin numbers from junked cars and use them on the application for plates. The DMV clerks never go to the car to check the Vin. They take the numbers you give them, and if the computer doesn't kick it out, you get your plates."

Tina nodded, as if satisfied with her explanation. She then added, "Next, we have to open the preformatted spreadsheet and start compiling a to-do list and a list of materials we'll need. Then, we plan the kill step by step. The Instigator wants certain conditions met and the job done in the next three weeks. It's normal to get specific instructions that we have to meet, and our planning has to consider the entirety of the instructions."

Kathryn retrieved the laptop and returned it to the dining room. She booted it up and opened the spreadsheet and familiarized herself with it. With her fingers poised over the keys, she said, "Fire away."

"Jot down a couple of obvious things first. Like my last hit, this job is in northeast Connecticut, and I stayed in the town of Thompson, so we shouldn't stay there again. You need to find a place to stay in Pomfret or Killingly, but not at an Airbnb. This hit mustn't be in the Mill building, and the intelligence I received from the Instigator was that the target plays Pitch on Tuesday nights after work until about nine o'clock."

"What the hell is Pitch?"

"Pitch is a trick-taking card game popular in England and the American colonies of New England during the Pre-Revolutionary period. It is still popular in New England. Anyway, he plays at the Cargill Falls Elks Club. Get on Google Maps and scout the location of the Elks and find a place where we can stakeout the building. According to the Instigator, he's staying in a rented condominium in Webster Massachusetts, and it's not a good place for a hit. We'll follow him from the Elks and hope he stops someplace on the way home. If not, we might have to kill him as he leaves the building or at his condominium. It's not ideal, but it might be necessary. In the meantime, I'm going to check out our guns. I'm thinking of silenced pistols. While I'm gone, print out maps of the area, that we can use to follow him. They should give us a wider view of area roads then we'd get on GPS. And they'll come in handy if we have an issue."

Kathryn printed four maps. The first was an overview of the Town of Cargill Falls and a part of Webster, Mass, including the target's condominium. The overview map also included the part of Thompson that they would pass through on the way to Webster. She also printed detailed maps of the area around the Elks Club, the targets condominium, and the old Mill building.

Tina returned momentarily. "Did you get the maps printed?"

"Yes." Kathryn showed Tina the four maps. "Did you decide on the guns we'll use?"

"Good work on the maps. I did decide. We'll use the Beretta M9A3. It's a 9mm handgun that holds a 17-round clip plus one in the chamber. It's suppressor ready. I have one for each of us and a hiding spot where they fit in the SUV. We won't drive more than three miles-per-hour over the speed limit to keep the cops away. There are a couple of things you'll need to take care of before we leave: you'll need to dye your hair and eyebrows black and hide those large, fabulous boobs."

"As long as I don't have to hide them from you."

"When we're alone, you can let those puppies free."

"I'm ready to do just that."

"Me too, but I want to go over the plan again. You'll reserve a room for us at a hotel in Pomfret or Killingly and do it as mother and daughter. You'll get your hair and eyebrows dyed black, and I'll do the same. After all, I am your mother for the duration. You'll figure out a comfortable way to corral your puppies. I don't have that problem. How unfortunate for you."

Tina continued, "Now back to work. I'll ensure the Berettas are well-oiled and reliable. We don't want a misfire. We'll stakeout the Elks Club on the first Tuesday, follow the target to his condo, and decide the best place for the kill. We'll be ready to act if he stops someplace on his route home that looks like a possibility. The Instigator doesn't want the kill connected to the Mill, which makes killing a bystander a possibility. I want you to be ready for that possibility and not freeze. Could you kill a bystander if the opportunity presented itself?"

"Yes, I think, I don't know. I guess I am just not sure." Kathryn was obviously concerned.

"Don't worry. One of us will do it if it becomes necessary." Tina said. She respected Kathryn's feelings and would handle it.

"We haven't planned the hit in detail yet. When do you want to do it?" Kathryn said, wanting to change the subject.

"No need to worry. We'll have plenty of time to plan as we drive to Connecticut and at night in our room. Let's spend the next couple of hours enjoying each other."

Chapter 17

When Noelle split up the group's information-reviewing responsibilities, Jim and Mary Ann received the Putnam Family records relating to the Mill. Phil and Rose received the information relating to the family itself. Both couples started reading. Their goals were the same, look for anything, no matter how insignificant it appeared, that might be a motive for murder.

Mike and Tess, on the other hand, received the drive that contained all the architectural information and various drawings. The assumption was that Mike's knowledge and experience with repairing buildings would increase the probability of finding anything that was amiss.

Phil and Rose divided their job by date, Rose reviewing the 1900s and Phil the 1800s. They read the documents every chance they had and wrote detailed summaries of the content. Jim and Mary Ann took a similar approach, Jim carrying most of the load. Mary Ann had decided to keep her job until they moved to Connecticut.

Mike and Tess chose to have Mike review all the architectural information and drawings, while Tess would transfer anything he found to a spreadsheet. They would then review and refine their notes. Different owners had made so many modifications and additions to the Mill that it was almost impossible to make sense of the drawings.

Because she had time to review it, Noelle kept copies of everything. She considered the Putnam Family information a boon to her role as the northeast Connecticut historian. The older documents would be especially valuable.

At first, the information on the thumb drives was more confusing than helpful. Then the more the couples read and the more they talked to each other, the more connections started forming. When Jim and Phil spoke on the phone, they began to piece together the history of the Mill. Rose would add details that Phil had overlooked, and Mary Ann would interject with information that Jim had missed. Mike and Tess worked hard to sort out a complicated tangle of changes to the building. The 1800s were particularly complex.

To speed up the process, the unofficial investigators met at Piccolo Sicilia in Oyster Bay. Even though the Hines' were the only ones from Long Island, everyone wanted to experience the food at Piccolo Sicilia. They reserved a table for eight at two in the afternoon, hoping to miss the lunch rush. They had one drink at the bar before the host seated them promptly at two o'clock, and then ordered a second drink when seated.

"Jim, I know you've eaten here, but Phil's the Italian, and I want his opinion on what's good, not yours," Mike joked.

"Hell, I can't even pronounce this stuff," Jim replied, grinning. "But I can definitely eat it."

"I'll order two tasting boards and some antipasti for the table, but I'll only consult on lunch," Phil added.

When their server delivered their drinks, Phil ordered Two boards, one featuring Prosciutto di Parma, Parmigiano-Reggiano, and Castelvetrano Olive, and one featuring Sopressata, Pecorino Toscano, and Cerignola Olive. He also ordered four plates of calamari rings fried with hot cherry peppers and served with a side of pepperoncini aioli, and an extra-large meatball, made from ground sirloin, veal, and pork, and topped with San Marzano marinara and ricotta cheese. It was garnished with Parmigiano-Reggiano cheese and fresh basil. Satisfied with his selections, Phil responded to Mike's request. "Now, for the main course, I suggest you decide if you want Pasta, Pollo, Carni, or Pesce, and I'll make a recommendation for you," he said.

The "Old Mill Investigators," a name they had all agreed on earlier, ordered two Gnocchi Alforno, which included homemade potato and ricotta dumplings baked in terracotta with a pink pomodoro sauce, Parmigiano-Reggiano, fresh mozzarella and basil. They added one Tagliatelle alla Bolognese: delicate golden noodles tossed with a genuinely classic Bolognese sauce made with pork, pancetta, sirloin, diced vegetables, tomatoes and a touch of cream, then topped with Parmigiano-Reggiano cheese. They also included three Gamberi con Timo, each of which came with four jumbo shrimp sautéed with garlic, vegetable purée, and fresh thyme leaves, served over a bed of creamy Parmigiano-Reggiano risotto. Their last request was one Brasato, a 12 oz. boneless beef short rib braised with garlic, tomato, vegetables, wine, and stock, served over Parmigiano-Reggiano risotto.

While waiting for the food, Noelle, the chosen leader for today's meeting, explained the agenda for the day and asked Phil and Rose to tell the group what they had found in their documents. Just as they started, their meals arrived, and the Old Mill Investigators agreed to eat first, then talk. The talking stopped, and the only sounds emanating from the table were people enjoying their meals.

After they all finished, Noelle asked Karen Parisi to update the group on the status of the state police investigation. Karen mentioned that she had received a text during her lunch break and had news.

"It's not much. The police have concluded that the Mill owners are no longer suspects and, as of last night, have no possible suspects. The police brass has officially suspended the investigation until they develop a lead to follow. My contact told me, and this will not surprise any of us, that they need a motive. The only conclusion they feel sure of is that a hired professional did the hit. And since pros don't come cheap, the motive involves money. I'll stay in touch with Connecticut and let you know if something breaks," Karen concluded.

Rose started speaking. "Phil and I have less than Karen. The Putnam Family supplied very personal family information pre-1940. I guess they figured the family members mentioned were dead or dying. Other than normal family matters, there wasn't much of interest to us in the information, except during the period after the Civil War through 1900. The amount of family conflict and intrigue increased dramatically. Family members disagreed constantly: usually about money, but nothing stood out. We noted numerous individual events from the documents. We summarized the information, but other than the post-Civil War period in the late 1800s, nothing stands out. Phil, would you hand out the summaries?"

Jim went next. "Our results were basically the same as the Messinas'. The Mill grew or changed constantly. The period at the end of the 1800s was particularly active. The difference was that the activity was not well-documented, and we couldn't make sense of some of the changes. We hope that Mike and Tess can help us understand."

Mike promptly replied, "I'm afraid we did not find anything that would help us determine a motive. What we did find, though, were numerous blueprints for various changes to the building that looked wrong. I think the Mill management intentionally messed up the blueprints to hide something or confuse someone looking to find something. I can't be sure of anything until I look at the building, especially the basement. Until I do, I have nothing."

They moved the meeting to Jim and Mary Ann's home and hung around until after rush hour. The five New Englanders left in Mike's large SUV, feeling that they had made little progress. Noelle gave the group hope by reminding them that she had not met Elijah Putnam yet. The old man could have some information that would help them.

Chapter 18

Larry Davidson was home for the evening, relaxing before another day of work. He had been much less anxious recently; his "business partner" had been less antagonistic and seemed more comfortable with him. They had talked pleasantly about Larry's discovery and the next steps they would take, and they talked about the problems in the old Mill. It was still too early to undo the steps he had taken to protect himself, but he would wait and see. He concluded that he was probably just being paranoid.

Larry put those thoughts aside for another time. Tomorrow night after work, he would play Pitch with the guys at the Elks. He always had an enjoyable time and stayed just sober enough to drive home. Larry smiled to himself as he headed to bed. *Friday night I have a hot date. Life is good.*

Tina and Kathryn were on their way to Connecticut, and they expected to check into the Holiday Inn in Killingly around noon. They planned to set up surveillance at the Cargill Falls Elks Lodge at seven that evening, giving them time to rethink every detail of the operation and ensure success.

"I think we should wear loose fitting jeans and oversized sweatshirts. On top of that, we should wear plain jackets and baseball hats with our hair tucked into them. The jackets are blousy enough to conceal our weapons. For shoes, we should go with plain white sneakers, which aren't particularly expensive or noticeable. What do you think?"

Kathryn replied, "Perfect. If a surveillance camera catches our images, no one will tell whether we're male or female. It works for me."

"The plan for tonight is simple. We'll wait outside of the Elks club, in their parking lot, for Larry to drive home and follow him. Our aim will be to gather information, but if we see an opportunity to finish the contract, we'll take it. If we see an opportunity to hit the target, we'll quickly assess the situation and only act if we won't put ourselves at risk. I know we'll have changed our appearances, but we have to remember there are cameras everywhere. Also, I think Larry will be a little tipsy, so his reactions will be slower. He drives a red Ford Edge, a small SUV, which should be easy to follow even at night."

"I think we have tonight covered. I'll visualize the operation this afternoon at the motel, and we can go over it again while we're on stakeout."

"Sounds like a plan," Tina said.

The first thing Larry Davidson did when he arrived at the Elks was order a draft beer and drink it in one swallow. The second thing he did was order another. The day had been full of problems and Larry was exhausted, but he was looking forward to a game of Pitch, a couple of beers, and good non-work-related conversations with his friends.

Larry and his friends played Pitch until eight o'clock, when he decided that he was too tired to continue. Larry told his fellow Pitch players that he would skip playing until next Tuesday because he needed rest. As he was leaving, however, a teammate said that there was a Pitch tournament on Friday and that the team was short one player, then asked if he was interested. After determining that it would be after his date, Larry said yes, and his Friday evening was full.

As he walked to his car, Larry noticed a tan SUV in the lot with out-of-state plates. He wasn't sure why it caught his attention, but it did. Maybe it was because he thought he saw movement in the car, but he was tired and in no mood to investigate. *Am I becoming paranoid again? Eh, I'll worry about it tomorrow.*

"Shit, he saw us! What do we do now?" Kathryn stuttered, flustered.

"Don't worry, he probably saw some movement or noticed the out-of-state plates. Either way, there's nothing to worry about," Tina said calmly, as putting her car in gear and followed Larry.

"Sorry, I panicked. I don't want to get caught."

"No problem. Now get to work and keep your eyes on the maps. We don't know his route home." Tina wanted to calm Kathryn down. She was not panicked, but she was worried enough about what Larry may have seen to do everything possible to complete the contract tonight.

Larry intended to go straight home. He called Mae and confirmed their Friday night date, told her how much he missed her and said that he was looking forward to Friday night. Mae said that she missed him, and that time would pass slowly until she was at his side. Hearing Mae's voice stirred his emotions, but all Larry wanted that night was to crawl into bed alone.

Larry took the backroads home and stayed off of I-395 to avoid the police. He had realized that he had too much to drink and did not want a DUI on his record.

Tina followed Larry as he drove down Edmund Street toward Grove Street. He surprised Kathryn when he turned right onto Grove Street instead of turning left toward the entrance ramp to I-395, the fastest route to his home. He drove into Cargill Falls, then onto Bridge Street, heading to Woodstock. They followed him past the Woodstock Fairgrounds, then onto Route 169 until Larry turned right onto Route 197 in north Woodstock.

Larry, with Tina and Kathryn tracking, drove through Dudley Massachusetts into the town of Webster via Route 197. Just before entering Webster, he was almost sure that he saw the same SUV that had been sitting in the Elks parking lot. Almost sure. He dismissed it. When he was passing through Woodstock, it was so dark that he only saw headlights following his car. And when he was driving through Dudley and into Webster, the car was too far behind for him to make out its features.

Tina stayed far behind Larry as he traveled on Main Street through the town of Webster. He continued it went under I-395 until he turned right onto "Arthur J. Remillard Jr. Way" and parked at his waterfront condominium. Tina continued driving until about a quarter mile from the target's condominium. She and Kathryn thought it best to give Larry time to get into his condominium before they headed back.

Larry would live another day.

Immediately after merging back onto, I-395 South, Tina called the Instigator. "He's still alive. We had no opportunity to complete the contract. We need info about his life after work. What does he do? Does he have a love life?"

The Instigator was quiet for a few minutes before saying, "I'll have to ask around. Give me a day or two. I'll call you."

For two days and two nights, Tina and Kathryn lazed around their hotel room. The Instigator had not called, and they became more frustrated by the minute. Tina feared that something had happened, like Larry panicking and calling the police, or worse, the FBI. Tonight, she would take Kathryn out for a late dinner, thinking that the restaurants in the area would not have many customers late on a Thursday night.

Tina and Kathryn had a delicious dinner at ANYA Restaurant in the town of Thompson, outside of Cargill

Falls. There were only four other diners in the restaurant, and they were at a table on the other side of the room. Though both women tried to relax, they could not totally control their feeling that something was wrong, and that the hit would not happen. Then Tina's phone vibrated. It was the Instigator.

By the time she disconnected the call, Tina had a wicked look on her face. "It's on for tomorrow night. The Instigator delivered. I'll fill you in when we get back to the room. Let's enjoy a drink before we leave." After sipping on one of ANYA's signature cocktails, they returned to the Holiday Inn.

Tina and Kathryn changed into their comfortable clothes before discussing the Instigator's information. Kathryn prepared two cups of tea while Tina took a moment to collect her thoughts. After several sips of tea Tina took a deep breath and began speaking. "The Instigator wasn't 100% sure of his info, but overall, believes it's worth pursuing. He wouldn't tell me his source, but I think we should follow up."

"We have nothing to lose and nothing else to do. So, why not?" said Kathryn.

"I feel the same, let's go over the Instigator's information in detail. Larry has been seeing a woman in the area and the relationship has become serious, and that he plans to see her tomorrow night after he plays in a Pitch tournament. She works at the Extra Mart on Route 12 in Thompson. Her shift ends at 9:30 PM. If the info is solid, we know Larry will be at the Elks after work, and we know he'll be meeting his girlfriend at the Thompson gas station.

We'll go out tomorrow, check the locations, and plan the Friday night hit in detail."

Friday started with a quick breakfast in the hotel dining area, then the two women showered and dressed for what they both hoped would be a successful day. They left the hotel and drove to the Thompson Extra Mart to buy gas and snacks, all paid for inside at the cash register. Before making their purchase, they slowly walked around as if to find the snacks they wanted, but in fact, they were checking out the store in preparation for the hit. Tina concluded that the one camera in the store was a dummy, and they could hit Larry without worrying about being seen.

Next, they drove around Cargill Falls and committed the roads and landmarks to memory. Their plan was simple: follow Larry from the Elks until he stops at the gas station, the preferred killing ground for Larry and his girlfriend. If that part of the plan failed, they would stay on Larry's tail.

Like clockwork, Larry exited the Elks and walked to his car. He had a spring in his step. Tina followed again and hoped that this time she knew his destination. Larry turned left onto Grove Street, then turned onto the entrance ramp for I-395 north, and Kathryn breathed a sigh of relief. She had expected Larry to do just that. Now, if he were to exit left onto the second ramp, their predictions would be confirmed.

Sure enough, Larry took the left exit. Tina slowed down and let him get farther ahead. The Extra Mart was about a mile north on Route 12 on the left-hand side. Tina drove past the station and, after seeing Larry's car in the parking lot, executed a U-turn and parked on the road just north of the store. The women exited their vehicle and walked toward the store.

On entering the Extra Mart, Kathryn walked to the shelving area and Tina walked past the counter where Larry and his date were talking. Tina slowly made her way to the back of the store where Kathryn was faux shopping. Tina whispered, "Her shift relief is running late and won't be here for twenty minutes. Now's the time. Remember, we want this to look like a robbery committed by amateurs, not professionals. So, you put three in the girlfriend's torso and one in the head. I'll take care of Larry… arm, leg, and head, maybe one to the heart if I need it. We empty the register and leave."

Larry and Mae were still talking when Mae looked up and got ready to cash out a customer. Larry heard a loud spit and saw Mae move backward. In the same instant, he felt a severe burning sensation in his left arm. Mae's body shook again, and Larry felt his chest open and blood rush out. Mae dropped to the floor and Larry's world went dark. Neither felt the next bullets that entered their bodies. Beautiful Mae died moments later, ending her days on earth at 9,277. Larry was the only living person to know the precise location of the Mill's treasure room, ending his days on this earth at 11,981.

The killers cleaned out the register, picked up all the cartridges, and casually strolled to their car and drove to the motel. They would check out of the motel after breakfast and return to Ogunquit. The only remaining tasks were to dispose of the guns and their clothing.

Twenty-three minutes after the murders, Jane, who was late for work as usual, entered the store. She spouted apologies until she saw the bodies and blood and threw up. Then she dialed 911.

Chapter 19

Noelle did not sleep well before meeting with the patriarch of the Putnam Family. Her pending conversation with him and his brother concerned her. She had never met either man, or did she know how to approach the subject of their treasure-hunting ancestor. Noelle believed that in the six hours before the meeting, she would produce the answer. While she made her breakfast, she listened to WINY. She loved to hear Harry O's voice deliver the news. Just then, Harry O's news report took on an urgent tone. His voice cracked as he said, "Robbers killed two people at the Thompson Extra Mart last night and escaped with cash and merchandise. Jane Jackson, a store clerk, found the bodies about ten minutes before ten, when she reported for work twenty minutes late for her shift. The State Police identified the murder victims as Mae Lamphere of Thompson, who was the store clerk on duty, and Larry Davidson of Webster, Massachusetts. Mr. Davidson was employed as the renovation manager at the Pomfret Cotton Mill. The police believe Lamphere and Davidson were in a relationship."

Harry O wrapped up his report with, "The police have nothing else to report this early in the investigation. Personally, last night's events baffled me. After years without violent crime in northeast Connecticut, we now have a virtual crime wave. I will bring you more news about the Extra Mart murders as it becomes available."

Noelle cried. Although she had not met either victim, she cried for them. But she really cried for the Quiet Corner, her home. She cried because she believed her home would never be the same. Noelle dried her eyes, called Phil, and left a message.

Phil heard the report on WINY and immediately called Jim, then filled him in on the events. Jim would wait for the Connecticut State Police to gather facts and then have Parisi follow up with her contact.

The caller ID on her phone read Elijah Putnam, so Noelle answered. "Hello."

"Ms. Lefevre, I am Carlton, Mr. Putnam's chauffeur. Mr. Putnam asked that I drive you to lunch. Is eleven-thirty acceptable?"

Noelle was shocked by the offer and replied, "That's unnecessary. I can drive myself."

"I am afraid that Mr. Putnam insists."

Noelle was about to argue, then thought that she might as well enjoy herself. "Okay. I'll be ready at eleven-thirty."

Wanting to dress appropriately for the lunch, she wore a form-fitting, designer blue dress, and broke out her best diamond jewelry. When she opened her front door, she stared at the Cadillac Limousine and at Carlton, decked out in full chauffeur regalia, holding the rear door open. She walked to the car. "Good morning, Carlton. Beautiful day, is it not?"

"Indeed, it is. There are refreshments in the refrigerator. Enjoy the ride."

Upon their arrival at the Putnam mansion, Carlton opened the car door for Noelle and then directed her to the front entrance. The exquisitely crafted mahogany double-door entryway exhibited cherubs and angels carved by an old-world craftsman. As Noelle approached the mansion, the right-side door opened to reveal a man dressed in a tuxedo. His left arm bent ninety degrees at the elbow with a folded cloth draped over his forearm.

"Welcome, Ms. Lefevre. If you follow me, I will lead you to the dining room where the staff will serve lunch. Right this way, please."

The interior of the mansion was almost exactly what Noelle had visualized. Dark, stained mahogany walls and parquet floors were coupled with towering fourteen-foot-high ceilings. Original artwork adorned the walls. The rooms were full of beautiful Victorian era couches, chairs and marble-top tables, contributing to the overall opulence. When Noelle entered the dining room, both Putnam brothers were standing. They looked in good health. In fact, they looked much younger than their actual ages. Elijah was ninety-two and Nathen was in his late eighties. Both brothers appeared fit.

Elijah walked toward Noelle, extending his hand to shake hers. He said, "I hope you like steak. We are a meat and potatoes family. I assure you that the steak will be among the best you have ever had."

"I love a good steak."

"Too bad I am not forty years younger. We would have made a great couple."

"I think we just might have," replied Noelle, smiling.

Nathan jumped into the conversation. "Watch out! He may be an old man, but he has the mind of a young man. And you are quite the fox."

"Now, gentlemen, I'm flattered, but I am here on a mission, and I am very focused on getting it done."

"We're just teasing. I guess you don't have a grandfather complex. James, please serve lunch. Noelle, this is your seat. Nathan and I have our everyday places. Again, please know that we were only playing and meant no disrespect."

Noelle typically would have been concerned that she put a damper on the meeting, but the brothers acted as if they took no offense. The staff served lunch right after they sat down, and it looked fabulous. Noelle turned toward the brothers and said, "I want to tell you why I'm here, but I would rather dive into lunch first."

The steak, potatoes, and string beans were all perfectly cooked, and all three diners seemed to enjoy the meal. A waiter stood behind each of the three as they ate, waiting to take care of their every need. That impressed Noelle immensely. Noelle was also impressed that there were still people who could afford to live this way. As a historian, Noelle had read about the golden age and the lifestyles of the upper class. Today, she lived it. She thought that she could get used to this kind of life.

During lunch, the three chatted about the towns in northeast Connecticut and the linear park, and mostly stuck to small talk. The Putnam brothers learned about Noelle, and Noelle learned about the Putnam brothers. The Mill, the main reason for the meeting, did not enter into the conversation until after lunch.

Before the staff served dessert, Noelle asked, "Did you hear about the murders at the Thompson Extra Mart?"

Both brothers said simultaneously, "No, what the hell happened?"

Noelle told them what she knew from the WINY reports, highlighting the fact that the male victim was managing the renovation project at the old Mill. She wondered aloud if the murders had anything to do with Bob Martineau's murder. After discussing possible connections to Martineau with the Putnam brothers, she realized that they did not have enough facts.

Noelle decided it was time to get to the main reason for the luncheon. She leaned over the table and said, "I have joined with three couples and a Long Island police detective interested in solving Martineau's murder, or at least in helping the State Police solve the murder. Jim Hines and Phil Messina solved the Purity Pharma murders about five years ago. The Robertsons own a commercial services company and know their way around buildings and architectural drawings. And lastly, Karen Parisi, a Nassau County Police detective, has been working with the Connecticut State police and sharing information on the investigation into Martineau's murder. Jim Hines is a retired Nassau County Police Commander. Phil Messina lives in Cargill Falls and is a retired pharmaceutical executive."

"An impressive group, but I don't see a reason for their involvement. But that's not for me to judge. If they help find the killer, God bless them," Nathan said.

Noelle continued, "I met with your younger family members, and they supplied a lot of history about your extraordinary family. We have scanned documents and drawings, each of which we reviewed in detail. For the most part, they didn't shed much light on the murder. However, the information about Isaac's interest in a treasure buried during the Civil War piqued our curiosity, as did the drawings on the Mill renovations in the late 1800s. The drawings weren't specific enough to help us. I have two questions for you: are we on the right track? And do you have any information that might help?"

Nathan gave Elijah a look that said, "We have the info. It's up to you whether or not we help."

Elijah smiled knowingly and replied, "You're on the right track. We heard stories about Isaac's hunt for Confederate Major Beck's treasure when we were young men. It was my favorite family legend. There was no agreement on whether he found it and, if he did, where he hid it. Nathan and I believed the legend and wanted to find the treasure to show the rest of the family that we had value. We studied all the info on Isaac and the hunt we could get our hands on, but to no avail. We believe that if the treasure exists, we will find it in the Mill. It is our belief that Isaac stored the treasure in the Mill because a box car with four sturdy locks installed on the doors remained on the train siding at the Mill for a long time in the late 18th century. However, as I've said, we studied the info and looked all over the Mill but never found a clue. I will give you all we have on one condition. You will come to us first if you find even the slightest hint that the treasure exists."

Noelle replied, "Deal."

"Now for dessert, after which Carlton will drive you to your home. I need my afternoon nap. As does Nathan."

Jim had arranged a Zoom call with the other members of "The Old Mill Investigators" at seven o'clock. All the Investigators signed themselves in by seven-ten.

Once the meeting began, Jim asked Karen what she had learned. Karen had spent most of the day on and off the phone with her contact in the Connecticut State Police. Her small picture on the screen said, "CSP is leaning toward a straight-up robbery at the Thompson Extra Mart. The evidence points to amateurs who entered the store to rob it and killed the victims. They're basing their theory on a couple of facts. The perps shot the victims multiple times, and not one was an accurate kill shot. Plus, they cleaned out the cash drawer. They think there were two perps but won't know until the forensics are done. I asked if they found any shell casings, and the answer was no. The police believe they may have used a revolver. If it was a semi-automatic weapon, picking up the casings isn't an amateur move, but they might have learned that from television."

Jim replied, "We'll see. Anything else?"

"The male victim, the renovation manager for the Mill, left a card game at nine and arrived at the store twenty minutes later. He was still there after nine-thirty, which is strange until you learn he was dating the other victim."

Jim took over. "We'll wait for the forensics. Noelle, how did you make out with the Putnam brothers?"

In her tiny Zoom window, Noelle adjusted her glasses and looked down at a legal pad. "Great. I have a lot of info and old drawings, but I need Mike to analyze it before I talk to the team. Mike, I'd like for you and Tess to come to my house for lunch and discuss the drawings."

Mike and Tess both confirmed.

Jim bid everyone a farewell and waited a moment for his friends to log off. Then, he ended the call.

Chapter 20

Mike and Phil met in the parking lot of the rest area on I-295 in Rhode Island, an access point for the Blackstone Valley Bike Trail. As usual, Mike was late, and Phil killed time by biking in circles around the parking lot. Mike was late because he had a business to run, and Phil was usually early because he was retired. It didn't matter to him that Mike was late. He enjoyed the time they spent together, their conversations, the banter, the sports talk, and the political arguments.

Mike arrived about ten minutes late and quickly readied his bike and donned his biking shoes, helmet, and gloves. The entrance ramp to the bike path from the parking lot required a biker to navigate six switchbacks and a short but steep drop. The ramp was a mile-long steep downhill, and most bikers, Phil included, were on the brakes a lot. Mike, however, pedaled to gain speed. Phil had concluded after their first ride that Mike was a daredevil. Once on the bike trail, Mike would put the derailleur in the highest gear and pedal as fast as he could for the entire ride.

Phil tried to keep up with Mike on the trail, but he couldn't quite stay with him. He didn't even bother trying to keep up with Mike going downhill.

The Blackstone Valley Bike Trail is nearly 20 miles long. For most of the twenty miles, it runs along the Blackstone River. Also running along the river is the raceway that supplied power for the many old mills along the river. The scenic trail crosses and recrosses the river, offering views of waterfalls, marshes, and wildlife. The old mills lining the Blackstone River are evidence of its impact on the Industrial Revolution, when it earned the title of "the hardest-working river in America."

Mike and Phil completed the 20-mile trail in under two hours and averaged a speed of twelve point four miles per hour for the ride, stopping only once to enjoy the view. They now faced the climb back to the parking lot, and with its steep uphill slope and multiple switchbacks, it seemed virtually impossible. Phil lost sight of Mike shortly after they started the climb. When he got to the parking lot, Mike had already loaded his bike into his vehicle, taken his biking gear off, and prepared himself to leave for a burger. Phil was too tired to move.

The best burger place close to the bike trail was the Hangry Burger, aptly named for the times when you are so hungry you are angry, therefore "hangry." Any hangry visitor could stack the burgers as high as he liked and would always be content after his meal. At least, that is what the Hangry Burger advertised. Mike and Phil had eaten there before and agreed that the advertisement was accurate.

Mike ordered a double burger: two five-ounce patties covered with American cheese and all the trimmings, curly fries, and a sixteen-ounce Sam Adams. Phil also ordered a double burger, but with cheddar cheese and onion rings, and a sixteen-ounce Yuengling. With their orders placed, they started the BS part of their Burgers, Beer, and BS outing.

Mike started the BS session. "You were a little pissed at me and Jim the other day when you jumped on us and told us you're not an oppressor and don't have white privilege. Hell, Jim and I could've told you that just being white is a privilege and backed it up with real stories."

"I have no doubt. The difference is that you aren't told you have black privilege. It's expected that you had a tough life and were denied opportunities because you're black. Of course, not all black people grew up in poverty, and not all white people grew up privileged. That's the issue when you assign people to groups and label the group: you're always wrong. It's easier that way, since you don't have to think about nuance. When you see a white male, you'll assume 'privileged' or 'white supremacist' or some other derogatory term. When you see a black person, you'll assume all kinds of negative things. And they're always wrong. Whether prejudging a person or a group, you're always wrong. That's why when I walked into the room and heard the term white privilege, I just went off."

"Tell me, Mr. White Privilege. How did you have it growing up?"

"I didn't have a life of comfort and had very little in the way of material things. I grew up in a house without running hot water. We had a bathroom with only a toilet; there was no sink and no bathtub or shower. We manually fed a coal stove to heat our house and cooled it by an open window. The coal stove sat in the middle of the kitchen. All the other rooms were chilly. That said, I thought of myself as rich. I was rich in family. I had thirty-one first cousins and lots of aunts and uncles, as well as grandparents living close-by. We would get together often."

"A sad story. I almost shed a tear."

"Fuck you."

"I was kidding. Jeez, you can't take a joke. I want to talk about a couple more things."

Their burgers arrived, and they both focused on eating.

Finally, Phil said, "Okay, what else is on your mind?"

"Have you ever heard of the George Hill Challenge? It's a timed ride of five hundred feet up George Street in Worcester. George Street is an eighteen percent grade, and you do it from a standing start. I did it the last two years."

"Good for you. You don't expect me to do it, do you?"

"I was thinking you might like to try it."

"I'll work on my legs and try to lose some weight, but I can only commit to watching as you ride up George Hill."

"The Challenge is in honor of Major Taylor. He was an American bicycle racer and was the world's first black sports superstar. He was world cycling champion in 1899, American sprint champion in 1900, and set many track cycling records. He was nicknamed 'Major' in his youth and later known as 'the Worcester Whirlwind.' He had to fight prejudice just to get on the starting line."

"That was over one hundred years ago. The prejudice he had to face must have been horrendous. It's amazing he got to race, let alone become the World Cycling Champ."

"Yes, it is. Next: our annual trip to Vermont for the Burlington Bowling Tournament is in early April and Dave Evans can't make it. Are you interested?"

Just then, Phil's phone rang. He picked up and heard, "It's Jim."

"Hello, Mr. Hines. I'm with Mike. We're just finishing lunch. You're on speaker."

"Mary Ann and I are moving to Cargill Falls. We don't want to live in the old Mill and are planning to come up for two or three weeks to house hunt."

Mike winked at Phil and scoffed, "There goes the neighborhood."

"Asshole."

Phil said, "Mike, you're in good company. That's what he called me the first time we met. At least, that's what Parisi told me."

Jim's voice came over the speaker. "She did, did she? We don't want to bother you and Rose, so we're going to stay in an Airbnb in Pomfret."

"You could stay at our house."

Mike jumped in. "Or with Tess and me."

"We knew you folks would offer, but we want and need the freedom to come and go in order to manage the hunt. I'll let you know our schedule."

"You're probably right," Mike responded.

"Before I hang up, did Noelle update you further on her meeting with the Putnam brothers?"

Phil answered, "No, not since the first report. I'm sure she wants to have Mike's input, get the details right, and keep everything well-documented. Give her a few days."

"And Mike, any progress on the blueprints?"

"You're like a friggen' pit bull with this case, Jim! And no, I need to connect with Noelle to see what she has, and

I'm sure I need to get into the building and look around. Right now, I'd say that the architectural plans don't make sense. I need to be in the building with the plans to have any hope of figuring out what's where."

"Jesus. Goodbye boys, I have to go." Jim hung up.

"All you need to know about the tournament for now is that you'll share a room with me. There will be ten of us going, and we'll meet in Worcester and head north."

"Tess said you snore and you're loud. Did I draw the short straw to get you as a roommate?

"Fuck you."

Chapter 21

Mike and Tess enjoyed a delicious lunch at Noelle's and chatted about the town of Cargill Falls and the Quiet Corner of Connecticut in general. Noelle filled them in on her lunch with the Putnam brothers, focusing on the food and service. Mike said, "One day, I'd like to live like that!" and laughed. After cleaning up the dishes, they got down to the business at hand.

Noelle had received mostly hand-drawn prints from the Putnam brothers. She explained to Mike that Elijah thought the answer was in the drawings, although he had never discovered it. They all pored over the prints and looked for a solution. Did Isaac find Beck's treasure and hide it in the Mill or not?

After a few hours, Mike suddenly grabbed a drawing he had already reviewed and placed it next to the one he was working on. He studied both intently before shaking his head and muttering to himself, "It doesn't make sense, it just doesn't make sense."

Tess said, "Mikey, what doesn't make sense?"

"I think there's a hidden room in the basement of the Mill, and part of the foundation hides it. It's a secret room, a room that no one has ever found or laid eyes on. If the stories about Isaac are true, he died suddenly of a heart attack. Maybe he had the room built, hid the treasure, and then died. I need an hour or so uninterrupted to study the drawings, and maybe I'll be able to make sense of the information."

While Mike worked on the drawings, Tess and Noelle engaged in small talk. Noelle said, "I don't know much about you. Are you comfortable telling me your history?"

"Definitely, and I'd like to hear your story."

Noelle replied, "Sure."

Tess Robertson thought for a minute before starting. "Like Mike, from my youth to adulthood, I lived in Worcester. My parents, Kathleen and Malachi O'Hara, were devoutly conservative and staunchly Irish Catholic. St. Patrick's Church was the heart of Worcester's Irish community and of my family. In its tightly knit community, traditions ran deep, and my family was no exception. I was the oldest of the eight O'Hara girls. My father described me as having a fiercely independent spirit and a beautiful smile. I mentioned that only because of Mike.

"When I was nineteen, I found myself immersed in a romance that defied the norms of my upbringing. I met Mike at a local bar. He was a charming and intelligent young man, and very black. I was immediately smitten with him. He was tall, dark, and handsome, and he sported a magnificent afro. As our connection deepened, we couldn't ignore the invisible threads pulling us together.

"When I introduced Mike as my boyfriend, my parents were shocked. My parents, stubbornly adherent to their traditions, found themselves grappling with the clash between their ingrained beliefs and the love that blossomed between their oldest daughter and Mike.

"Caught between love for my family and my growing affection for Mike, the tension at home grew. The evening dinners became silent battlegrounds, where unspoken words hung in the air. Despite the disapproval around me, I refused to let go of the man I loved.

"Things started to change during the Saint Patrick's Christmas Bazaar, a time when my family celebrated their unity and faith. Torn between my loyalty to the family and my love for Mike, I decided to take him to the Bazaar. As we strolled hand in hand through the festivities, whispers followed us like shadows.

"In a moment of courage, I decided to address the elephant in the room. With my family and seemingly the entire Irish Community watching, I stood up and spoke about the power of love and acceptance. My words echoed through the crowd, challenging the prejudices that had silently thrived in their community.

"My family, initially stunned, felt a collective shift. My parents, torn between their conservative values and the love for their daughter, began to see my strength and conviction. Slowly, they started to reevaluate their preconceived notions.

"My love for Mike became a catalyst for change. As the seasons changed, so did the hearts of the people. The O'Hara family, once divided, found a way to bridge the gap between tradition and acceptance, realizing that love could be a powerful force for transformation.

"My father said I was courageous, and my speech didn't just break down barriers; it paved the way for a more inclusive and understanding family, where reason triumphed over prejudice. My father accepted Mike and the more he got to know him, the more he liked him. Now, Mike is his favorite son-in-law and the first call he makes when he needs help."

Noelle reacted, "That's one hell of a story. And judging by the way you and Mike treat each other, it's a story with a happy ending. Unfortunately, my story doesn't end as happily for me and my husband. Don't get me wrong; I'm happy, but I miss him every day."

"I'm sorry. If you'd rather not tell me, I understand."

Noelle, lost in thought, said after a minute or two, "I'm fine. I just like thinking about Earl. I'm good to go. Like you, I'm from a large family, but unlike you, my father abandoned the family after his sixth child was born. I was an excellent athlete when I was young and parlayed that into scholarships at the best high schools in the area. I was outstanding at baseball and basketball; my basketball skills secured me a scholarship at UConn. Earl was a hockey player at UConn. It's where we met. I studied history and Earl studied business.

"We dated in college and for a little while afterward, then we married. Earl worked for a major insurance company with offices in Hartford and I taught high school history to juniors and seniors. Our lives were idyllic. Eventually we had two children and settled on a lake in Thompson where we looked forward to raising our family. Earl used the lake house as home base, but his job required him to travel fifty percent of the time. I taught at a high school in Thompson, close to the lake. When our kids were in their teens, Earl was on his way home from a business trip on Christmas Eve. He was traveling east on Rt. 44 when a FedEx truck crossed into his lane and hit him head-on. He died from his injuries on my birthday, Christmas Day, at Day Kimball Hospital.

"We received a good settlement from FedEx and have survived very nicely financially. The kids were able to afford college, and I was able to quit my teaching job and start a small genealogy business. In my spare time I study the history of the Quiet Corner. I love my life and hate what propelled me here. I just want Earl back."

Tess asked, "Are you named Noelle because you were born on Christmas Day, and is Lefevre your Maiden name?"

"Noelle and Christmas go together, so my mother named me after something related to the holiday. My Maiden name is Kitka. I kept Earl's name because I knew I'd never remarry. I just can't see myself in a relationship again."

"You're one strong woman."

"Thanks. I think it's time to see how Mike is doing."

Tess walked into the room where Mike was working and asked, "Any progress?"

"Yes. I've learned I don't know enough about the Mill. I have ideas and theories, but nothing for sure… and I don't even know whether, if I had access to the Mill, I could even find the room that I believe is there. I want to assemble the

Old Mill Investigators and talk about the room, the possibility of what might be in it, and decide what we'll do.

Noelle added, "And we'd best do it fast. Remember, we've heard there's another offer on the Mill."

Chapter 22

Kathryn was lying in bed, already awake, when Tina stirred. Kathryn rolled onto her side and smiled as Tina struggled to fully wake up. "Come on sleepyhead, rise and shine!" she exclaimed, lightheartedly shaking Tina's shoulder.

"Let's just lay here a while and talk. Okay," Tina replied, yawning.

"Sure. I wanted to talk about our last kill. I feel like we're free and clear. It's been a while and the police have shown no interest in us."

"I hear they're not connecting it to the Mill, but it's being treated as a robbery instead."

"The perfect crime."

Despite the sleep in her eyes, Tina scowled. "Don't get too sure of yourself. If you think you can commit the perfect crime, you'll get sloppy in your planning and execution."

"So, you don't believe the perfect crime can happen?"

"No, I don't. A few years back, my control organization asked me to develop a scenario for the perfect crime. An extremely wealthy woman wanted her husband killed because he was cheating on her with multiple women. If she divorced him, he'd get half of her wealth since she, rather stupidly, did not demand a prenup when they were married. She'd be the suspect if we killed him, and she didn't want the embarrassment."

"Did you figure out a way?"

"I figured out a very low-risk way. The issue with killing someone is disposing of the body. If the authorities can't find the remains, it's almost impossible to gather enough evidence to convict anyone. At first, I thought cremation and scattering the remains over a large area would be the answer. But that was risky. Someone might smell it and report it, and if anyone found the ashes, maybe a forensics team could use DNA to identify the victim. Then I thought coming up with a way to have the body cremated by a funeral home was the answer."

"Sounds like a simple solution. You'd just have to figure out a way to get the body into the furnace while the funeral home is legitimately cremating another body. You could bribe or threaten the mortician to prevent him from talking."

"Unfortunately, it's not that simple. Law enforcement professionals had already anticipated that it might be a clever way for a killer to dispose of a body. There are procedures and regulations to monitor the cremation process at funeral homes. Gas supply lines that feed the crematoriums can measure and automatically record the precise amount of gas used for each body, and the funeral home has to record the body weight of every cremation."

Kathryn was confused and blurted out, "But you said you figured out a low-risk way to kill someone, and I assumed you had to get rid of the body."

"I did just that. But it was expensive. Fortunately, the woman that wanted her husband killed had hundreds of millions of dollars at her disposal. I told her how I planned to kill her husband and dispose of his body. Then I let her know how much it would cost, and she gave me the green light. I found the director of a funeral home who was in deep financial trouble and who I believed had the balls to execute the plan. The funeral home he owned had a moderate number of weekly cremations, enough to work. I explained my plan and told him it meant a big payday for him. I also told the funeral director that if he told anyone about our conversation, he would die an unpleasant death. That got his attention and he committed to the agreement."

"How did you pull it off?"

"Our client called and told me her husband planned to go out that night to meet his current mistress. She told me she also wanted his mistress killed, and she wanted it done in front of him. She would happily pay an extra three hundred thousand dollars for the mistress. I shadowed him when he left the house and eventually trailed him to a luxury motel. His wife also told me he would probably order room service, and I waited until they delivered his food, then knocked on his door, said I was from room service, and that we had forgotten part of the order. His mistress opened the door, and I pushed her into the room and closed it. I quickly slapped a piece of duct tape over her mouth and ordered her to kneel. Minutes later, he walked out of the bathroom to see her kneeling on the floor, trembling in fear, and gagged with duct tape. I used a Glock 9mm with a suppressor and shot her between the eyes. He immediately focused his attention on my gun and his mistress's body. He looked confused, his knees buckled, and he collapsed into my arms. That gave me the opportunity to inject him with heroin; I had prepared the syringe in advance. I kept him sedated until two in the morning, then drove him to the funeral home."

"At the funeral home, I injected him with a massive dose of heroin, and he died instantly. We replaced his blood with embalming fluid and cut him into twelve pieces. The next morning, we placed his head and hands in with a body scheduled for cremation. It only took eleven days to cremate all his body parts. The weights recorded for each cremation were within normal range for one person, despite the added body part in each casket. The gas consumption was also within the normal range for each person cremated."

Tina added, "I watched the funeral director for a while after the cremation. I noticed that he was drinking heavily, and I worried he wouldn't keep what we did secret. I decided to use an overdose of heroin to kill him."

His days on this earth ended at 19,231.

"The perfect crime," said a smiling Kathryn, "but how did you get rid of her body?"

"I left it in the room. She was a high-priced call girl, and she reserved the room in her name, my target's name was not used."

Tina continued, "It was perfect only because I prepared for every contingency and had a plan to take care of the funeral director if and when he became a problem. And it helped that the authorities were lazy and assumed he committed suicide because he was despondent because his business was failing."

Kathryn asked, "If he's gone, how will you handle it if you have to get rid of a body in the future?"

"I've had a couple of contracts that wanted the body disposed of and have a very reliable funeral director on retainer."

Kathryn's reaction to the gruesome details of the story she just heard bothered Tina. The first time she had seen a body cut into pieces it took Tina several days to overcome her feeling of disgust. She knew her family abused Kathryn, but still wondered how she could be so amoral.

Tina looked Kathryn in the eye and asked, "Your lack of reaction to what I just told you concerns me. How did you feel as you heard the story?"

"I didn't feel a thing. I have a way of detaching from the reality of a situation and moving outside of my body. I only felt he deserved to die and have his body cut into pieces. It's how I deal with things."

Tina, although concerned for Kathryn's mental health, said nothing.

Chapter 23

Jim rolled to his side, and looked over at a still-sleeping Mary Ann. After all these years, Jim hardly believed that a beautiful woman fifteen years his junior would want to marry a sixty-year-old retired cop. Mary Ann kept her youthful figure by working as a server in a busy Long Island diner. He remembered the night she shared her story with him – every word of it – and knew he would always love her.

Mary Ann and her older sister Vanessa shared a close bond that extended beyond a typical sisterly relationship. Growing up in one of the best neighborhoods in Brooklyn, New York, they navigated life together. Despite Mary Ann's inherent shyness, she looked up to Vanessa as a role model, aiming to emulate her sister's choices, both the wise and the unwise ones.

Vanessa, being the older sibling, served as a trailblazer for Mary Ann. From childhood games in the backyard to teenage escapades, Mary Ann often found herself following in Vanessa's footsteps. Vanessa's charisma and confidence were qualities that Mary Ann admired, hoping to absorb some of that self-assurance herself.

As they ventured into adolescence, Vanessa made various life choices, both good and bad, and Mary Ann was there to witness and sometimes join in. Whether in navigating school, friendships, or relationships, Mary Ann sought guidance and inspiration from her sister's experiences.

As Mary Ann entered her late teens, a subtle but profound realization settled within her: she and Vanessa were growing apart. The differences in their values, preferences, and aspirations became more apparent, particularly when it came to material possessions and the circles they frequented.

Mary Ann discovered that she held a distinct perspective on life, one that didn't prioritize expensive belongings or associations with well-heeled individuals. Her contentment stemmed from appreciating the simple joys of life and forming connections with people who, like her, found fulfillment in the essentials rather than extravagance.

Her choice to surround herself with like-minded individuals allowed her to build connections based on shared values and mutual understanding. While Vanessa pursued a lifestyle that resonated with her own aspirations, Mary Ann found fulfillment in a community that embraced simplicity and authenticity.

The drifting apart of the sisters was a natural part of their personal growth. As Mary Ann embraced her uniqueness and appreciated the beauty of a less materialistic existence, she carried the lessons learned from Vanessa's influence into her own distinctive journey. The sisters married and their differences increased, but they remained connected by the shared memories and the profound impacts they had on each other's lives.

Mary Ann's marriage to Jared began with the belief that they shared similar values, creating a sense of happiness and connection. Jared worked hard and became an asset to his employer and received several promotions. The more money he earned, the more he changed. The two grew apart and divorced. These unexpected twists and turns led Mary Ann back to her parents' home after the divorce. Initially, she saw this return as a temporary measure, a period of recovery and regrouping after the end of her marriage. However, life had other plans for her.

Life changed dramatically when Vanessa, now a single parent to two young children, overdosed on heroin, an addiction she had effectively hidden from her family. Vanessa's ex-husband had left New York right after their second child was born and his whereabouts were unknown. Mary Ann's parents adopted Vanessa's children, and Mary Ann committed to living at home and raising them until they moved out.

Mary Ann loved her new life. Living with her parents simplified her life and helping out with her nephews gave her life a purpose. It was the perfect balance. Not only did she love her home life, but she loved her job, especially the people she worked with. She loved every aspect of her life. Mary Ann, in her early twenties, settled into a life free of the complications a relationship created. She vowed to herself that she would only get involved with a man she judged worthy of her love.

She remained at home after her nephews grew up and moved out, and when both her parents passed, she continued living in the home. She was alone most of the time but not lonely. She had her work, she saw her co-workers on occasion, her nephews visited and eventually their families came by on holidays, and she enjoyed reading. So, Mary Ann a young and beautiful woman chose to live the single life and had no desire to have a man in her life. She was happy and content. Then she met Jim Hines.

Jim looked over at her one last time before asking, "Are you awake yet? We have a lot to do today."

Mary Ann groaned. "Now I am, you jerk. I was in the middle of a dream about Denzel, and you ruined it."

"I'm glad I did, or you would have been useless for the rest of the day. We should talk before the realtor picks us up. Phil told us most people in this area were good people and racists were few and far between. Now we'll have the chance to see for ourselves. I know where the upscale areas are and have found some homes for sale in those areas that we can easily afford. We'll see if she plans to show them to us. If she hasn't scheduled any, we'll ask to see them tomorrow. I've studied the housing market and I know what areas are desirable, and I have Phil's opinion on different areas and towns. We'll know after a few days whether we want to live here. Or do we think the people are not ready for black neighbors?"

"Good, because I don't think people will readily accept us, no matter what Phil says. He hasn't seen the prejudice we have. The cop and the server and black to boot."

They relaxed in bed for a little while, organizing their first day of house hunting in Northeast Connecticut, before they had breakfast and chatted over a cup of coffee while waiting for the realtor. She arrived promptly at nine.

"Good morning. Can I come in and go over the homes I scheduled for today? Based on the information you provided, I'm sure you won't have a problem affording any home you want. We'll see homes in the upscale areas in Pomfret and Woodstock today. Here's the information on them." She placed a hefty packet of papers in Jim's hands.

Jim and Mary Ann looked over the homes that Jane, their realtor, had scheduled for the day and smiled. The homes were the same ones they would have picked. Jim said, "I like every home you picked. You did an excellent job understanding what we want and need. Any issues arranging the showings?"

"I'm not sure what you mean, but no, there were no issues," Jane replied.

"Just wondering if anyone changed their mind about selling? Or decided not to sell?"

"No. Nothing like that."

"Let's get started, then," Mary Ann said. "I want to see our new home."

After a busy morning of house hunting, the trio stopped at the Vanilla Bean restaurant for lunch. After they placed their orders, Jane told them a little about the area. "Just down the road there are two of the top private schools in the country: the Pomfret school and the Rectory school. They are attended by children of some of the wealthiest families in the country. Pomfret is a wonderful community and a delightful place to live. It's less rural than Woodstock, which you'll see this afternoon, but Woodstock has a charm all its own. I think you'll like it. One home in Woodstock is on the market for forty-five million dollars. I didn't think you would be interested in that one."

Mary Ann asked, "What is a forty-five-million-dollar home like in this area? On Long Island's gold coast, you can buy a large mansion with that kind of money."

"It's a castle. Literally, it's something out of medieval times with a Disney World look. It is nestled on one hundred and twenty-six acres, complete with an enormous moat, animals that roam the property, and for a while had old B-52 bomber, but the owner disposed of it. I thought it might be a little out of your price range."

"I would love to see it. Can we do a drive by?"

"Sure. It's in a remote area, but it's not far."

"First thing this afternoon, we're going to Woodstock Hill to see a grand old home, if that's okay with you. It doesn't fit your specs, but it is an interesting home with fabulous views. Woodstock Hill is the town center and is home to historical properties, an orchard, an area high school, and many beautiful homes. Is that okay?"

"Absolutely," replied Mary Ann, nodding.

An hour or two later, Jane put on her tour guide hat and started her much-practiced speech. "Woodstock Hill may be the center of town, but it is a quiet center." Jane had parked in front of a large Victorian Mansion set on two acres of land that the town's people lovingly referred to as the Bubblegum House. "The property is now a state historical site. It was originally owned by Henry Chandler Bowen, a businessman, philanthropist, and publisher who was born in Woodstock, but made his fortune in New York

City. He returned to Woodstock later in life. Built in 1846, the house is a fine example of Gothic Revival architecture. It features a colorful exterior, a stunning garden, and a collection of original furnishings and artifacts.

"Next, we'll see the Woodstock Academy, one of the oldest secondary schools in the country, founded in 1801. It has a rich history and a distinguished alumni list, including politicians, artists, and writers. You can visit the campus and see some of the historic buildings, such as the Academy Building, the Hyde Cultural Center, and the Center for the Arts."

Jane continued, "There are a lot of attractions in the area. Palmer Arboretum, for example, is a beautiful park that is home to over 200 species of trees and shrubs, as well as a variety of flowers and plants. You can stroll along the trails and admire the scenery or sit on a bench and relax. The arboretum also hosts events and programs throughout the year, such as concerts, workshops, and festivals. Another is Taylor Brooke Winery, a family-owned winery that produces award-winning wines from grapes grown on their own vineyard. You can sample the wines at their tasting room or buy a bottle to take home. They also offer wine tours, events, and a wine club."

Mary Ann grinned and said, "That's exciting! A winery close by!"

Jane replied, "Actually, the Connecticut Wine Trail cuts through the area. There are wineries all along the trail. And Woodstock is home to one of the oldest and largest agricultural fairs in New England, attracting thousands of visitors. The Woodstock Fair takes place every Labor Day weekend."

Jim interjected, "Jane, if you don't mind, I'd like to talk to Mary Ann in private for a little bit. We won't take long. Mary Ann, let's step away."

They walked back within a few minutes. Mary Ann explained, "Jim and I agree that everything you showed us today met or exceeded our expectations and was right in line with what we asked for. We just didn't realize how rural the area is and how citified we are. We've decided that we want to live in Cargill Falls, preferably on Grove Street. Close to Phil and Rose."

Jane smiled sympathetically and replied, "Nothing is currently for sale that would fit your minimum needs. However, I've heard that a house that is perfect for you both is coming up on the market in a month or two. The sellers, a couple, are building a house in Naples, Florida. The house is four doors up from the Messina home on Grove Street. Let's take a look at the castle, and then we'll take a look at your future home. I know the owners personally."

The castle was absolutely amazing, a gothic version of Disneyland. And the Hines's' loved the house on Grove Street.

Chapter 24

It was a dark and rainy early April morning. Phil cruised north on I-395, carrying four bowling balls and a duffel with a weekend's worth of clothes and toiletries. His destination this morning was Denny's Restaurant in north Worcester. He would be meeting seven bowling buddies for breakfast, then drive to Burlington, Vermont, to compete in the 'Lanes on the Lake' bowling tournament. The eight bowlers planned to travel to Burlington in two SUVs, which would accommodate all their bowling balls and duffels. Mike, Tim Brookings and Craig Lathrop, Phil's teammates, would ride to Burlington with him. They filled the rear of Phil's SUV with twelve more bowling balls and three more duffels. Kevin Sullivan and John Duffy would complete the ten-man team for the tournament, were driving together and would leave around eleven o'clock after work.

The bowlers each ordered a large breakfast, with eggs, bacon, toast, and waffles or pancakes. Over breakfast, they talked about sports, bowling, and the lanes for the tournament in detail. Their averages were all higher than Phil's this season. But all agreed that finishing his first year with a one-eighty-two average was great, considering that he had started the season with a one-forty-seven average. Mike had told Phil that the same group had bowled in the tournament for at least twenty-one years. Mike had also explained that the oil pattern used for the tournament was much more difficult than Phil had ever seen. The lanes had oil on the outside 6 inches for fifty feet, and if his shot was right of target, it would not hook and would slide into the six-ten. In the middle, the lanes had heavy oil for thirty-five feet, which caused the bowling ball to over-hook when the bowler missed the target to the inside. The lanes required perfection.

They loaded Phil's MDX and headed out. Phil took I-290 east to I-495 north, then picked up Route 3 north through Nashua and Manchester. North of Manchester, he picked up I-93 north toward Concord, where just south of the town, Phil got on I-89 north. And that is when the rain became freezing rain. As I-89 climbed steadily to Montpellier, the roadway iced over, and travel became treacherous. The Tuttle Post team decided it was worth the risk and would push on until they could not move anymore. Sitting around at the motel later, though, they would all admit to being worried, even scared.

Phil drove between forty and forty-five miles per hour and the MDX felt solid, glued to the road. Maybe the eight-hundred-plus-pounds of humans, the two-hundred-forty-pounds of bowling balls, the traction control, the Super Handling All Wheel Drive, the anti-lock braking system, the even weight distribution, or all of the above provided the necessary traction to climb I-89 north. Along the way, they saw a couple of eighteen-wheelers off the road and ten or twelve cars with hazards on. None looked like they were in serious trouble, and in all cases the police had already responded. The drive from Concord to Montpellier, despite the traffic being almost nonexistent, took three hours and fifteen minutes instead of the slightly less than two hours it would normally take. Once they passed the Montpellier exit off I-89 and descended toward Burlington, the freezing rain changed to rain again.

They arrived at the motel with plenty of time to register, unpack, and relax for several hours before their first event. The second SUV, carrying the other bowlers from Denny's, arrived an hour later, and Sullivan and Duffy arrived thirty minutes after them.

The singles competition was the only event scheduled for Friday night, the ten best pinfall totals for the three-game series would receive prize money. Phil had a horrendous series and bowled well below his average. Mike rolled a good three-game series but considered his score only acceptable. Mike could not stop reminding Phil, once every five minutes, how poor Phil's performance was.

Dinner was at a Japanese restaurant with a hibachi grill. The bowlers enjoyed shrimp, scallops, and steak hot off the grill and washed their meals down with a flood of drinks. On returning to the motel, the inebriated group sat around Steve Gardner's coffee table, talked about the tournament, played Texas Hold 'em, and drank even more.

Phil had more fun with his bowling buddies than he ever had with the dull, pharma execs in his old life.

When he and Mike called it a night and returned to their room, Mike started talking immediately. It was clear that he had been fixating over the Mill plans and the treasure. Mike stared at the ceiling and growled, "I've studied the drawings until I can't see straight, and I've considered every possibility and come to one conclusion. I ask myself if I'm sure there is a treasure, and the only answer I come up with is, 'I just don't know.' But in my gut, I genuinely feel like it's there. If I can get into the Mill, I will find it."

"We need to do everything we can to find it once and for all. Now, I can't hold my liquor like you, so I need to get to sleep."

The bowlers faced nine games and three unique events on Saturday: singles, doubles, and team. The team event started at nine the next morning, with most guys ready and wide awake. Phil bowled better than before. He wondered whether he was just becoming familiar with the lanes and the surroundings. Mike was on fire and bowled all three games above his average. Maybe he was thinking about finding the treasure and living 'the good life'.

The doubles event paired Mike and Phil. Even though Mike liked Phil, he would have been happier if he drew a partner with a higher average. Phil, much to Mike's surprise, bowled well above his average for the first two games. Mike also bowled above his average, and their pinfall for the first two games was a combined eight hundred and fifty-seven, in range to place in the money in the doubles competition. Mike had coached Phil through the first two games, explaining how the oil pattern was changing and how to target his shot. Now, at the start of the last game, Mike took his coaching to the next level.

"Phil, I want you to start from the left side of the approach and target between the third and fourth arrows, then over the short, dark targeting board forty-five feet down-lane. If you hit both targets and keep your ball speed up, you'll get some strikes. Not to make you nervous, but if we can roll four-ninety combined, we'll be in the big money."

"Thanks for telling me. I'm not at all nervous. You bastard."

Phil followed Mike's instructions and struck in the first frame, then followed with four more strikes. The last strike was lucky. It was not a solid pocket hit, but it carried.

Mike got in Phil's ear. "Move three boards left with your feet, target the same arrows, and stay on the targeting board. The oil carried down the lane is changing the shot. And for God's sake, keep your speed up."

Phil was feeling confident. "I will. We'll be in the money."

Phil threw four more strikes – nine in a row – and needed the last three for a perfect game. Mike was bowling great and had a chance at a big game, too. They were already in the prize money, now it was a matter of how much.

Mike rolled the first two strikes in the tenth frame and then left a ten pin to finish with a two-sixty-six game.

Phil had seen guys throw the first eleven strikes and not carry the twelfth because they panicked. Their knees weakened, they lost focus on their approach, or they fell prey to some thousand other reasons. Rolling three strikes in the tenth frame was more difficult than rolling the first nine.

Phil's first ball in the tenth was a solid pocket hit for a strike. He did not have enough lift on his second shot, and the result was a light pocket hit, but he got lucky again and had enough pin action to carry the strike.

As he stepped up to the approach, everyone in the neighboring lanes stopped talking and the entire building went silent. Phil had anticipated this reaction. He believed that a staring audience was what unnerved other bowlers on the brink of a perfect game. He put his fingers into the ball and visualized the perfect approach, the ball drop, the backswing, his foot speed, the release, and the follow-through. He then executed the shot just as he had visualized it and rolled his first perfect game at just the right time.

After the celebration subsided, Mike explained to Phil that they had taken first place in the doubles competition for the tournament. The other guys declared, in unison, "You're buying tonight."

The singles competition was a blur and Phil did not care that he bowled below his average. He and Mike had won the doubles, and he had bowled a perfect game. What more could he want? Mike, obviously more competitive than Phil, bowled a great game and finished in the money.

As was their long-standing tradition, the gang went out for Chinese food. Before ordering massive amounts of appetizers, they ordered drinks Phil thought were interesting, like Frog Cutters and a Scorpion Bowl. The best part of the night was the laughter and camaraderie. Phil's momentous day ended gloriously.

Singles was the only event scheduled for Sunday; it kicked off at nine with a ten-minute practice session before the event started. Both Mike and Phil were hungover and bowled accordingly. Mike rolled a five-fifteen series and Phil's pinfall for the three games totaled four-ninety-four. Both were well out of the money.

Phil felt he was in no condition to drive and asked Mike if he felt up to driving back to Connecticut.

Mike replied, "Sure. But if the police stop me for DWB, I'll tell the cop that I'm chauffeuring you three white guys home because you're all too drunk to drive."

Chapter 25

Gathered at Mike and Tess's home in Worcester were all the "Old Mill Investigators" except for Karen, who was working. Mike kept whispering, "there's treasure in that there Mill!" He believed the input from Elijah and Nathan Putnam and had concluded that the old treasure's presence was likely. Isaac Putnam's obsession with the Virginia mountains also contributed to Mike's reasoning. The question before the group was: would they be willing to bet money on Mike's analysis?

Mike started the meeting by saying, "Tess and I have been analyzing the drawings Noelle gathered and the information from the Civil War. There's a lot of info on Major Beck and Brigadier General Isaac Putnam online. None of it is absolutely conclusive, but it's enough to reach a tentative conclusion, and I conclude that we can find all or some of Beck's loot in that there Mill!" He seemed excited, slamming his fist down on the table. "I just need to examine the physical foundation walls and compare them to the drawings. I want to walk around the building and measure. Well, what do you think?"

Jim's furrowed brows made him look skeptical. "How do you propose to get permission? You don't have a warrant. And if you find a treasure, do you turn it over to the owners? We don't own the Mill."

"I know," Mike responded. "I just have this feeling that we'll find a treasure from the Civil War in the Mill. And I want to be the guy who found it! I'll be the guy who was smart enough to find the Civil War Treasure. Let's buy the Mill."

Jim, wide-eyed and believing that Mike had lost his mind, countered, "Good idea. All we have to do is come up with about twenty-five million dollars. Okay, everyone! I'm ready to risk it all on Mike's gut feelings! I'll toss in half a million. Just twenty-four and a half to go." He folded his arms and stared condemningly across the table at Mike.

Mike scowled. "Let's just walk away from a fortune because it's complicated. I, for one, believe that if we think hard enough, we can work it out. Remember: Noelle said the elder Putnam brothers said they wanted to know if we found anything, and those guys are loaded. We should talk to them."

Noelle replied levelheadedly, "They're extraordinarily rich, they're interested, and they tried to find it but couldn't. As far as I know, no one here has near enough money to compete with the Putnam's. They could buy the Mill out from under us, and it would leave us with nothing. It's our discovery."

Phil, who seemed lost in thought, was unusually quiet. He eventually asserted cautiously, "Maybe there's a way everyone can get a fair share."

That caught everyone's attention. Mary Ann offered, "I hope you're right. If you have a way to deal with the issue, it'll break the logjam and we can move forward."

Phil inhaled deeply. "I haven't worked it all out yet, but I'll do my best to explain what I am thinking. Then you can poke holes in it. The LLC that owns the Mill has an asset worth – let's assume for the sake of this discussion – twenty-three million dollars, and they have about nineteen million in liabilities, leaving about four million dollars of equity in the Mill. We believe there's an asset hidden in the Mill, we think we can find it, and we'll hazard a guess that it's possibly worth millions of dollars. That's not a sure thing, though. But we believe in Mike's instincts and believe he can find the treasure if anybody can. We also have the Putnam brothers, who can bring a chunk of money to the deal if needed. We approach the current owners with an offer to buy a piece of the Mill for a price to be determined. If we can bring an asset to the deal, we'll work out a fair stock distribution based on the appraised value of our asset. If we don't find anything valuable to bring to the deal, the deal is off."

The Old Mill Investigators all sat deep in thought, and the silence was deafening. Phil tried to guess what they were thinking but could not. No one moved. While the rest of the party stared into space, Noelle broke the silence. "How do we dispose of any treasure or asset Mike finds?"

"Legally, it'll depend on what we find and what it's worth. The agreement has to be as clear as possible on that point, and really on everything. A legal agreement will cost us. Lawyers are expensive. And an agreement this complicated will require a lot of back-and-forth negotiations."

Looking a little uncertain, Jim expressed his hesitation. "Mary Ann and I are in the middle of buying a house in Cargill Falls, which limits what we can commit. Mortgages are sometimes difficult to get for black folk."

Mike chuckled and replied, "You can probably buy three or four houses here for the price of your house on Long Island. I think we should get Elijah and Nathan involved and structure a deal to present to the owners. Phil, how would you structure the offer?"

"I'd incorporate our investment group and offer to match the current owner's equity in the Mill as fifty-fifty partners. The deal would be contingent on Mike getting complete access to the Mill to search for the 'treasure.' Whether we proceed with the deal would be Mike's call. We then pay four million dollars, or the equity value, and receive shares of stock in an amount equal to that of the current owners. Unless I'm totally misreading the situation, we need the Putnam brothers. Our offer will be the basis for negotiating."

"What if they want to look for the 'treasure' without us? Also, I hear an offer is coming to buy out the current owners. What if they decide on the other offer?" asked Rose.

"Another offer will complicate things for us, but we'll make our best and fairest offer and hope they're smart enough to take it. We'll make sure they know the Putnam brothers looked for the 'treasure' and failed. We can only hope they realize how unlikely it is that they will find it," replied Phil.

Tess interjected, "It can't hurt to try. I say we push ahead, write up an offer, get with the Putnam brothers, and see if they're interested. Any of us could back out before we sign if we think it's too risky. Do you agree, Phil?"

"Tess is right. I'll do a draft of the offer we can all read. When we're all in agreement, Noelle, Mike, and I will present it to the Putnam brothers." Phil excused himself and said he would be back with copies of the first draft.

Investment Offer
Draft

We, the undersigned representing the Old Mill Investors Group, bring this offer to the Putnam Group, owners of the Pomfret Cotton Mill. To show that we proffer the offer in good faith, we fully disclose the reason for the offer. We have recently discovered documents, drawings, and testimony which we believe prove there is a Civil War era treasure hidden in the Pomfret Cotton Mill. Further, we believe we possess the knowledge and skills necessary to find said treasure. If we are incorrect or simply fail to find the 'treasure' this agreement will be null and void.

If we believe there is a high probability the 'treasure' exists, the Old Mill Investors Group will invest an amount equal to the equity of the Putnam Group in the Pomfret Cotton Mill based on a fair appraisal. Subsequent to executing the partnership, all assets found by the Old Mill Investors Group will be an asset of the partnership and immediately belong to the enterprise.

Members of the Old Mill Investors Group will have access to all parts of the Mill, always accompanied by a member of the Putnam Group.

Representatives of The Putnam Group agree not to, under any circumstances, divulge anything about the existence or possible existence of a 'treasure'. The penalty for revealing the existence, or possible existence, of a 'treasure' is the loss of all claims to the 'treasure.'

Phil delivered copies of the draft to everyone at the meeting and emailed a pdf to Karen. He gave them a half-an-hour to recommend changes for the others to consider. Phil sat down and closed his eyes and waited.

Jim and Mike had a couple of changes to the Draft. But Rose, Tess, Mary Ann, and Noelle working together, had thoroughly examined and changed the Draft and significantly improved it. Phil incorporated all the changes in the Draft.

Investment Offer
Draft Modified

We, the undersigned representing the Old Mill Investors Group, bring this offer to the Putnam Group, owners of the Pomfret Cotton Mill. We certify to the Putnam Group that the offer we make is in good faith by fully disclosing the reason for the offer. Through our research we have recently discovered documents, drawings, and verification which we believe prove there is a Civil War era treasure hidden in the Pomfret Cotton Mill. Further, we believe that we possess the knowledge and skills necessary to find the treasure. If we are incorrect or simply fail to find the 'treasure,' this agreement will be null and void.

If we believe there is a high probability the 'treasure' exists, the Old Mill Investors Group will invest an amount equal to the equity of the Putnam Group in the Pomfret Cotton Mill based on a fair appraisal. The investment shall only be used to pay down the current liabilities of the Putnam Group. Subsequent to executing the partnership, all assets found by the Old Mill Investors Group will become assets of the partnership and immediately belong to the enterprise.

Members of the Old Mill Investors Group will have access to all parts of the Mill, always accompanied by a member of the Putnam Group.

Representatives of the Putnam Group agree not to, under any circumstances, divulge the existence or possible existence of a 'treasure', or that the Old Mill Investors made an offer of purchase. The penalty for revealing the existence or possible existence of a 'treasure', or of the offer to purchase, is the loss of all claims to the 'treasure.'

Everyone agreed with the changes and Phil said, "I will run the Offer by the Putnam brothers. Assuming they buy in, and I mean literally buy in, the next step is our lawyers. Then, and only then, we will present the offer to the Putnam Group."

Suddenly, the prospects of finding a 'Treasure' started becoming more likely in the group's collective mind.

Chapter 26

Noelle assumed responsibility for arranging a meeting and providing Elijah and Nathan an overview of the purpose for the get-together. She told them about Mike's research, his conclusion, and the proposed offer to purchase a fifty-percent stake in the Mill.

Over the phone, the Putnam brothers sounded excited about the possibility of investing in the Mill and of having three guests over for lunch. They told Noelle that they wanted to get to know some of their potential partners. If they were to invest in the deal, they would want to determine whether the other partners in the investment group met their standards, both of ethics and competence.

While they waited for their ride to the Putnam Mansion, Noelle filled Mike and Phil in on what to expect. "The Putnam brothers are interested, but because they're wealthy, they're concerned about being scammed. They'll question you in order to learn about your knowledge of investing and, Mike, your familiarity with construction, particularly of old mills. And all the while, they'll assess your honesty and ethics. Since we'll need a lot of money, their opinion of you two is critical. I myself have already made a good impression."

Mike cringed and looked at Phil. "No pressure."

Phil responded, "If they have issues with us, too bad. We'll find other rich people. They had their opportunity to find the 'treasure' and failed. They can't do it without us, and you in particular, Mike."

"You scare me, Phil. Don't be so rude," Noelle warned, then continued to prepare them for what to expect on the ride to the mansion and at lunch. She gushed about having an individual server to take care of your every desire.

"This poor black boy is coming up in the world!" Mike cheered. "Soon Tess and I will be living high on the hog."

"Do you even know what that means, or where it came from?" Phil nagged.

"No, I don't, you wise ass. But I'm sure you're going to tell me."

"I am. It's an old slave saying. Normally, slaves ate the stomach, guts, and intestines of a pig for dinner, while the slave owner dined on the good meat: pork. Now and then, when the owner felt generous, the slaves got to dine on the good meat, the meat that came from high on the hog."

Noelle glared at Phil. "Do you know what you're talking about, or are you just making it up? Trying to make fun of Mike?"

"When I worked at McKenzie, way back when, we attended courses on black history. And that information was part of the lessons, along with some other tales about slavery. Most of the others were horrific and described the dreadful treatment endured by slaves. It's nothing to joke about."

"You know more about my history than I do. Not fair!" Mike complained.

"Not really. You lived it."

Noelle looked out of the front window. "Our limo has arrived."

The ride to the Putnam brothers' mansion was just as Noelle described, but the mansion itself was beyond description. It was enormous, ornate, but the real impression it made on Mike and Phil was that every element fit with each other elements of the architecture. It was perfect. It was not a home as much as a masterpiece of human craftsmanship. When they passed through the entrance, the opulence – the massive foyer, the grand staircase, the oil paintings adorning the walls – rendered them dumbstruck. Mike, finally able to speak, said in amazement, "Noelle, you understated the magnificence of their home. It's astonishing."

When the trio entered the sitting room, Elijah and Nathan greeted them generously. "We are excited to hear what you have uncovered, what your plans are, and how we are involved. Noelle, please first tell us what you know of Mr. Robertson's and Mr. Messina's background."

"Mr. Robertson – Mike, from here on – owns a large service business that maintains commercial buildings throughout Massachusetts. Their services include routine maintenance and repair of all building systems, outside maintenance including snow removal, and consulting on new construction projects. Mike lives in Worcester and has been married to the former Tess O'Hara for over thirty years. They have one son, Dr. Michael Robertson, MD.

"Mr. Messina – Phil, from here on – held a senior management position in a large multi-national corporation. He worked for the corporation's Medical Diagnostics and

Pharmaceutical business units. By the time he retired, he had become Director of Business Resources for the Purity Pharmaceutical Company. The company stonewalled the police investigation into the murders of several executives. The police lieutenant working on the case asked Phil to get involved, and the two solved the case together. It was national news about five years ago. Phil has been married to the former Rose Bartolomeo for over twenty years and they have two children: Ann, a customer service manager for a major credit card company in Delaware, and Tony, who is a mechanical engineer working for BMW in South Carolina. Jim Hines, the police lieutenant who solved the case with Phil, is also part of our group."

"I followed the case," Elijah noted. "I was fascinated. In fact, Nathan and I both were. Why did the company attempt to stop the investigation?"

Phil responded, "Long story. Jim and I will fill you in on all the details sometime over dinner. There were lots of twists and turns that people in the company's high places didn't want the police to discover. That especially included the covert operations occurring in production."

Lunch was magnificent. Waiters served grilled pecan-crusted salmon, smashed potatoes, and perfectly cooked mixed vegetables from shining platters. Ice cream parfaits in crystal glasses followed for dessert. During lunch, Elijah and Nathan took turns probing Mike and Phil's character and competence. Satisfied that the offer was not fraudulent, they adjourned to Elijah's office and got down to the business at hand.

Mike opened the presentation. "I began studying the layout of the foundation with late-1800-era architectural drawings that Noelle received from your family. They just didn't make sense when I compared the detail drawings to the overview. Then, when I examined information on the current configuration of the foundation, which you provided to Noelle, the documentation made no sense. Couple that with the stories of Isaac Putnam, his fascinations, and his trips to the mountains of Virginia. I believe that there's 'treasure' in the Mill. I also believe that I can find it."

"We looked around the Mill for years and didn't find a clue to the 'treasure.' Why do you think you can find it by looking around maybe once or twice?" asked Nathan soberly.

"My analysis of the drawings from the late 1800s has provided some clues. If they pan out, we'll find the 'treasure.' If not, it's not there," Mike answered.

Phil outlined the proposed offer. "The Mill renovation is in financial trouble. The owners can't keep up with the payments and they keep falling further into debt. We have heard, in good authority, that they're seriously considering selling. However, we want to be one hundred percent honest with the current owners, and we plan to tell them about the possibility of finding a Civil War treasure in the Mill or on Mill property. The offer states that if we find a treasure of any value, we'll partner with them, and if we don't, we'll withdraw the offer. All they have to do is accompany Mike as he roams around the building looking for clues. The Mill is worth approximately twenty-three million dollars and is around nineteen million in debt. To partner with the current owners, we need to match their equity of four million dollars. We've drafted an outline of the offer. If you agree, we'll have an attorney draw up a legal Letter of Intent." Phil gave Elijah and Nathan a copy of the second draft.

After a few minutes of reading, Elijah spoke. "I see some holes in the draft, for example how do we proceed if we find treasure worth less than four million dollars? The issues I see are minor and my attorney will easily fix them. Now, let's talk about money. If Mike either finds the 'treasure' or feels good about finding it, then we will need approximately four million dollars. How much will Nathan and I have to contribute?"

"Each of the families on our side will put in half a million dollars. Noelle will put in two hundred thousand dollars, and Karen Parisi will put in fifty thousand dollars. Parisi is young and still works as a detective for Nassau County PD. That leaves you and Nathan with two million, two hundred and fifty thousand dollars."

Nathan and Elijah talked among themselves for a couple of minutes, and finally, Nathan gave the verdict. "We are in. We will also cover expenses from here on and will kick in whatever we need to close the deal. We like the way you plan to deal with the current owners. Very ethical."

Mike, who had to take care of his business, left Phil and Noelle to discuss the results of the meeting with the Putnam brothers. After a brief review, they felt positive about the brothers' willingness to proceed with the deal and to produce their share of the money.

Noelle, with a stern face, asked Phil an unrelated question before his departure. "Phil, the way you and Mike talk to each other has been bothering me. I'm not sure you like each other. Are you guys' friends?"

"I've known Mike for less than a year and I'm closer to him than I am any human on earth, except Rose. Mike and I go on long bike rides together. He's helping me improve my bowling average. But most importantly, we can talk to each other, say anything to each other, and don't have to worry about the other guy taking offense. We consider each other brothers, and I consider Mike a once in a lifetime friend."

Noelle sighed in relief. "Thanks. I feel better."

Chapter 27

Dorian Gregson had been roaming around the lower level of the Mill since Robert had hired him, examining the foundation and trying to find a hidden Civil War treasure. His predecessor had supposedly found it, but Larry Davidson had either lied about the location to protect himself or had simply made a mistake. Whatever the reason, the location of the treasure was still unknown, and Robert was extremely angry. And he expected Dorian to find it. Dorian, the new renovation manager, possessed all the latest high-tech equipment he needed to do the job. All he needed to do was find a clue, a simple difference in the foundation walls.

While overseeing a small crew preparing for renovation by clearing debris, he noticed a minor variation in the foundation wall. The stones were a little smaller, and the cement filling between the stones appeared newer. Yet regardless, the foundation was different. He carefully recorded the location in a small notebook. Dorian had thought that he had found the location several times in the past, but each time, his suspicions had failed him.

Dorian returned after the crew had finished for the day, lugging the equipment he needed to check out the location. He inserted a long carbide drill bit into a power drill. He firmly pressed the bit against the cement between the stones at about chest-level. Hoping that he would hit wood eventually, he slowly drilled a quarter-inch hole into the cement and stone. After about fifteen minutes, the drilling required less effort and Dorian knew he had reached wood. The carbide bit made quick work of it, completing the first step in the process. Next, he unpacked his specialized camera equipment and opened the app on his phone. The camera and a bright LED light were mounted on the tip of a flexible but somewhat rigid cable. It would easily snake through the quarter-inch hole that he had just drilled. After being fed through the hole, the camera would send video to the app so Dorian could observe the other side of the foundation wall. It would also record the video.

Once he had set up all the equipment, Dorian opened the app and looked behind the foundation wall. In the bright haze of the LED, he beheld an approximately two-foot by four-foot room that held two wooden boxes. The ancient boxes had hinged lids, just like the treasures he had seen in the movies. Dorian worked the cable to maneuver the camera, trying to capture the entire room. Before removing the camera, he watched the video until he felt like he knew what was behind the wall.

He removed the camera, filled in the hole, and packed his equipment. He marked the wall to make sure that he could find it again. Then, he policed the area to ensure that his drilling had left no telltale signs. Despite knowing that Robert was capable of murder, he called to alert Robert before arriving at his house. He explained that he had found the location of the treasure and wanted to show him video evidence.

Robert was thrilled and watched the video five times before handing Dorian's phone back to him. "They are just as Davidson described: old treasure boxes. You found the treasure. The jut-out in the foundation is about two feet deep and four feet wide, just as Larry said it was. I'm positive it contains treasure. Now all we have to do is buy the building. I'll make sure you share in the profits for finding it. Let's drink to our future."

Robert poured drinks, and the two relaxed in the living room and contemplated the future. They spoke about their plans to buy the Mill and speculated over how they would get the treasure past State taxes. And finally, they pondered how they would sell the various pieces. Robert decided that he would call his other partners after checking on Amanda and getting her settled for the night.

Amanda had survived the accident, but her life plans with Robert would never materialize. The weight of the sheetrock panels had catastrophically damaged her legs, and she would never walk again. She sustained a severe concussion, and her doctors eventually diagnosed her cognitive problems as chronic traumatic encephalopathy (CTE), which was more commonly caused by repeated blows to the head. Amanda's skull must have struck the floor exceptionally hard. After the doctors had done everything possible, Robert and Amanda learned that she would be permanently crippled and would have cognitive issues for the rest of her life.

Their health insurance refused to pay for Amanda's medical bills because they had resulted from an accident. For years they suffered through multiple lawsuits and civil trials, enduring debt that towered over a million dollars high, with no guarantee that they would receive anything. When the courts finally acted, they held that the company that had renovated the mill would be liable for Amanda's injuries. The judge required the company to pay all her medical bills. The Sullivans' short-lived joy died when they learned how the family that owned the company had bled it dry. They had paid their lawyers unwarranted amounts in legal fees and stuffed their own shirts with large bonuses as the trial dragged on. The courts quickly intervened and awarded the company assets to Robert and Amanda. Robert swore to himself that if he did nothing else with his life, he would take care of his beloved.

Robert soon found that selling the company's assets would not generate nearly enough money to sustain Amanda. So young Robert, with no management experience and little knowledge of how to run a construction business, appointed himself CEO. With an inexperienced helmsman, his company flirted with bankruptcy many times in the first years. But he always found a way to save the business: an unexpected job, a new client with a building to build, a payment from a delinquent account. Robert's commitment to Amanda kept the company from failure by helping him see opportunities to turn the business around. After a while, the financial pressure dissipated, and business was solid.

Then a year ago, the country entered a recession. To make matters worse, clients struggled to pay their invoices on time. New business dropped dramatically, and as a result, the company's revenue dropped twenty-five percent. Amanda's medical bills, on the other hand, steepened and her condition deteriorated. Robert groped blindly for funds for ever-rising insurance payments. Despite the dire circumstances, he knew that he had to succeed to keep his commitment to Amanda. If he did nothing else with his life, he would take care of her.

The Civil War treasure would ensure their financial future.

Amanda had not fallen asleep yet and said something incoherent to her loving Bobby. When he was with Amanda, he was Bobby again. He smiled, smoothed her pajamas, straightened her covers, and kissed her goodnight. Her haggard appearance concerned him, and it had for some time. Amanda was failing and her doctors knew nothing of why, let alone how to treat her. Bobby swore that he would not rest until she was healthy.

Robert updated the State Senator and the Director on Dorian's findings and supplied the video evidence of the treasure hidden in the Mill. They would meet next week and prepare a Letter of Intent to purchase the Mill. They also would plan how to convert the treasure into cash – tax-free cash. Robert ended the conference call and looked in on Amanda. Her breathing was shallow. He felt like he was watching a rose wilt to death.

Bobby suspected that she would not last a month. Even though her doctors had administered every test that they thought necessary, they had no answers for him. Bobby thought about artificial intelligence. As a last resort, he went online and found several sites that claimed they could search all the medical information known to humankind, accurately diagnose every patient, and create an effective treatment plan. Although skeptical, Bobby entered every bit of information he had on Amanda: doctors' after-visit summaries, eighteen months of blood and urine tests, recent PET scans, MRI scans and CAT scans. Bobby waited over an hour for an answer, hoping the whole time for a diagnosis and treatment plan that would work for his precious Amanda.

When the answer finally came, it simply said, "It appears the patient has given up. Diagnosis: Failure to Thrive." Bobby threw his laptop into the fireplace and cried.

Chapter 28

A week later, Robert sat with a new laptop in the living room while he pondered the restructured offer to purchase the Mill. It had been his evening's work, and he intended to present it to the Mill owners on the following afternoon. He was close to completion. He just wanted one last look.

Before he did, he needed a break. He would check on Amanda again, tuck her in, and then finish the offer. In the morning, he would review it with the other investors and polish it before meeting with the Putnam Group. Last week's artificial intelligence diagnosis had terrified him, and this new offer was his only ray of hope. The money he would profit from selling the treasure could – maybe, possibly – prolong Amanda's life until medical science could find a cure. The only thing that could save her was money. The only opportunity he could see was the treasure. He gripped the sides of his new laptop tightly and watched the blood drain from his fingers. Nothing would stop him. He would remove any obstacle in his way and kill anyone who threatened his success.

He was Bobby again as he walked into Amanda's room, plastering an artificial smile on his face. He said cheerfully, "Time to get some sleep! I'll tuck you in for the night."

As he leaned over her with gentle hands, Amanda's eyes seemed to lock in on him. She mumbled what he thought was "I love you" as she passed. He became Robert again and cried.

When he regained his composure, he began making Amanda's final arrangements. The offer could wait.

Dorian's success in finding the treasure had excited the Director. His share of the treasure would increase his net worth, especially if he could avoid paying taxes. He knew that he would likely never have the amount of money he had as an executive of a fortune ten company. Also, his reputation had died with his position. He would never work for a major corporation again. Only small companies, small money, were his fate now. He knew who to blame for his downfall.

The Director had just learned that the Old Mill Investors Group had made an offer on the Mill contingent on finding the treasure. A paid informant had relayed the information to him. If the Mill owners accepted the offer, the Old Mill Investors would have access to the Mill. It shaped the perfect time for their demise. He simply had to convince his co-conspirators to eliminate the competition, permanently.

A week after Amanda had passed, Robert finished the draft of his investor group's offer and called a meeting. Although the wound of Amanda's loss was still raw, he wanted to control the treasure and begin securing his future. "You will be done reviewing the draft offer soon," he said. "I'll return in five minutes, and we'll get started on finalizing the offer."

Five minutes later, the co-conspirators regrouped. Robert summarized the offer. "We, the Cargill Falls Mill Company, are offering to purchase all the assets of the Putnam Group for $24.5 million. As you are aware, that is $1.5 million over the appraised value. I have already filed the incorporation papers, so I hope you are okay with the name," Robert said. The others nodded. He continued, "There is a significant difference between an asset purchase and a stock purchase when buying a company.

"In an asset purchase, buyers purchase the specific assets and the specific liabilities of a company. There is no transfer of ownership. In a stock purchase, buyers purchase a company's stock and gain their share in the assets and the liabilities of the seller company. In an asset purchase, the assets and any included liabilities move to the new entity. The stockholders of the old company (and any assets or liabilities it still owns) must dissolve the company. In a stock purchase, the buyer purchases the entire company, including all assets and current and future liabilities."

The Director added, "There's also a difference in tax treatment. The tax implications of an asset sale versus a stock sale can vary significantly. Buyers typically prefer asset sales, while sellers usually prefer stock sales. In a stock sale, the seller pays capital gains tax on the difference between the selling price and the original purchase price of the shares. In an asset sale, the buyer purchases individual assets of the company, such as equipment, intellectual property, and customer lists. The seller pays ordinary income tax on the gain from each asset sold. Capital gains tax is around twenty percent, while ordinary income tax could be as much as forty percent."

"I am glad you two are so well versed in the ins and outs of acquiring a company, but how do we buy the Mill?" the State Senator said.

The Director replied, "We offer an asset purchase. It's what any buyer would do. Then we negotiate."

They all agreed, and Robert said, I'll have a Letter of Intent drawn up."

The Director chimed in again. "Before we call it a day, I have something I want to discuss. I understand that a well-funded group is going to make an offer and let the current owners know about a possible treasure. They also want to have access to the Mill to try to find the treasure. If they find the treasure, we lose."

"What!" The Connecticut State Senator jumped in. "Do you have a plan to deal with it?"

"All we have to do is find out when the other buyers are going to look for the treasure. We have Tina in place, and she kills all of them. Eliminate the competition. It's that simple. I have a way to get all the intelligence we need."

Within a week of Robert hiring Dorian, The Director had worked out a deal with him. Ever since, the Director was getting information right after Robert. The Director's experience enabled him to ask better questions and get more detailed information. He would know not only the schedule, but also the route and who was part of the tour.

"I think we should prepare Tina for another kill," said the Director.

"I'll do that," Robert replied. "But I won't tell anyone to go until we meet again and make the decision."

The Director knew that he would get his way.

Chapter 29

The stockholders of the Putnam Group, LLC gathered at the Mill to discuss the two Letters of Intent they had received last week. One Letter of Intent, signed by Robert Sullivan, represented Cargill Falls Mill Company. Phil Messina had signed the other Letter of Intent. In attendance were Crystal Martineau, who was Bob Martineau's widow, Janet Howell, and Greg Adams. Collectively, they owned one hundred percent of the outstanding shares in the Putnam Group.

The trio decided that Janet Howell would lead the meeting, as she had the most business experience and knowledge. She had prepared for the meeting by putting the major points of each offer into a Power Point presentation.

"Before I get into the specifics of the offers, I feel that it's important for you to understand the tax and liability issues involved in the sale of a business. The current Federal and State laws governing the sale of a business allow for two types of sale: an asset sale and a stock sale. The type of sale we accept will have as much impact on how much money we net as the sale price. If the final deal we negotiate results in a stock sale, we will pay capital gains tax and have no future liability, period. The buyer accepts all current and future liability. Any questions?"

Janet looked at each of the others and added, "It's better to also understand the implications of an asset sale so we can compare the offers. Agreed?"

The other owners nodded.

Janet resumed, "In an asset sale the buyer and seller agree to the specific assets purchased and the specific liabilities assumed by the buyer. The seller is responsible for taxes on the increased value of the assets sold and to pay off any liabilities not assumed by the buyer. The seller remains liable for anything that happened while they owned stock in the company. If the company violated any laws, or if a lawsuit is brought for something that occurred while we owned the business, we remain liable. I've analyzed both Letters of Intent and concluded that we negotiate each."

Greg Adams said, "I've also read the LOIs, but will you give us your overview?"

"Sullivan is offering to purchase the assets, and I calculate that we'd net around three million and risk future liability. Messina, on the other hand, is making a contingent offer to buy half the outstanding shares of stock. The contingency is that his group will look around the foundation walls and move forward only if they find a 'treasure,' or if they're convinced enough that this treasure is in the Mill to want to keep looking. We need to aggressively question Mr. Messina. The really interesting thing about our second offer is the contingency. The buyers are right up front about their belief that hidden in our mill is a treasure that dates back to the Civil War. They think they can find it, too. But if they're wrong, the deal is off."

Greg started to speak, but Janet raised her hand to stop him.

"Hold on. I want to mention a few more things. then we can talk. They want access to the Mill with one of our people in attendance. And finally, their money offer is to match our equity. Assuming they find the treasure, it becomes an asset of the business. I repeat, they offer to buy fifty percent of our shares for an amount equal to our equity based on an appraisal of the value of the Putnam Group, not counting the treasure. They will become equal partners in the Putnam Group. We will also own half of any treasure. Okay… questions?"

After a lively discussion, they decided to schedule negotiations with both buyers to better understand the offers. It was obvious to all, however, that they preferred Messina's offer.

Janet called Sullivan and Messina and told them the Group's decision. At the other end of the line, Robert Sullivan imagined the worst scenario: that the Putnam Group had chosen the competing offer and were keeping him dangling in case it fell through.

Robert called The Director at once, shared his concerns, and asked him to start planning the hit with Tina. He explained that he was still depressed and couldn't deal with more death. In fact, Robert was tumbling into a deep depression brought on by Amanda's death. He had started drinking heavily and taking OxyContin in ever-increasing amounts.

The Director assumed the role of Instigator with a smile and called Tina. Tina was relaxing at home when the call came. She did not recognize the number and let it go to voice mail. When her phone dinged, she dialed her voice mail and listened to the message. The caller said that he was her new Instigator and gave her a number to call that night at eight.

The Director and Dorian spent the time before eight PM planning the route that the buyers would take in their quest to find the treasure. Now that Robert no longer wanted to be the Instigator, the Director did not need to conceal his conspiracies with Dorian, and he knew Dorian would lead the search as the designated Putnam Group participant. The Director understood his great luck and felt that the chance of success was high. They also planned Tina's route through the Mill. Dorian would control the other buyers' movements such that Tina would enter the main hallway from the side, approach behind the group, and kill them before they knew she was there. They were in the middle of a celebratory drink when the Director's burner phone vibrated.

He explained the plan to Tina in precise language. He explained that she might have to kill as many as four people, then texted their pictures directly to her phone. The most likely scenario was that three buyers would be in the group:

Mike Robertson, Jim Hines, and Phil Messina. He made sure that Tina understood that all three had to die in order for her to get paid.

Tina asked questions until she was sure she had memorized the details of the plan, including her escape. Only then did she say, "Call with the date and time at least four days in advance. I'll manage my end."

After hanging up, the Director said to Dorian, "One can never start the planning process too early."

Chapter 30

For two full days, Tina ignored Kathryn and mulled over the next hit. It was a delicate process. Killing three men simultaneously was nearly impossible, especially if one was a retired cop – he would definitely have a gun – and there's a chance the other two might also. The risk of injury or death was enough that she did not want Kathryn involved. In reality, one woman killing three men just did not work, unless everything went exactly as planned. That rarely happened. Tina begrudgingly admitted to herself that she needed Kathryn's help. With Kathryn involved, they would succeed.

Tina stepped into the living room and found Kathryn stretched out on the couch watching TV, or at least looking in that general direction. "Did you think I didn't love you anymore?" Tina asked.

"Not for a minute. I'm secure in our relationship and know you can't live without me," Kathryn said coyly, grinning. "I know you by now. You were wrestling with a problem – most likely a new contract – and you aren't sure you want to involve me. You're afraid I will get shot or even killed and you're not sure you can live without me. How am I doing?"

"Amazing. You're exactly right. I – we – have a contract to kill three men, one a retired police commander."

"All for a huge payday?"

"The client is paying for three hits, full price."

"Let's make some tea. Then we can sit down and talk. I'll tell you everything I know."

They both sipped their tea and looked – no, stared – over their teacups at one another. Both had little smiles on their faces. Even a casual observer could tell that they loved each other.

Tina looked up at the ceiling and gathered her thoughts before starting. "If all goes as planned, our targets will be searching for a Civil War treasure in the Pomfret Cotton Mill in Cargill Falls, Connecticut. Dorian Gregson will be leading them around. Gregson is working with the Instigator. We'll have access to the Mill from a different entrance and a place to stay out of sight in a hallway that intersects with the route our targets are taking. We step out behind them after they go by, kill the targets, and graze Gregson."

"When you say 'we,' does that mean I'm included?"

"That's what I've been thinking about for two days. This hit is dangerous, extremely dangerous. We'll be in tight quarters with at least one target, armed, who can shoot straight. I'd prefer doing it alone, but one of the targets kills me no matter how I plan the hit. With the two of us, the odds favor both of us coming out alive. Gregson being on our side really stacks the odds in our favor."

"If you think we'll be successful with me helping, we'll both survive."

"We have to do more than just survive. We have to plan the whole operation – every step – to ensure that we don't wind up in jail. That ranges from getting to Cargill

Falls, determining where we stay, and entering the Mill to executing the hit, making sure we leave no evidence, and finally getting home. Every move we make needs to be precise. If we don't predict everything that can go wrong and plan for how to deal with it, we're either on the chopping block or rotting in cells for eternity. First, we should make sure that our vests are in good condition and will protect us."

"Do we have enough time?"

"The Instigator said that we should have at least three weeks to prepare. We'll have time if we focus."

'Okay. Let's start, times-a-wasting."

Chapter 31

As she stood in front of her new house, Mary Ann felt like bawling. Yesterday she had said goodbye to the girls at the diner, most of whom she had known for twenty-five years. They had cried, she had cried. Mary Ann had been saying goodbye to people for weeks, but none of her farewells were as hard as those to her fellow servers. Anxiety bubbled up inside her, too. She loved the new house, but she knew that moving in and making it her own would surely involve heavy work. She could manage it, she knew. But could she handle the pressure that Jim would apply?

Just then, she heard car doors opening and slamming shut. She turned around and saw Rose, Tess, Noelle, and Karen dressed in their work clothes. Noelle yelled out, "Mary Ann Hines your problem is solved, your friends are here to help!"

Ten minutes later another car arrived, and Jim, Phil, and Mike tumbled out. Mike looked at Tess and grinned. 'What? We stopped for a quick beer! We're gassed up and ready to work." Tess just shook her head and smiled.

As the day progressed, they put the furniture in place in no time, hung clothes in closets and placed items neatly in drawers, hung pictures, filled and organized the kitchen cabinets, mounted shelves, put away tools, and cleaned the mess moving in caused. Mary Ann looked around and judged the house livable with little to do. Her anxiety faded, and if she was crying, her tears were tears of joy. The house was her home.

With the job done, it was time to relax and have a drink. Eventually the talk got around to dinner, but it seemed like everyone was tired and wanted to order takeout. Before they decided, the doorbell rang. To Mary Ann's surprise, the Putnam brothers, dressed in expensive tailored suits, were standing in her doorway.

Nathan asked, "May we come in? We brought dinner." Before even receiving a response, the brothers parted and the G Seven catering crew marched up the steps, hoisting a massive amount of food and dozens of portable gel-fuel burners. They had steak and all the trimmings, the same for chicken and pork, a variety of pastas, and beautiful, delicately decorated desserts. Dinner was beyond fabulous. When everyone had eaten their fill, Elijah pointed to the bar the caterers were setting up. Mixed drinks and digestifs like limoncello, Frangelico, and amaretto were all on offer.

Mike whistled and exclaimed, "Damn, I could live like this. All I need is money."

Several days before the Hines' moved to Cargill Falls, the Putnam Group agreed to the offer Phil Messina had presented. "If you find the treasure, you'll live better than this," Elijah laughed. "Mike, now that both parties have signed our offer to purchase the Mill, and we can begin our search for the treasure, what is the plan for the search? We should be less than a couple of weeks away, yes?"

"We're scheduled for next week. Phil and Jim are also going, and Dorian Gregson is representing the seller and will take the lead on the tour. I know where I want to look, and I'll make sure I get there. I have a bad feeling about Gregson, I'm not sure why but I don't trust him. We're all going in armed. I have all the equipment I need, and I'm prepared," Mike replied.

Rose said, "I'm worried, really worried. The Mill CEO, Bob Martineau, is dead. The former renovation manager is dead. His girlfriend is dead. I don't want my husband to be next."

Tess agreed. "I wish there was another way. Mike, if you get yourself killed, I'll never speak to you again."

That caused a little laugh, but it was a cautious, worried laughter, especially for Mary Ann.

Nathan seemed sympathetic. "We have tried to figure out who the other buyers are but have been unsuccessful. We have had Dorian checked out. He is clean. We will stay on it."

"Karen, I am curious about the state of the investigation into Bob Martineau's murder. It happened a little over a year ago and there has been no arrest, nor even a person of interest identified. Is there any progress?" asked Elijah.

Karen replied, "Officially, the State Police have made no progress, but the investigation is still active. Unofficially, the police have given up. They're just not saying it. Several weeks ago, I found out there are two detectives that have a theory they think will lead to the murderer. But their higher ups are not allowing them to work it. I talked to them, they shared the theory with me, and I think it's possible, especially now that we think there's a Civil War treasure in the Mill. They conjecture that a person or group of people hired a professional to kill Martineau and scare the current owners into selling. They also theorize that Larry Davidson was killed because he knew something he shouldn't know. Davidson was a loose end and his girlfriend, the store clerk, was collateral damage. If they pursue the case, we, along with the other buyers, would be prime suspects."

Chapter 32

Mary Ann Hines decided to host lunch for Rose Messina and Tess Robertson so that they could discuss the dangers their husbands would face while searching the Mill. The other ladies had arrived, and as Mary Ann began setting the table, Tess took a seat. "I told Mike to triple his life insurance," she said, "because I want to travel the world after he's killed. He laughed. He told me not to worry, because Jim's a good shot and that he and Phil would be armed and maybe even hit something. He's being a real asshole." She rested her face on her palm in exasperation. Rose, who had just pulled out a chair, patted Tess on the back.

Mary Ann brought out a quiche, a pot of tea, and several small plates. As she served her guests, she said, "Jim played the 'I was a cop for over thirty years and never got shot' card. I reminded him that it only takes a second to change everything. He told me I was worried for no reason, and the only issue was whether they would find any treasure. He said he was going to protect Phil and Mike if someone wanted to cause trouble. He's going no matter what I say." Her voice quavered a little bit.

Rose spoke her peace. "Phil and Jim survived almost being killed by the assassin five years ago. Phil said he was scared to death, and they only survived because Echo got overconfident and let Phil manipulate him. Phil's scared now, but there's no way I can talk him out of it either."

Tess asked, "Mike told me a little of that story, but he didn't know the details. Please tell me."

Mary Ann looked at Rose and said, "I would like to share what Jim told me. Is that okay?" Rose nodded.

Mary Ann explained, "Jim and Phil were investigating the murders of four executives of the Purity Pharmaceutical Company. Jim was acting for the Nassau County Police and Phil as Jim's insider. They were interviewing the Purity CEO when the assassin, Echo, entered the office, gun drawn. He was surprised that Jim and Phil were there and decided they should witness his confrontation with Bob Cohen. Echo ordered Jim and Phil onto their knees and began accusing Cohen of covering up problems with one of Purity's drugs.

"Phil knew Echo, who was a previous Purity employee, and complained that his knees hurt and asked if he could stand. He was standing in front of a bookcase that held a solid crystal replica of Washington's Capitol Dome. Phil threw the chunk of crystal like a football and hit Echo in the neck. Echo's gun fired, but he missed everyone. Jim said Phil saved everyone's lives."

Rose added, "Phil told me Jim was off his knees in an instant and charged. He grabbed Echo's gun hand and deflected the second shot, which hit Echo in the head. He died in the hospital."

"Holy shit," Tess exclaimed, wide-eyed. "Maybe they can take care of themselves. But I'm still worried."

Tina and Kathryn decided to drive to Connecticut three days early so they could discuss the hit's final details, relax a little, and enjoy some time together. Their first stop was Worcester, Massachusetts. Tina wanted a good steak dinner at One Eleven Chop House, which was arguably one of the best steak houses in Massachusetts. Kathryn wanted to stop at La Enchantress, a nightclub that catered to gay women, before checking into what would be their home for the next few days.

On the way to Worcester, they discussed the weapons they planned to use and the tactics they would employ if things went wrong. They arrived at the restaurant just as it opened. Tina ordered a fillet and Kathryn ordered a ribeye. Both were delicious, as were the garlic smashed potatoes and roasted zucchini.

At La Enchantress, they danced and drank lightly, but despite the crowd, they kept to themselves and left early. They were sufficiently certain that they did nothing the Enchantress clientele would remember.

They had rented a house in rural Ashford, Connecticut. After arriving, they spent the next three days cleaning guns, looking over drawings of the Mill, planning their entry and exit from the Mill, discussing how best to dress, selecting body armor, and reviewing contingencies and tactics. When they were satisfied and felt they had everything under control, Tina summed up their strategy.

"We have a well-thought-out plan for the hit, and we've planned for things that may go wrong, but we still need to stay alert the entire time we're in the Mill. Anything can still go wrong," Tina said, then added, "When the contract is complete, we'll have no more obligations to the Instigator. We can live as we choose. But before that can happen, we need to kill Phil Messina, Jim Hines, and Mike Robertson."

Chapter 33

Mike Robertson's brain was at war with itself. Conflicting thoughts were fighting for his attention and attempting to dominate his actions. It was very unusual for Mike's brain to resist his efforts to be in charge, but he had lost his ability to influence his own thinking. His mind was out of control. Mike was excited that the search for the Civil War treasure was about to begin, and at the same time, he was terrified that it would end in death.

He wanted to find the treasure, he wanted his efforts and skills recognized, and he wanted to be rich. He also realized the risk he was taking, and worse, he knew that he was putting Phil and Jim's lives in peril. Jim believed that the Civil War treasure was a myth and had only agreed to participate on the grounds of friendship. Mike suspected that Jim wanted to protect the group in case his wife's fears became reality. To minimize danger, Mike had analyzed the reams of old drawings, reconciled the conflicting information, and determined where the most likely location of the treasure was. They would be in and out.

After spending the morning courting new clients for his business in Northborough, he was now driving down I-395 to meet with Jim and Phil in Cargill Falls before starting the search. They planned to review, for what seemed the hundredth time, the old foundation drawings so that they could make a beeline to the supposed treasure room. Just before the Cargill Falls exit, Mike lost focus and nearly collided with a tractor-trailer merging onto I-395. A massive blare of the truck's airhorn shook him back to reality. His brain had failed him. Unbelievable.

"I hope I can make it to Grove Street without getting into an accident," Mike grumbled to himself.

While Mike was making his way to Phil's house, Jim and Phil were trying to make sense of the mess of drawings littering Phil's desk. Phil rubbed his temples and said, "I give up. I only see contradictory information and nothing relevant to a treasure."

Jim replied, "I'm with you. Mike says he sees several possible places to store the treasure and wants to check them out. So, I'll support him, I just hope it doesn't get us killed. Mary Ann will never speak to me again."

Phil's face hardened and he said seriously, "Are you really worried? Do you think we're in danger?"

"Martineau's murderer is still on the loose and the State Police still have not zeroed in on the killer or killers. If there's a conspiracy behind the murder, the State Police have no idea of what's going on. It's been over a year and the police don't know the motive, nor do they have suspects or even a person of interest. My cop senses are on high alert. So, yes, I'm worried. Very worried."

"The choice we face is to look for the treasure or to concede the Mill to the other investors. They said they'll drop their offer if the current owners give us a second chance to look for the treasure. They claim they're sure the treasure is a myth, and they simply want the Mill as an investment property."

"We don't even know who they are! It's possible that they're manipulating us and want the treasure for themselves. Maybe they had Martineau killed and agreed to let us search the Mill one time so they can kill us in it. Puff! No more competition."

"Good Lord! Your police work seems to have made you suspicious of everything and everybody. You don't really believe it's possible?"

"I do."

Just then, Mike walked in. "Jesus Christ, I was almost killed!"

"What are you talking about?" Jim said, glancing at Phil.

"My mind wandered, and I almost missed the exit. I jumped into the exit lane, and I heard a loud airhorn. It scared the hell out of me. I looked in the rearview mirror and saw an eighteen-wheeler filling my mirror, the driver shaking his fist. He was full on his brakes and looked like he was getting back into the exit lane from the shoulder. I obviously ran him off the road. I got on the gas and lost him. That's how I almost died."

"What were you thinking?" Jim followed up.

"Not about driving. I was wrestling with what's happening today. It's a high-risk day with only my word, my opinion, that there's probably a reward at the end of it. And I think that both of you are taking a significant risk based on my judgement, and I don't want that. I want to conduct the search, and I want both of you to stay out of it. I'm responsible if anything happens to either of you. I don't want that."

"Tough shit. We've already decided that we're going with you. We know the risk and accept it, so shut up and get on with it. Show us where you think the treasure is and the best way to get there, and we'll get in and get out fast," Phil said, then looked at Jim, who nodded in agreement.

"You're afraid Tess will kick your ass is all," Jim added.

"Yeah, I guess I am. None of our wives want us in that Mill and they're worried – extremely worried. But if we're going to do this, let's get on with it. I'll show you where I think the treasure may be."

They adjourned to Phil's desk and Mike pointed out the area of the foundation that could not be accurate. He gathered the drawings that documented each addition, then drew a sketch that showed the same area of the foundation. Mike explained that the sketch was the only possible layout of the current foundation and pointed to three areas where he believed Isaac Putnam could have hidden the Civil War treasure.

They had gathered early, so Phil gave Dorian a call to warn him that they would arrive at the Mill in ten minutes.

Dorian panicked. His job was to time the visit so that the contract killer would have it easy coming in from behind to kill the targets. He would have to think of a way to delay the search. He texted the number that the Instigator had given him in case of a problem. The timing had to move ahead about twenty minutes for it to work.

Tina and Kathryn were already behind schedule when the text from Dorian arrived. Fortunately, Tina had built a safety cushion into their plan. She told Kathryn to drop whatever she was doing and finish dressing. They were leaving now. They had loaded the SUV, and the house was clean and wiped down to eliminate fingerprints. The last thing to do was load the weapons into the SUV and head to the Mill.

Kathryn yelled, "Tina! I can't get my body armor vest on right and secured. I need help!"

Tina rushed to Kathryn's room, found the problem, and fixed it, but it took a few minutes. She was certain that they were late. She texted Dorian, "running behind, delay as long as you can, be there in thirty minutes."

Tina and Kathryn gave the house another once-over before getting into the SUV. "Check the guns while we drive," Tina ordered. "Before you say it, I know it's risky, but it's a risk we have to take."

As Dorian waited in the Mill lobby, he mentally reviewed his responsibilities. Most importantly, he had to ensure that all the targets would not pass the corridor where the hitman would hide until after he was in place. Secondarily, he wanted to pick Mike's thoughts on the treasure's hiding place just in case there was another room hidden in the foundation walls. And finally, if for some reason the killer only wounded Phil or Jim, he would have to finish the job.

Dorian lingered in the lobby until Mike and company arrived. After a perfunctory greeting, he immediately started to question Mike about how he had determined the treasure's location and why he believed that it actually existed. Mike ignored the question and announced, "Let me show you where I want to go." He then unfolded a hand-drawn sketch of the Mill foundation and pointed to the destination.

Dorian intuitively knew that he would need to delay the search to give the killer a chance to get into position. He repeated that he wanted to know how Mike had settled on the location. Mike curtly replied, "I don't have all day. Let's go. Just show me the fastest way to get there," and started walking. Then, looking over his shoulder, he added, "When I get there, it won't take long for me to determine if the treasure exists."

On the way Mike sensed that Dorian was looking for ways to slow them down. He would periodically stop walking to point out features of the Mill and discuss the operation in the space above them. Mike was not interested, but Phil obviously was, given the number of questions he asked Dorian. Mike looked at the drawing and knew that they were getting close.

As Tina and Kathryn snuck down the corridor, Tina glimpsed a group of men walking down a perpendicular hallway. She knew that they were her targets but couldn't tell how many men were in the group. She and Kathryn would have to hustle to get into position for the kill. Tina grabbed Kathryn's arm and started to jog.

When they reached their designated hallway, Tina whispered, "Look down the hallway to your left and tell me how close we are to the targets. And draw your gun."

Kathryn peered down the hallway and saw no one. Just then, she heard someone shout, "DROP YOUR GUN!"

Jim disliked Dorian's delay tactics. He had to take a piss, and bad. His urge to urinate had been happening more often as he grew older, and he promised himself that he would see a doctor soon. Spotting a restroom off the corridor, he stopped short. "Guys, I need to stop. Finish the search and I'll catch up to you." He charged toward the bathroom like a bull looking for water. Dorian quickly explained that the group should wait for Jim, but Mike gave him a look that said, "we're not waiting for Jim. We're moving on," and Dorian got the message.

Jim rushed into the restroom and found the urinal, but instead of a stream, he got a trickle. He felt like he had to piss like a racehorse, but after he stood at the urinal for what seemed like an eternity, the floodgates never opened. He zipped up still feeling like he had to go.

As he returned to the hallway, he saw an opening where another hallway entered from the left. A woman leaned out, looking left, with her gun drawn. Jim drew his weapon and yelled, "DROP YOUR GUN!"

Jim intuitively recognized the danger in her movements as she turned and leveled her gun at him. He fired, and she fired an instant later. Jim's bullet struck her in the chest, and she crumpled to the ground. Her bullet missed him by a couple of inches, and he heard it hiss as it passed by.

Just as Jim breathed a sigh of relief, another woman popped out of the side hallway and fired at him. This time he fired second, just as Tina's bullet hit him in the gut. He fell backward and quickly scooted behind some wooden pallets. He worried that she would try to finish him, but she did nothing.

The gunfire alerted Mike and Phil and they ran toward it. Tina heard their footsteps and helped Kathryn to her feet, happy that the vest had done its job. After almost-dragging Kathryn through the halls and out of the Mill, Tina loaded her into the SUV and headed north.

Mike and Phil made a beeline to Jim, who sat wheezing and clutching his belly. Blood flowed over his fingers. Mike tried to staunch the bleeding with pressure. Jim cried out in pain. Phil called 911 and demanded an ambulance and police presence as quickly as possible, citing a gunfight in the basement of the old Pomfret Cotton Mill. He then put

Dorian on the phone and told him to guide the EMTs to Jim. Dorian was secretly relieved that he had no chance to finish the job. He knew that he lacked the guts to do it.

Dorian guided the Cargill Falls police to Jim and stayed on the phone, and he did the same for the EMTs and eventually the State Police. Two Cargill Falls police officers arrived seconds before the EMTs, recognized the seriousness of the victim's wounds, and worked quickly to secure the scene. They hastily confiscated three guns, separated the three men, and told the EMTs to start treating the victim. Only then did they interrogate the three men. They established that Mike and Phil were part of the group planning to purchase the Mill and that Dorian, who worked for the Mill owners, was in the process of conducting a tour. Jim, the victim, had stepped away from the tour briefly and was not with them when they had heard the gunshots. By the time they found Jim, the shooters were nowhere in sight.

Having no information on the perpetrators, the State Police immediately called in the Mobile Crime Lab and began the process of reconstructing the shootout. They also sent out a general alert – a BOLO (Be on the Look Out) for anyone suspicious – but the officers knew it was a long shot.

The EMTs wasted no time on Jim. They started by checking his airways, breathing, and circulation. Jim was conscious and talking nonsense, so his airway was intact. They identified his short, rapid breaths as wound-induced tachypnea. Next, the EMTs listened to the sounds of Jim's heart and lungs and established that they were not damaged. They then started an IV of normal saline and administered a hundred micrograms of fentanyl. The fentanyl acted quickly, and Jim's body relaxed. The EMTs tore through his clothing with scissors and performed a head-to-toe check, front and back, for entrance and exit wounds. They found one of each, indicating a single bullet, and placed a thick ABD pad on each wound. They wrapped his abdomen with cling wrap as a pressure dressing to control bleeding. Once Jim stabilized, they placed him on a long board and lifted him onto a stretcher. One EMT rode in the back of the ambulance with Jim, while the other drove and updated the emergency department physician. He told Doctor Debra Collins that the patient was a sixty-year-old male with a gunshot wound to the abdomen and indicated what they had done to control the bleeding. He added that the patient's BP was dangerously low – ninety-four over fifty – and his heart was racing at one-twenty-two BPM. His respiratory rate was slightly elevated, and he was awake but delusional.

Within fifteen minutes, Jim was in the Day Kimball Hospital Emergency Room in the capable hands of Doctor Debra Collins. As she conducted her initial exam in the ER, Dr. Collins tried asking Jim what happened, but his response was unintelligible. Dr. Collins listened to his heart, lungs, and abdomen for bowel sounds. She removed his bandages to look at Jim's wounds and redressed them. She ordered the nurses to bonus normal saline two thousand liters and start Rocephin one gram and Flagyl five hundred milligrams to treat fecal matter that might be spilling into Jim's abdominal cavity. She ordered two units of O-negative PRBCs (packed red blood cells) stat, and she also ordered two units, typed and cross-matched, placed on hold for the operating room.

Dr. Collins called the surgeon, Dr. Jacobs, and briefly explained the extent of the patient's injuries and explained his immediate need for exploratory surgery. The surgeon then set about assembling the operating team and an anesthesiologist.

As Dr. Collins spoke to Dr. Jacobs, Jim's body began to shut down. He was decompensating. Dr. Collins intubated him, and since his blood pressure dropped, she put in a central line and started Levophed to increase it.

Chapter 34

When Kathryn fell, Tina's first reaction was to check on her. Her second was to protect her. She moved to the end of the corridor, peeked around the corner, and saw Jim slowly approaching, his gun drawn. Tina used all the skills she had honed over the years and with astonishing quickness aimed and fired. She watched Jim hit the floor. She then helped Kathryn to her feet and quickly walked her to the SUV, which she had parked close to the Mill. Kathryn was in remarkable condition for someone who had just taken a bullet to the chest. Tina was unsurprised. Kathryn was young and strong. After she loaded Kathryn into the SUV, she pointed the vehicle north toward Ogunquit, Maine.

Outside of the Mill parking lot, Tina's vehicle was just another SUV on Kennedy Drive heading to I-395. Once on the interstate, she set the cruise control to seventy-two miles per hour and figured that they would be home in a little over two hours. About an hour into the trip, Tina grew concerned. Kathryn had grown pale.

"Are you feeling all right? Do you have any pain?" Tina asked.

Kathryn smiled weakly. "My chest hurts a little. I feel like something's torn, and the pain's moving between my shoulder blades. I'm weak and a little nauseous, but not bad for someone knocked on her can by a bullet."

"I have a doctor on retainer in York Beach and want him to take a look at you. He's good and will get you fixed up."

Tina said it with a smile, but she was worried. Kathryn looked bad and was looking worse by the minute. Tina increased their speed, then called the doctor so he would clear the final patients out of the waiting room and prepare to treat her. When they arrived, Tina struggled to hold Kathryn up and to walk her to the doctor's office.

It took their combined effort to get Kathryn on her back on the exam table. She was looking up at Tina when her aorta ruptured. Tina watched as life drained out of her, and in minutes, Kathryn was dead. She ended her days on this earth at 7,610.

Tina begged the doctor to do something – anything – but he just shook his head. He placed his stethoscope in various places on Kathryn's chest and listened. He finally said, "A slight tear in her aorta ruptured, and she bled out fast. The impact of the bullet probably caused it, even though she wore a vest. Maybe she had an underlying heart condition. I need a CT scan to be sure. What do you want to do?"

"She's dead and that's not going to change, and I don't want an official record of her death. Help me get her into the back seat of the SUV and I'll manage it from there. I don't want you involved." Tina was crying, and her whole body was shaking. The doctor wondered whether extreme sadness or extreme rage was the cause, but looking at her eyes, he suspected rage.

When Kathryn's body was in the back seat and well-covered, Tina got back on the Maine Pike and headed to Portland.

Tina could not shake the thought that she was responsible for Kathryn's death, the woman she loved was dead because of her, her and Jim. If Jim survived Tina vowed, she would kill him.

Harry O was minutes from going live on WINY. He knew that word of the incident at the Mill was spreading through the community; he would have a large audience. He needed his report well-organized and understandable for the majority of his listeners. He took a breath, reached for the microphone, and spoke.

"Today there was a shootout in the basement of the old Pomfret Cotton Mill. Today, three potential buyers were touring the Mill as part of their due diligence when the shooting started. One victim is currently in serious condition at Day Kimball Hospital. Doctors are treating him for a gunshot wound. I will not identify the victim until I am sure that the police have notified his next of kin. The perpetrators were able to escape, unseen and uninjured.

"An unknown assassin executed Bob Martineau, the Mill CEO, in his office in the old Mill over a year ago. That execution remains unsolved to this day. Connecticut State Police, with their vast resources and funding, failed to solve the case and simply stopped investigating. They left the northeast corner of the state with an unsolved murder, continuing their practice of ignoring us. I believe that this shootout would not have happened if the Connecticut State Police solved Martineau's murder. I also believe that the State of Connecticut's government has a propensity to discount us, which is the only explanation for the arrogance of the State Police simply deciding to stop investigating a crime as serious as murder.

Responsibility for a shootout occurring in downtown Cargill Falls squarely rests with the State. But I also bear responsibility. I did not do all I could have to keep the case in front of my audience and call out the incompetence of the State Police. That, I assure you, will not happen again."

Robert Sullivan had become Bobby again. All he could think about was Amanda and their life together. He blamed himself for the accident which ultimately, after years of suffering, took her life. She was gone and would not return, no matter his efforts. Amanda's needs had propelled his actions for as long as he could remember. He had scrounged the money to pay her medical bills, given her a comfortable place to live, and provided the myriads of things she needed to get some joy out of her life. He had driven her to appointments. He had even had Bob Martineau killed when the financial going became difficult. Now she was gone, and any hope for their dream had died with her.

Bobby had the TV tuned to the local Massachusetts CBS station when it reported the news about the shootout in Cargill Falls. Through his drug-and-alcohol-induced mental fog, he knew that the shooter was Tina, and that the victim was one of the three targets whom the Director had wanted killed. The next thought that penetrated the fog was that Robert Sullivan, who had planned to live a life that was above reproach, had failed. He had made a mess of his own and Amanda's lives and committed brutal crimes in the process.

He decided that his life must end, and that it must end immediately. To pay for Robert's sins, Bobby would be the one who must end his life. He needed to kill himself to pay for the damage he had done to Amanda and for the murder of Bob Martineau. He would end it with an overdose of Oxycontin and alcohol. The rest of the world be damned. He would leave no will, nor tell anyone how to dispose of his estate. The only person Bobby had cared about was Amanda. Everyone else be damned. He washed down a handful of pills with a tall glass of whiskey and felt euphoric for a time. He wondered that he might even see Amanda, and then his world went black, ending his days on this earth at 15,844.

Mike and Phil decided that they wanted the "Old Mill Investigators" together at the hospital to wait for word on Jim and to plan their next steps. When they finished with the police, Mike drove Phil to the hospital. On the way, Phil called Rose and briefly explained what had happened to Jim and asked her not to tell Mary Ann. Mike would do it face-to-face, then drive both her and Mary Ann to the hospital. Mike called Tess, told her about the shooting, and asked her to come down to the hospital. He also told her that he would give Mary Ann the news. Phil called Parisi and Noelle and advised them about Jim. Both said that they would be there.

Mary Ann did not cry when Mike told her about Jim. She froze. She stared at Mike without really seeing him. He suspected she saw nothing, really; her mind and expression were completely blank, and he assumed that she was in shock. Rose was already in the car when he led Mary Ann out of her house. Rose quickly decided that it would be best if she let Mary Ann talk when she was ready, and simply smiled as she got in the car.

The Nassau County police brass authorized a helicopter to take Parisi from police headquarters in Mineola, New York to the landing pad at Day Kimball Hospital. Karen arrived in less than an hour, surprising the Old Mill Investigators.

Before meeting Jim, Mary Ann had been content – maybe even happy – with the way her life had evolved so far. She had been married and divorced. Her mother had warned her that black men break down under the subtle pressures of racism. She maintained that those pressures could lead young black men to drugs and alcohol, abuse, or depression. Mary Ann's husband had lived down to her mother's theory. By age twenty-three, she was divorced and had decided that she would live alone for the rest of her life.

After marrying Jim, Mary Ann began to believe that her mother's opinion of Black men was out-of-date. America had changed for the better. Black people were, for the most part, accepted. There would always be racist people, and there would always be people who saw a racist behind every tree. But Mary Ann experienced it less and less.

The only thing she cared about at this instant was Jim's condition. Mary Ann had found and married her perfect man; she was as happy as she had ever been, and Jim was the reason. After his wife had died, he had eaten dinner almost every evening at her diner. She had decided to try and talk to him once because he looked like a lost puppy, and she felt sorry for him. Mary Ann's life changed for the better that night. At the hospital, Jim would not only be fighting for his own life, but he would also be fighting for hers. She needed Jim. She needed to grow old with him. If Jim were to die, Mary Ann would die along with him.

Chapter 35

The Emergency Waiting Room at Day Kimball Hospital housed a solemn gathering of Jim Hines' friends. Despite the room's occupancy, an eerie quiet permeated the air, each person wrestling with his own thoughts and concerns. Mary Ann, consumed by the gravity of Jim's situation, remained silent, lost in contemplation. Phil and Mike, burdened with guilt, harbored self-blame for Jim's unfortunate fate. Tess and Rose, casting accusatory glances at Phil and Mike, held them responsible for Jim's predicament. Noelle, quietly hopeful for Jim's recovery, clung to optimism.

Karen Parisi's unexpected arrival stunned everyone. Swiftly recounting her helicopter journey and the heightened concern from higher-ups, Karen conveyed the collective well-wishes of those who respected and admired Jim. Attempts to comfort Mary Ann fell on deaf ears, the weight of the situation rendering her unresponsive. The group lapsed into silence until Jim's doctor entered the room.

Dr. Collins provided an update, stating, "We have stabilized Mr. Hines and prepared him for surgery. The bullet caused substantial damage, and the surgery, which could last two to three hours, is crucial. Survival odds are fifty-fifty, but personally, I'm optimistic. His strong heart and overall constitution give us hope. The next few days will be critical, but I believe in his resilience."

Mary Ann did not hear a positive word the doctor said. After a minute or two Phil asked, "We're all present, which is rare. There are no other people in this waiting room, and we have two or three hours until we find out about Jim. We should plan our next steps. I have a lot of questions. Who in hell shot Jim? Jim got two shots off, so did he hit anyone? Will they come back?"

Rose interrupted, "Great questions. Hopefully, the police will get to the bottom of the shooting. The first question I'd ask: what are the current owners thinking and planning now that there's been another shooting? My second question is: even if there is a Civil War treasure in the Mill, will it be worth anything? What did people in the 1800s have of value?

Mike replied, "They may just sell it to the other group, and we may be out of luck. We have to talk to them, and fast. Jesus. We could lose our chance to find the treasure."

"A treasure that may be worthless…" Tess responded.

The operating team's job was to open Jim's abdomen and find and repair all the damage done by the bullet. They would thoroughly inspect the entire intestine and bowel system, removing what the bullet had damaged or moving anything that blocked their view. Since the bullet had entered Jim's abdomen in the upper-right quadrant, it likely had injured his liver or spleen.

First the team flushed Jim's abdominal cavity to rid it of any fecal matter and blood, then proceeded to look for and repair any damage. Once the team had made all the needed repairs, they put segments of the bowel back together, a procedure referred to as anastomosis. They began another abdominal cavity flush and a final inspection for any bleeding before closing.

Noelle said, "I know what valuables people and families had in the mid-1800s and what they might be worth today. I did some research when I found out there might be items from that period hidden in the old Mill."

That gave everyone pause and the room quieted until Phil said, "Well, let's hear it."

Noelle replied, "Okay. I'll try to give you an overview. Remember that years – like over one-hundred-fifty – have gone by.

"In the 1860s, the possessions of a wealthy family in America would reflect their social status, lifestyle, and access to resources, as they would today. America was prosperous in the years leading up to the Civil War, and there were more wealthy families in America than most people would guess. Wealthy families often owned substantial amounts of land with grand estates or mansions as their residences. Rogue soldiers, both Confederate and Union, would rob and pillage these wealthy Americans during the Civil War. Their homes would contain high-quality, often handcrafted furniture made from expensive woods like mahogany or cherry. The rogue soldiers probably would not take larger furniture, but they would take smaller pieces, and elaborate sets of silverware and fine China used for dining and entertaining. The soldiers would also steal valuable paintings, sculptures, and antiques that had aesthetic appeal or historical significance.

"The homes of the wealthy would also have expensive clothing and luxurious fabrics such as silk, satin, and velvet. Their garments were often made with intricate lace, embroidery, and other finely constructed details. The wealthy would adorn themselves with high-quality jewelry, including gemstones, diamonds, and precious metals. They also wore fine watches and accessories."

"Stop for a minute, please. I, for one, am convinced that if there's a treasure hidden in the Mill, it could certainly be valuable. Noelle, could you just list the rest, please?" Karen asked.

"Sure. High-end musical instruments; rare and valuable books, often in leather-bound editions; fine wines and spirits; stocks, bonds, and other financial instruments."

"Are we agreed that it's worth pursuing the Mill and the treasure?" Mike asked.

Just then, the Putnam brothers, Elijah and Nathan, walked in. After a quick look around, they went straight to Mary Ann. Elijah patted her on the back and spoke. "What happened to Jim is horrible. I can't imagine what you are going through."

At the sound of Elijah's voice, Mary Ann came out of her trance and cried, "I don't want to live the rest of my life without Jim. He can't die! My life has been so much better since I met him."

Nathan interjected, "Dr. Collins and Dr. Jacobs are excellent and will take superb care of him, and I assure you that he will make it through the procedure. I have a good feeling about it."

Mary Ann did not hear the last statement as she returned to her thoughts.

Elijah asked the group, "Did you hear Harry O's report on the radio? We should recruit him. He could help."

Tina had three things on her mind as she drove to Portland: Kathryn's death, the disposal of her body, and revenge. She had a funeral home in Portland on retainer for just such a situation. Tina called ahead and advised Paul Derrick, the owner, that she would need his services. He would not have to prepare the body. Paul told her that the Huntington room was ready and that the key would be in the normal place. Since learning of this method of disposal, Tina's controllers had made it a routine part of their offerings, albeit an extremely expensive part.

Tina had heard a news report that Jim Hines had survived the shooting and was in surgery, she hoped that he would survive so that she would have the pleasure of killing him. She would wait a day or two before acting.

Tina was pleased with the condition of the Huntington room. Paul had thoroughly cleaned the concrete floor, the tools were clean and neatly laid out, and there was plenty of room in the freezers. The first step was to drain all the blood from Kathryn's body and wash it down the drain.

Next, Tina severed Kathryn's limbs and cut her legs in two. She then separated Kathryn's head from her torso and cut the torso in half. Tina wrapped the body parts in plastic and carefully loaded them into different freezers. Most people might think what she did was ghoulish, but Tina, however, thought of it as an act of love.

Tina left the Huntington room as she had found it and started for home. On the way, she formulated a plan for how to end Jim Hines life: this time, a plan that would work.

While waiting for the results of Jim's surgery, the Old Mill Investigators planned their next moves. Phil volunteered to recruit Harry O to help get the story out. Mike and Phil would meet with the Putnam Group and determine how they wanted to proceed. They also intended to find out as much information as possible about the other buyers. Karen would reestablish contact with the Connecticut State Police and determine whether they were active in the case, then subtly push them to provide her information. Rose, Tess, and Noelle would look after Mary Ann and hopefully stay on top of Jim's recovery. More importantly, they would learn all they could about Civil War treasure and its value today.

Elijah and Nathan believed that the treasure could only be in the Mill if Isaac Putnam had found it and brought it there. They would reread all the information on Isaac and look for a clue.

The group had finished planning for the night and found themselves staring into space, waiting for word on Jim's condition. They were worried. He had been in surgery for almost three-and-a-half hours.

Instead of relief, a feeling of dread descended on Jim's friends when the doctor finally walked into the waiting room. Dr. Jacobs appeared grim and genuinely concerned. "Mr. Hines has a strong constitution, a strong heart, and a will to live," he said. "He will need to muster every bit of his strength to make it for the next few days. The fact that he survived the surgery is almost amazing. The bullet that the shooter used was meant to kill. It literally exploded on impact and did major damage to his internal organs. We repaired all the damage we could find. His blood pressure is good and holding, so he is not bleeding internally. As long as he doesn't start bleeding in the next day or two, he will survive."

"We will have Mr. Hines under constant observation in Intensive Care until we feel he's stable. It should take about three days," he added.

Mary Ann planned to spend the night in Jim's room and Tess would stay with her. Mike and Karen would stay at the Messina house and Noelle would go home. The Putnam brothers would also go home. Everyone was exhausted.

Major Beck

Adam Beck enlisted in the Confederate army at the onset of the Civil War, initially serving as a private in the Washington Mounted Rifles. The Partisan Rangers Act, passed by the Confederate Congress, allowed him to form Beck's Rangers after proving his mettle as a skilled scout and intelligence gatherer. In 1863, with approval from his commanders, Beck took command of the 43rd Battalion Virginia Cavalry, operating as part of the Army of Northern Virginia. His unit, however, operated outside the conventional norms of regular army cavalrymen, living among civilians and avoiding camp duties.

The unconventional cavalry unit, stationed in central Virginia, wreaked havoc on Union positions. Beck's Rangers employed guerrilla tactics, slipping behind Union lines under the cover of darkness to capture soldiers and supplies. Known for their blistering attacks, they destroyed rail lines and bridges, dispersing into the woods afterward.

In a daring 1863 raid near Fairfax Court House, Beck and his men infiltrated Union lines, capturing General Edwin H. Stoughton without firing a shot. The Rangers left town with prisoners, horses, and reportedly a substantial treasure, which was valued at around two hundred thousand in gold, silver, jewelry, and family heirlooms taken from Southern homes.

Beck, following a distinct treasure-hiding strategy, claimed an abandoned wolf den and stored the spoils deep within. Legend suggested that this treasure could be worth fifty million dollars today. Even General Robert E. Lee applauded the heist, stating, "Hurrah for Beck! I wish I had a hundred like him!" Conversely, President Abraham Lincoln, upon hearing of the raid, expressed more concern for the loss of horses than his general, remarking, "I can make brigadier generals, but I can't make horses."

Beck's rapid promotions to captain and then major in March of 1863 underscored his military prowess. Despite continuing his operations in north-central Virginia until the war's end, Beck met his demise during an attempt to retrieve the hidden cache. Near the war's end, a reconnaissance team in search of Major Beck and his men prowled the hills of Virginia. They found their prey, and a firefight ensued. With superior tactics, the union soldiers overcame Beck and his men. When Beck lost hope, he ordered his men to scatter. A Union major followed Beck, and after a protracted chase and running gunfight, the union major discovered Beck's lifeless body.

Before his death, Beck allegedly lamented that there was more valuable treasure hidden in the Virginia countryside that he wished he had obtained. To this day, there is no record of anyone finding the treasure, leaving its existence shrouded in mystery and legend.

Chapter 36

The Director harbored deep concern, bordering on anxiety. His attempts to reach Robert Sullivan the previous day, spurred by the shootout at the Mill, had yielded no response. Determined to address Robert's apparent despondency and redirect his focus to acquiring the Mill, he embarked on an hour-long drive to Robert's house.

Upon arrival, a sense of dread filled the Director even though he spotted Robert's car in the driveway, indicating his presence at home. The house appeared to be empty. Though eager to find out Robert's condition, he opted not to call 911, as he knew it would be unwise for the authorities to connect him to Robert. He knew that Robert's neighbor helped him care for Amanda and that she had a key to the house. The Director would wait for her to act.

That afternoon, Mabel Theodor decided that it was time to check on Robert, as she had not seen him in two days. She retrieved the key and headed out. Robert's house seemed eerily quiet. Mabel rang the doorbell, then knocked. When Robert failed to answer, she knocked harder. Finally, she put the key in the lock and twisted it.

Inside the house she called Robert's name over and over, hoping a grim discovery did not await her. She mustered the strength to look in Robert's bedroom, where she found his lifeless body. She dialed 911.

Within thirty minutes, the police arrived, offering apologies for taking so long. Mabel explained the reason why she had a key and how she had found Robert's lifeless body in the house. Next, she detailed her concern about Robert's mental state, prompting the sergeant to conduct a thorough examination of the other entry points, all of which were securely locked. He ruled out foul play and reported Robert's death as a suicide.

As soon as he heard a news report on Robert's death, The Director called his coconspirator, the State Senator, to deliver the disturbing news of Robert's suicide. "Robert was the face of our investor group and the sole member known to the Mill owners. We need to meet tonight and strategize our next moves. I must gather information from both Dorian and Tina on what transpired at the Mill. This situation could escalate into a significant problem for us."

The State Senator, considering his schedule, responded, "I'm tied up throughout the day. How about meeting at 7:30 in Rhode Island? Siena works for me."

"Great, see you there," said the Director, affirming the urgency of their meeting.

Tina had meticulously planned to end Jim Hines's life that very night. Having finalized the details, she set out to acquire everything required, including a nurse's uniform and a quantity of Fentanyl. Departing for Day Kimball Hospital at noon, Tina was determined to arrive before the three PM shift change. She managed to reach the hospital a little after two, giving her plenty of time to observe the activity around Jim Hines before changing into her nurse's uniform and executing her plan.

In the ICU waiting room, Tina found herself alone until Mary Ann, Rose, and Tess walked in, taking seats within earshot. Apparently, Jim's blood pressure had dropped a little, causing enough concern among the staff to prompt a thorough examination. A team of medical professionals worked diligently, checking vital signs, listening to chest sounds, and drawing blood for analysis. The medical team working on Jim asked Mary Ann and her friends to leave.

Jim's progress in the last two days had been slow and steady. Mary Ann remained worried yet hopeful. She communicated with her friends, expressing her appreciation for the positive impact he had on her life. Mary Ann spoke passionately about Jim's character, her disdain for the person who shot him, and Jim's rightful presence in the Mill. Tina listened intently, processing Mary Ann's sentiments.

Tina's rage at Kathryn's death intensified as she observed Mary Ann's suffering. *Just wait,* she thought, *he's alive and has a chance at life. Kathryn's dead and gone. I'll never see her again.* Despite her blinding wrath, the thought ran through her mind that Jim Hines had not set out to kill Kathryn. She and Kathryn were in the Mill to kill Jim and his friends, and Jim had shot Kathryn in self-defense. As the three women continued to converse, Tina realized that a CNN televised debate on Hamas and Israel was airing in the waiting room. The question at hand was, "Who is responsible for the death of Palestinian civilians?" Tina absorbed arguments from both sides before concluding that Hamas had initiated the conflict with a terror attack on Israeli civilians, and that Israel had the right to defend itself. Tina blamed herself for Kathryn's death but realized that the Instigator was also responsible for her death, not Jim. She had entered the Mill with the intent to kill Jim, Phil, and Mike, while Jim had no intention of causing harm to Kathryn.

During the drive back to Maine, Tina solidified her belief that the responsibility for Kathryn's death rested squarely on the shoulders of the Instigator.

Tina faced the challenging task of uncovering the identity of the Instigator, a formidable undertaking. The organization responsible for orchestrating contract killings diligently guarded the anonymity of those who commissioned them. Tina knew that unveiling the mastermind behind her current contract would be an arduous endeavor, yet she clung to the hope that it was not insurmountable. Once she arrived home, her immediate focus would shift to meticulous planning.

Phil found himself running about ten minutes behind schedule for his meeting with Harry O. The radio host had squeezed Phil into his tight schedule, leaving only thirty minutes, now reduced to twenty, for Phil to present his case. As Phil entered the office, he noticed Harry O sitting at his desk with his eyes closed.

Harry O remarked, "I had a late-night last night."

Not wasting time, Phil got straight to the point. "I'll be quick. I'm part of a group investigating Bob Martineau's murder, hoping to uncover something the State Police might have missed. We're searching for that crucial piece of evidence to crack the case open. There are eight of us in the group. Jim Hines, the guy shot while touring the Mill, is a retired Nassau County Commander now living in Cargill Falls. Karen Parisi, an active Nassau County police detective, is our liaison with the Connecticut State Police. My wife Rose and I, along with Mike and Tess Robertson and Mary Ann Hines, are investigators. Noelle Lefevre assists with the investigation and provides historical context as needed."

Interrupting, Harry O asked, "Wait a minute, didn't you and Hines solve that case down in Long Island?"

Phil confirmed, "Yes."

Curious, Harry O questioned, "Why me?"

Phil explained, "After hearing your comments about the shoot-out, we believe you're highly motivated and could be a significant asset. You could get information to the community and misinformation to the killers."

Expressing concern, Harry O noted, "I'm very busy with the radio station and not sure how much time I have."

Phil assured him, "I'll keep you updated personally via email or text, and you can do the same with me. You can attend meetings when your schedule allows. In today's world, communication is easy."

After some consideration, Harry O agreed, "I'll give it a try."

"Great," Phil replied, appreciative of the support.

Located in Smithfield, Siena stands out as one of the finest Italian restaurants in Rhode Island. The restaurant draws its inspiration from the Palio, a renowned horse race held thrice annually in Siena, Italy. Scattered around the restaurant are bronzes of bareback rider-and-horse duos and paintings of the race. The Palio is unique to Siena and is quite a spectacle. Three times a year, the Italian city of Siena transforms its central plaza into a dirt-covered oval racetrack surrounded by stands.

Teams representing the seventeen neighborhoods of Siena each sponsor a horse and rider. Each duo competes fiercely, racing around the oval track three times. Notably, the riders guide their horses bareback, and the race unfolds without any specific rules to constrain their actions. Siena, the restaurant, captures the essence of this exhilarating event, providing a unique and immersive dining experience.

Seeking privacy, The Director and the State Senator had reserved a booth in a small dining area. The Director broached the conversation, expressing his concerns. "The most significant issue we have is money. Robert raised one-point-five million dollars by leveraging his construction company, and that money is no longer available to us. We need to replace it in order to acquire the Mill. I don't have that kind of money."

The Senator weighed in, "I'm using campaign contributions for my share as it is. It's illegal, and I can't risk using more. While one of my donors could easily fund the entire deal, he's a real prick. He'd want to control every decision, and if things got tough, he'd betray us without giving it a second thought. What about a bank?"

The Director considered, "I don't think we have the collateral, but I'll give it a try. I have connections with a large Boston bank, and I'll see if I can squeeze them a little. However, I'm not optimistic about them lending us the money."

"Maybe Robert left us the money in his will?"

"I doubt it. He never liked either of us, or even if he did, settling his estate would take months, if not years. I think our best choice, if the bank says no, is to approach your big donor, even if he's a prick. We need to structure a partnership agreement that limits his influence as much as possible. The big question is – how much do we tell him about the treasure? He could buy the Mill without us."

As they savored their meal, the discussion shifted to the matter of who would replace Robert as the face of the investor group. The options on the table were a disgraced executive or a crooked politician. They weighed the pros and cons of each potential candidate, recognizing the significance of selecting someone who could navigate the complexities of the situation and not panic the sellers.

The Director still wanted Jim Hines and Phil Messina dead but kept that thought out of the conversation.

Isaac Putnam

In 1861, Isaac Putnam joined the Union Army, eager to wage the moral battle against slavery. His commanding officers quickly recognized not only his imposing physical presence but also his strong moral values. It took a little longer for them to acknowledge his superior intelligence and leadership abilities. Nevertheless, Isaac's ascent through the ranks was swift, and he reached the distinguished rank of Brigadier General by the time of his discharge.

Throughout the Civil War, Isaac Putnam distinguished himself in numerous battles, proving to be an exceptional soldier. From his early involvement in the victory at the Battle of Hoke's Run in Virginia to leading Union troops to triumph as a captain at the Battle of Fort Anderson in North Carolina, Isaac's prowess was evident. In 1864, as a Brigadier General, he secured victory for his troops at the Battle of Peebles' Farm. Acknowledging that not every battle ended in triumph, Putnam believed that he learned more from defeat, becoming a better leader with each subsequent engagement.

Near the war's end, he led a reconnaissance team in search of Major Beck and his men in the hills of Virginia. A firefight ensued, and with superior tactics, he overcame Beck and his men. When Beck lost hope, he ordered his men to scatter. In pursuit, Putnam, after a protracted chase and gunfire, discovered Beck's lifeless body. Among Beck's possessions were two seemingly meaningless maps, which he kept as a souvenir.

Isaac, hailed as a hero, returned to New England after the war. He settled in Cargill Falls, Connecticut. His military background attracted job offers from burgeoning manufacturing companies in town. Cotton goods manufacturing dominated Cargill Falls's growth, and Putnam chose to work at the Pomfret Cotton Mill, eventually rising to the position of General Manager upon Edward Cutler's retirement.

Living frugally, he invested heavily in the Pomfret Cotton Company, guiding it to prosperity and accumulating wealth. He married Sara Wheelock, and together they raised three intelligent and happy children. Despite his newfound success, either Isaac's humble upbringing or his thirst for intellectual challenge led him to invest in various industries.

The Cargill Falls Woolen Company, organized in 1878, witnessed Putnam's investment and consultation, thriving under the management of his father-in-law, E. A. Wheelock. Isaac's involvement extended beyond, as he assisted in the startup and operation of new mills and invested in emerging industries. The latter half of the 1800s saw rapid industrialization in northeast Connecticut, with Isaac contributing to the introduction of silk goods and modern shoe manufacturing.

As industries flourished, so did every town in northeast Connecticut, providing abundant employment for carpenters, masons, and workers in wood and stone. Over the years, Isaac Putnam amassed a considerable fortune through his management and investing skills, ensuring the well-being of his wife and children. Yet the more prosperous he became, the more he sought new challenges. His thoughts wandered back to Major Beck and the mountains of Virginia, spurred on by rumors of buried treasure hinted at by the maps he had so long disregarded as souvenirs. If he found a treasure, he would use it to secure the lives of the people of northeast Connecticut.

Chapter 37

Jim's doctor was no longer pessimistic about his chances of recovery, but she was not overly optimistic either. He was making progress. The many repairs the surgeon made to his internal organs were holding. Jim's doctor even allowed his friends to see him, albeit one at a time for ten minutes each. Phil was currently with Jim while the other members of the "Old Mill Investigators" relaxed and engaged in small talk in the ICU waiting room.

On returning to the waiting room, Phil said, "I talked to Jim, but I suspect that he didn't really hear me. He's still heavily sedated, but the doctor said talking to him will help his recovery. We should take the time to all go in and see him and talk to him. Mary Ann, do you want to go now, or do you still want to wait?"

"I'll go last so I might get away with spending more than ten minutes," she replied. While Phil visited Jim, Mary Ann had received a detailed update from Jim's doctor. Her face portrayed the good news the doctor shared about Jim, and a broad smile adorned her face as she rejoined the group.

Everyone wanted to hear Jim's prognosis, but the doctors could only tell Mary Ann. She obliged the group. "They started weening Jim off his pain medication this morning and are monitoring his reaction. They hope to have him completely off in two or three days. Once he's drug-free, he should be able to talk about the gun battle and describe the person that shot him. The doctor said his recovery is remarkable."

"The police are waiting for Jim's head to clear and give them something to go on. So far, they have nothing," Karen Parisi said.

After everyone spent some time visiting with Jim and a nurse finally asked Mary Ann to leave, they decided to head to the Courthouse Bar and Grill for a mid-afternoon lunch and to discuss their next steps.

The only customers at the Courthouse Bar and Grill occupied the bar and Sheila, the owner, seated the group far enough away from the bar that they could conduct their meeting in private.

The group spent hours discussing their individual findings, suspicions, and theories. They were determined to uncover the truth behind the shooting at the Mill and to bring justice to Jim. As the day wore on, they made plans and assigned tasks, ensuring that each member played a crucial role in the investigation.

The camaraderie of the Old Mill Investigators persisted, a bond forged through shared challenges and triumphs. They knew that they were up against a formidable opponent, but their determination and unity remained unshaken. The Courthouse Bar and Grill witnessed not only the exchange of information but also the strength of a community bound together by a common goal.

Tina, still despondent over Kathryn and angry at herself for deciding to involve her in the contract, thought about revenge. The anger at herself emanated from the logical part of her brain. The emotional part of her brain wanted the Instigator dead. Maybe she would feel closure if the Instigator paid with his life. She knew that acquiring his identity would be exceedingly difficult. It might cause her handlers to put a contract on her head, but it would be worth the risk. She needed a plan: who to ask, the reason for asking, and a way to explain what she planned to do with the information. Tina had thought of nothing else since returning from Portland and she could only come up with what was, in her mind, a weak plan. But a weak plan was better than no plan.

Tina looked intently at her cell, then said to herself, "What the fuck, the worst thing that could happen is they kill me." She punched in the number.

"Saul, it's Tina, how are you today?"

"Busy. What's on your mind?'

"Saul, I'm sure you know by now that I ran into a problem completing the hit the Instigator of the Mill contract wanted."

"We're working with him to come up with a resolution. There's nothing for you to do."

"I figured that, but when he called me, he was adamant that I successfully execute the contract. I want to explain to him what went wrong and why the timing was bad."

"My reaction is no. But this kind of thing does not happen often, especially to you. I'll run your request passed Herman and get back to you. Anything else?"

"I feel bad about the screw-up, so it's important to me that I talk with him. Please let Herman know how important I think it is."

"I will. I sense you might have an ulterior motive for getting his information, though. I'm sure you realize what will happen if you do, and it won't be pretty."

"My only motive is keeping my reputation intact and my rating perfect."

"Goodbye, Tina."

"Bye, Saul."

Tina ended the call and ran it through her mind again. She thought that it went well, except for Saul's suspicion that she might have an ulterior motive. That could be a problem. It was true, however, that her track record was pristine, and she hoped that Saul would believe her justification.

Next, Tina decided to search the internet for information on Phil Messina and Jim Hines to see if there would be a reason for someone wanting them both dead.

Chapter 38

The Nassau County police department officially placed Karen Parisi on a paid leave of absence to work on Jim Hines's shooting. The explanation given by the higher-ups was, "We hate it when a retired Nassau County cop is shot, and it's not going to go unpunished." Unsaid was that the Nassau County Police department believed that the Connecticut State Police were incompetent. It should never take over a year to solve a murder. The Mill CEO's murder had happened over a year ago and remained unsolved. The Nassau County executives would be damned if resolving the shooting of a retired Nassau County Commander would take that long. Karen would stay with the Messinas and work on the case for the duration.

The only item on Karen's agenda for the day was a meeting with Connecticut State Police Captain Sal Belardi. Captain Belardi was the lead investigator in the Martineau murder and had been since the beginning. Karen's first liaison on the case, Lieutenant James Rasmussen, retired effective immediately. Karen had heard that he had cancer. She hoped that Captain Belardi would appoint her new liaison promptly.

Karen decided on a professional, but slightly sexy outfit, a tight-fitting blue pant suit and a low-cut blouse. She wore white two-inch heels; at five-foot-six, she did not want to be too tall. *Hell, he's Italian and might be short. I want to look him in the eye*, she thought.

Captain Belardi, decked out in his Connecticut State Police Uniform, was waiting at the Mill entrance when Karen pulled up and parked her rental. He looked handsome and distinguished, and she felt her heart skip a beat when she stepped out of her vehicle and saw him fully. "Captain Belardi, I assume?" Karen said as she walked toward him with her hand out. "I'm detective Karen Parisi, Nassau County."

Belardi looked her over once, then again. "Yes, I'm Captain Belardi. Nice to meet you Ms. Parisi."

"You also, Captain, and please call me Karen."

"Only if you call me Sal."

"Okay, Sal. I hope you have lots of information for me on the shooting, and a new liaison for me to work with."

"I'll be your new liaison and I have information to share today. We can talk over a coffee at the Saw Dust Café. It's close, we can walk."

As they walked across the Route 44 bridge, Karen commented, "God, the falls are beautiful and right in the middle of town. And people can see them from most areas of Cargill Falls. Gorgeous."

Sal thought, *So are you*. He then said, "They are beautiful. I'm staying at an Airbnb in town until we get this case solved. When are you heading back to Long Island?"

"Same as you. I will be in town for the duration. I'm staying on Grove Street with the Messina family."

After ordering coffee, they settled into a secluded table. Sal started. "We've interviewed the Mill owners at length and have unearthed a lead. A man named Robert Sullivan committed suicide the day the perps shot Jim Hines. Sullivan had presented the competing offer to acquire the Mill before your team. Whether or not there is a connection between Sullivan's suicide and the Jim Hines shooting I just don't know, but we're looking into it. Sullivan's wife recently passed. They had been together since elementary school, so that may have motivated his suicide. We want to find his other investors, because we're thinking they might be involved with the shootings at the Mill. Questions?"

"Thanks for the update, and for what it's worth, you have a solid lead. Anything else?"

"We want to know the reason for the Mill tour. We think your team was looking for something and that something may be important to the case. The Mill owners wouldn't tell us. They said it was part of a confidential contract. I'd like you to tell me what it is you're hoping to find?"

Karen thought for a minute and replied, "Phil Messina is handling contracts and business dealings. I need to ask him before I say anything. I'll make sure he knows how important it is."

"Good. I want this to be a two-way street. We told the Mill owners to hold off on any activity related to selling the Mill for a minimum of two or three weeks. It could take us that long to get a subpoena and search phone and computer files to find Sullivan's contacts."

Karen nodded. "One more item before we're done. The two men that were with Jim in the Mill felt like Dorian, their guide, behaved like he had another agenda.

Sal wrote a note and responded, "Thanks, we'll sweat him and see what he knows. That's what I meant by a two-way street. How about we finish our coffee before we leave? I have a personal question." Sal hoped to get to know Karen better.

"Okay," said Karen. "I'll bite."

"Judging by your name, I assume you're at least part Italian. Have you looked into your ancestry, like where in Italy they came from, what towns? And their names? I'm curious because I don't know anything about my ancestors and want to find out."

"Both my father and mother have their roots in Italy. A couple of years ago, my father put together a fairly extensive family tree. My father's family, Parisi, is from a small hill town in Calabria, San Nicola dell'alto. His mother's maiden name is Rossi. My mother's family is from a small hill town in Umbria, Gubbio. Her Maiden name is Cardoni, and her mother's maiden name is Baldi."

"You know a lot about your family. I'll have to start researching my last name and my mother's maiden name, Orsini." Sal did not want to go back to work but knew he must, so he closed their conversation. "You'll get to me on the reason your team searched the Mill, and I'll keep you updated on our progress. Deal?"

"Deal."

Chapter 39

"Jim, do you remember who shot you?" Mary Ann asked.

"A woman, I think. She looked like a man, but I think it was a disguise. Two women – there were two women – I shot one, she shot at me but missed. The second woman showed up and pointed her gun at me and fired without aiming and hit me. All my years as a cop and the first time I get shot is after I retire. She was a real marksman," Jim said as he fell asleep.

Worried, Mary Ann called the nurse, who checked Jim promptly. "He simply fell asleep," she said. "His meds must have kicked in. He really has improved in the last day, and we've started weaning him off painkillers. He should be fully awake tomorrow. He's strong for a man of his age." Mary Ann breathed a sigh of relief.

Tess and Rose were in the waiting room and Mary Ann could not wait to tell them. "Jim told me there were two women in the Mill! One of them shot at him and the second one shot him. He said they looked like men, but they were women. He felt sure. The nurse said he was strong and would be fine soon."

Tess said, "Women. Jesus Christ, what has this world come to? Women hitmen. What else did he say?"

"Just that he thinks he shot one of them," replied Mary Ann.

"There was no evidence that Jim shot someone, no blood," Rose said. "But all of this definitely means that Jim is coming around. We need Phil and Mike here tomorrow morning, ready to ask questions. Let's wait for another hour or so to see if he wakes up. Okay, ladies… we can spend an hour talking."

After about fifteen minutes, all three seemed talked out. Mary Ann looked at Tess and asked, "What's Mike's story? Jim told me some of his background, but I would like to know more."

Rose nodded, adding, "So would I."

Tess gathered her thoughts and spoke. "We were nineteen when we started dating. I didn't know Mike before then, but he told me about his life growing up and I remember his story like I remember my own.

"Mike grew up in the heart of Worcester and faced challenges that shaped his journey to adulthood. Worcester is a diverse city and provided the backdrop for Mike to grow into the good man he is today. The city is full of unique communities, and Mike grew up in one that was tight-knit and mostly black. His family emphasized the value of education and hard work. Mike's parents were poor but proud, and they worked tirelessly to support their family. Mike learned the importance of resilience and determination from them. He looked up to his older brother and sister as role models.

"In high school, Mike experienced both the warmth of mostly supportive teachers and the harsh reality of racial disparities. Worcester exposed him to various cultures and perspectives, fostering a sense of openness and understanding. Mike still holds those values dear today.

"He only got there by struggling through his challenging teenage years, though. Mike dealt with the complexities of identity and belonging that teenagers face. Along with his brother and best friend Jamal, he started experimenting with alcohol and illegal drugs, lost interest in school, and focused on partying. Concerned, their parents intervened and emphasized the realities of life and the potential consequences of their actions.

"While Jamal struggled with the grip of addiction, Mike internalized the teachings of his parents and chose a different path. Engaging with community organizations and local mentorship programs, he found solace and guidance from role models who understood the unique struggles faced by young black people in Worcester.

"Mike used local community centers and sporting events to stay focused. He discovered a passion for sports, particularly football, and was the star wide receiver on the high school team in his junior and senior years. He continued to neglect his studies, though, and wasn't prepared for the work world despite above-average intelligence.

"Jamal secured a job for him at the foundry where he worked. Mike had to overcome the obstacles of stereotypes and oppression both at that job and elsewhere. When a stray bullet killed Mike's sister while she was shopping in downtown Worcester, he became angry at the world. Angry that his sister was a victim of a random act of violence. Angry that he was working at a miserable job: a hot, dangerous, dead-end job. Mike thought his future wouldn't change. He thought about returning to drugs.

"On a lark, Mike started to read the teachings of Martin Luther King Junior. Drawing inspiration from Dr. King's teachings, he learned to channel those experiences into self-advocacy. He became a positive force for himself and, later in life, his family.

"The lessons of his upbringing and the resilience instilled by his community changed Mike's life. Despite the challenges, he became a testament to the strength and potential of a young black man.

"Then we met, fell in love, and faced the problems I already shared with you. Fortunately, we overcame the issue of being an interracial couple at a time when people viewed it as wrong."

Mary Ann responded, "Unfortunately, Mike's story is still too common in the black community. He survived and prospered. That's not always the outcome."

Tess addressed Rose, "Mike said Phil had it tough growing up. Do you know his story?"

"Yes, but before I talk about Phil, I want to say that Mike had you as motivation. And I feel like Jim survived his first wife's death because he found Mary Ann. And after I tell you about Phil, I hope you'll feel I helped," Rose said.

"Phil's parents were first generation Italians. His grandparents immigrated around 1905 and settled in Jessup, Pennsylvania. His maternal grandmother immigrated with her parents, two brothers, and a baby sister. Phil's great grandfather, Carmine, worked and died in a coal mine. The accident happened in 1916, when a mine car full of coal ran over both him and his older brother. The mine supervisors loaded both bodies into a buck-board wagon and unceremoniously dumped them in the front yard of the house they shared.

"America didn't have a safety net at the time, and as a result, the families struggled. Phil's grandfather, Adolpho, and his great uncle, Alfredo, also worked in the mines. His grandmother and aunts worked in the garment factories that dotted the area. The factories were classic sweatshops: hot and dirty in the summer, cold and dirty in the winter. The cloth fibers filled the air in the factory, clogging the workers' noses and lungs and settling on their skin.

"The families eked out a living, raised their children, and managed food, clothing and shelter. When the children came of age at ten or eleven years old, they quit school and worked in the sweatshops. No one in the family earned a lot of money, but somehow, the next generation included Accountants, Engineers, Meteorologists, and Executives. Quite a change.

"When Phil was a teenager, he worked a number of jobs including two summers in a sweatshop. Phil worked a lot of hours, and he played for a lot of hours and didn't have time for school. He gave no thought to college and his grades reflected his attitude.

"Then we married, and Phil changed his attitude. He went to Penn State and then became successful at work for the McKenzie Company.

Tess responded, "Mike and Phil's backgrounds are similar. No wonder they like each other and get along so well! Mary Ann, since we're really getting to know each other by talking about our men, what do you know about Jim's early life?"

"A lot, really. Jim and I talked about his life many times. He wondered why he and Phil saw the world so differently. He said Phil always focused on the individual as opposed to me, who always focuses on the group. As for his early days, he was born in Alabama.

"When Jim was seven years old, his family moved to Harlem. His family included his mother, grandmother, and younger sister. In Alabama, Jim's father worked as a handyman for a well-to-do white family. The local police showed up on his day off and accused him of raping and murdering the wife. That day she was home alone, her husband was in Mobile on business, and her son was on a school trip. Jim's father was home with his wife. There was only a little circumstantial evidence, mostly fingerprints, tying his father to the crime. Jim's father easily explained the fingerprints since he worked around the house. Unfortunately, DNA testing didn't exist yet. The state had an eyewitness who saw a black man around the house, and despite his mother swearing her husband was with her all day, the jury convicted his father and sentenced him to death. The white woman's family was well-liked, and in the eyes of the town, Jim's family was the family of the man who killed her. So, they moved to New York City.

"Life in New York took its toll on Jim's mother. She was sixteen when he was born and twenty-three when they moved to New York. She worked two low-paying menial jobs, and Jim's grandmother took care of Jim and his sister. I've seen pictures; his mother was a beautiful woman. And she attracted the attention of many men. Unfortunately, one man in the neighborhood became obsessed with her, and when she spurned him, he killed her. Shot her in the face, then stuck the gun in his mouth and pulled the trigger. She was dead at twenty-six."

"You don't have to continue if the story is too painful," said Tess gently.

"Yes, I do. A beautiful woman, a good woman who worked hard to take care of her family, shot in the face by a lunatic. Jim's grandmother stayed in Harlem a while and then moved to Hempstead and lived on welfare. She swore that Jim and his sister would make it in the world, that they'd get a good education and good jobs. She pushed them constantly. She tried to keep them away from the street life, away from drugs, and away from the lazy good-for-nothings that stayed out late at night and skipped school. She made sure they knew that no matter how far they got in life or how much money they made, they should never lose sight of the black community. She drilled into their heads that without help, black people would always be poor and not respected by others in the world. Jim listened, graduated high school with honors, and went to Hofstra. He got a degree in Criminal Science and joined the Nassau County Police Department. He succeeded.

"His sister couldn't resist the street and wound up addicted to drugs. She died from AIDS fifteen years ago. Jim's grandmother died not long after, and before she did, she said Jim made her proud. She also told him he was strong and had to take care of his weaker brothers and sisters."

Tears filled Mary Ann's eyes and trickled down her cheeks.

Rose said, "We married good men. They all had little in the way of material things growing up, but they all had guidance and love."

Chapter 40

Tina's eyes felt irritated. They were, in fact, red, watery, and itchy. The days staring at a computer screen did that to her, and when those days were unproductive, Tina's eyes felt worse. And the last few days had not been productive. Her only lead was that Jim and Phil's success in solving the Purity Pharmaceutical murders could have driven the current Instigator to want to kill them.

Solving the murders had exposed their underlying conspiracies, and exposing those conspiracies resulted in Purity stopping production of Relieve® and losing a billion dollars of revenue. This resulted in hundreds of employees losing their jobs or suffering career damage at all levels. Purity Pharmaceutical demoted executives and reduced their salaries, and they also fired executives that were involved in the conspiracy. Since the Purity Pharmaceutical Company was a joint venture between the McKenzie Company and the Saga Pharmaceutical Company, high-ranking employees – mostly executives from the parent companies that were involved in the creation of Purity – lost their jobs and careers. A literal disaster. Tina found their names.

She dug deep into the life of every single executive on the list and came up empty. Her frustration was a testament to the security her handlers afforded their clients.

It was time to decide on her next steps, but she was tired and needed rest. The only thing she could think of was to contact Phil. Contacting Phil was the last thing she wanted to do, but it might be the only thing she could do. For now, she would close her eyes.

The Director called the State Senator to give him an update on the status of their efforts to purchase the Mill.

"Mr. Senator, how are you today? I have information on a number of fronts regarding the Mill."

"Okay, I'm all ears."

"I have some interest in the investment from a wealthy banker. He wants to stay in the background, be a silent partner. I didn't tell him about the Civil War Treasure, I just said there's something of value hidden in the Mill. If he buys in, we'll have enough money to fund the purchase. I need to do a little research to see if he is trustworthy."

Everything the Director told the Senator about the investor was a lie.

"Good news. Is there any negative news? There is always negative news."

"Well, you happen to be right, but it's not really that bad. Dorian stopped by and told me the State Police consider Robert Sullivan a prime suspect in Martineau's murder and are looking through email and phone records for his contacts."

"Hold the hell on. We emailed and talked on the phone. Sullivan said both were secure."

"I called Tina's handlers, and they assured me that as long as we used the phones and email addresses they provided, our communications are untraceable. I checked to make sure all my communication with you and Robert used their phones and email system. I did. Did you?"

"I'm sure I did, but I'll check. How reliable, how professional are the handlers? Can we take them at their word?"

"Give credit to Robert, they're the best. Tina doesn't know Robert's name, and now that I'm the Instigator, she doesn't know my name either. She has an untraceable phone preprogramed with the number of my untraceable phone. They compartmentalize all information. If Tina is arrested, she can't implicate me or the company. Are you okay so far?"

"Yes."

"The State Police asked the Mill owners to put on hold all efforts to sell the Mill until they check Robert's contacts, and the owners agreed. I figure we have at least three weeks to vet the banker and to come up with someone to present our offer to purchase the Mill."

"If the handlers are so secretive, how do prospective clients find them?"

"The dark web. I don't understand it, but apparently it works. Put your thinking cap on and check your communication with Robert. I'll call you."

Phil called the Old Mill Investors to order. "We have some important items to cover, so let's start. First, Jim's getting better, and fast. His doctor said his cognitive abilities are back to 100%, he's talkative, he makes sense, and he seems to remember everything. He's not completely healed physically, but his risk of internal bleeding is low as long as he rests and doesn't do anything too strenuous. Mike and I are going to see him later this morning and hear his take on the shoot out in the Mill. We're looking forward to hearing what Jim has to say. Karen, you're next."

"Good morning, all. I'm staying with Phil and Rose until we solve this case. I have a new liaison with the State Police, Captain Belardi, and he's in charge of the investigation. He now sees a certain Robert Sullivan as a person of interest and is searching his devices for contacts and communications. He called me this morning and said he contacted the NSA to ask for any data they had. The CSP – that's the state police – asked the Mill owners to hold off on acquisition talks for a month. Now for the big request: CSP wants to know what we were looking for in the Mill basement. The owners stonewalled them, saying they were contractually bound to stay quiet. My question to you is: do we risk telling CSP about the treasure?"

Mike reacted first. "If we say something to the State Police, they'll blab it to the press before you can say assholes."

Everyone nodded in agreement except Phil, who said, "What if we simply say that there may be an item of unknown value in the Mill? Or something that nonspecific."

After a heated discussion, the majority agreed. Mike didn't, until Phil added, "We'll also say that if it leaks, we won't assist them again."

Mike did not want to give the police any information, but he withdrew his objection. The Old Mill Investors moved to the next subject: Harry O.

"Wait," Karen said, "I told my liaison about Mike and Phil's concern about Dorian and that he acted strangely on the tour, as if he had another agenda. He committed to including questions in his upcoming interview and will try to confuse Dorian into a slipup. That's the last item I have."

"Any discussion?" asked Phil. "Okay, next item. Harry O does not have the time to join us. He said he'd vet any information we wanted to make public and make it a news item. That may come in handy in the future. Lastly, Jim. His doctor decided to move him out of the ICU and into a private room, and his nurses are getting him ready for the day. Mike and I want to talk to him before the State Police do."

Mary Ann said, "I want to go and hear what happened."

Mike replied, "Okay. I'll drive."

Chapter 41

Mary Ann talked the whole time on the short ride to the hospital. She was excited. Today her husband would be mentally whole, and he would start down the road to complete recovery. That, at least, was what Dr. Collins had told her on the phone. Mary Ann felt comfortable with Dr. Collins and had asked her to stay involved in Jim's case. She also informed Mary Ann that Jim would soon move out of the ICU and into a regular hospital room. Mary Ann hoped and prayed that Jim would be home shortly.

As they walked into the hospital Mary Ann said, "I want to see Jim first and spend some time with him. I have a lot to talk to him about, but mostly I want to see for myself if he's back to normal mentally. I know that physically he'll take longer to heal, but the last time I was with him I was scared. He was so out of it; he couldn't think straight. I need a half an hour at most."

Mike replied, "No problem, take all the time you need." Then, he said to Phil, "Let's relax in the waiting room and plan our talk with Jim. Then we'll find Dr. Collins and ask her if we have to be cautious with Jim."

A broad smile stretched across Jim's face when his wife walked into the room. "Mary Ann! You look great. Come over here and plant a big kiss on my lips. I'm ready for you to hop up onto this cot so I can jump your bones," he said, grinning deviously.

"My God, Jim, did you overdose on Viagra? You haven't been this horny in months."

"I feel great. Whatever they're giving me is working. In all seriousness, I know I have to be careful until my risk of bleeding is history, but I feel super."

Jim and Mary Ann discussed the shooting and the effect it had on them both. They talked a lot and cried a little. Then, they just held hands and enjoyed each other's company.

"I'll round up Phil and Mike," Mary Ann said when they were ready to part. "They're anxious to hear what happened."

Phil and Mike were talking with Dr. Collins in a secluded spot in the waiting room when Mary Ann found them. Dr. Collins gave Mary Ann a brief hug and said, "He's doing remarkably well both physically and mentally, and we'll release him as soon as we feel he's ready. With the speed at which he's healing, I feel certain he'll be home in a couple of days or so."

Mike replied, "Good news. And doc, thanks for your advice on how we should handle Jim. We won't aggravate him. Now let's go."

After a little small talk and some apologies from Mike and Phil, Jim said, "I was with you of my own free will, and me getting shot is the bitch's fault. I don't want to hear it again, and I don't want you two dummies treating me with kid gloves. I want to analyze what happened."

Jim took a moment to collect his thoughts before explaining, "I separated from you because I had to piss. Let's start there, okay?"

The others nodded.

"When I finished, and it took a while, I started after you guys. As I walked down the hallway, I noticed another hallway opening to the left. A person dressed like a man – a woman, I think – was in the opening looking to the left, pistol pointed in the same direction. That would be where you guys were. I'll refer to the gunwoman as "she" even though I'm not one-hundred-percent sure. I yelled, 'DROP YOUR GUN.' She turned in my direction and brought the gun around. I fired and scored a direct hit to her chest; she got off a shot that just missed my head. Another woman, also dressed like a man and holding a gun, appeared in the hallway and turned and fired with unbelievable speed. I fired and missed; her bullet tore up my guts. Questions?"

Phil asked, "If they both looked like men, why do you think it was two women?"

"The way they moved. Their movements were smooth and limber. I can't describe it exactly, but my brain registered women."

"You're an old man and can't tell the difference between a man and a woman?" Mike scoffed sarcastically.

Phil said, "Mike, don't be an asshole. I know that's hard for you. Jim, there was no blood in the hallway. Mike and I heard four shots, but the police only found three bullets."

"Mike, you are an asshole. I guess mine was a thru and thru, lucky for me. The fourth is in the perp's body armor. Have the State Police ever heard of body armor, like a vest?"

"Are you boys having fun," Mike responded, "Or is it you can't take a joke? No matter. The big issue for Jim is what he should tell the State Police about why we were in the Mill. We decided not to tell the Police about a Civil War treasure, but only to say that there may be an item of unknown value in the Mill. And we'll add, if necessary, 'if it leaks, we won't assist you again.' Are you good with that response?"

"Or I could tell them what I think. Mike had this crazy idea that someone hid an item of value in the Mill with no proof. I went along for the ride and wound up in the hospital. No good deed goes unpunished," Jim replied.

Phil, lost in thought, said, "Let me see if I have this straight. The shooters were women. The Martineau killing only required one shot, one shooter. If the Extra Mart murders were in fact related to the Mill and Martineau, two shooters were involved. And Jim, you put two shooters in the Mill, both women. The police already suspected a connection between the Extra Mart and Martineau. And now we're thinking that there are two female assassins killing people related to the Mill. Shit. We don't have a clue as to who they are. Any holes in my theory?"

"Before we answer your question, let's tell Jim about Robert Sullivan," Mike said.

Phil replied, "I forgot. Go ahead, you tell him."

"We learned that a guy named Robert Sullivan committed suicide the same day you were gut-shot, and he also happens to represent the other investors trying to acquire the Mill. He presented the offer to the Mill owners. The police think there may be a connection and are analyzing his contacts and conversations. They asked the Mill owners to hold off on any negotiations until they're done."

"That might work. They should interview the person who reported the suicide. I really hope that this is the break we've been waiting for. Anyway, I'm getting tired. Why don't you two go out to lunch and leave Mary Ann here to keep me company, then come back after lunch to drive her home?" Jim asked.

"Will do. See you in an hour," Mike said.

Marcy Sharp was already employed by the contract assassin management company when the company hired Tina. Because Tina and Marcy were close to the same age, management appointed Marcy as Tina's controller. Both women were young and attractive and in violation of company rules, they engaged in a personal and sexual relationship that ended badly. Both women faced termination when company management learned that they had violated the rule, which would typically be career-ending. Their boss, however, for some unknown reason, decided that they were young and deserved another chance. Tina went on to become the top money-earner in the company, based on her stellar performance as an assassin and because she introduced the company to a perfect way to dispose of bodies. Marcy progressed through the ranks and landed a high-level management position. Both heeded the warning; management would not forgive them again.

In the more than ten years since their breakup, Tina and Marcy had never spoken about the end of their affair; they only talked business. Since dealing with Phil would be a last resort, Tina decided to try to involve Marcy instead. Tina's company phone, which was untraceable, contained the numbers of everyone in management. Tina called Marcy.

"Hello, Tina." Marcy sounded annoyed.

"Marcy, hi. I have a major favor to ask."

"I hope it's not the name of the Instigator on your project. You already have your answer, and it's a hard no."

"Give me ten minutes to explain what happened. I think you'll understand why I want to talk to him face-to-face."

Marcy didn't respond immediately, but after what seemed like an eternity to Tina, she said, "I'll listen, but I don't think I'll change my mind."

"Thanks. I followed the Instigator's instructions to the letter and was in place for the kill. Dorian, the Instigator's man, had one job, which was to keep the three targets together. But he only had two with him, and the third was on the other side of my hallway. He saw me and pulled his gun. I turned and fired and hit him. The others started yelling and running toward me. They had guns, so I decided to run and finish the job another day. I'm worried Dorian won't tell the Instigator the whole story, and we'll look bad. I have a reputation to uphold. My record of accomplishment is perfect until now."

Marcy thought about what Tina had said and responded, "I'll run it up the line again and call you in a week. I hope you realize what'll happen to you if you go rogue. Bye."

Tina knew what would happen and did not care. She wanted to avenge Kathryn's death.

Chapter 42

Karen Parisi sat alone in a booth at the Courthouse Bar and Grill waiting for Sal Belardi. They had briefly talked a few times in the past week about the State Police's lack of progress on the case. As she mulled over what to order, Sal pushed the front door open, saw Karen, walked over to the booth, and sat opposite her. His first words to her were not "Hi, how are you," but rather, "Good God, am I frustrated."

"We can't find any communication or contacts on Sullivan's devices that connect him to the Mill, nor to Dorian. Considering that he made an offer to acquire the Mill representing a group of investors, that's strange. Extremely strange. There are no emails, texts, DMs on Instagram or Facebook, nothing. It's like the group involved in the Mill never existed. The next item: is there something of value hidden in the Mill? And the last item for today is our interview with Commander Hines. Is he ready?"

A server appeared and took their order. They placed identical food orders: cheeseburgers and fries. Karen ordered a Molson and Sal ordered a Heineken.

"Hines is almost ready, but he still needs a few more days. As for something hidden in the Mill, the answer is maybe. Mike Robertson believes, based on his research, that there's an object of some value hidden in the Mill. Hines doesn't agree. So: our answer is that we don't know, but we want to look for it."

"Pretty vague."

"On purpose, and if your team leaks that there's something hidden in the Mill, you won't get any more information from us. It's important for our investors and the Mill owners not to create a rumor."

"Okay, I got it. What do you think about Sullivan's lack of presence on the internet?"

"Very strange. The only thing that comes to mind is the dark web. But I don't know much about it, except that its where dishonest people hide their illegal endeavors. Maybe you have to assume he is – or was – dirty and find someone who knows about the dark web."

Their food arrived and both were quiet before Sal said, "The burger is really good, and I like the fries."

Karen nodded in agreement.

"Karen, tell me about yourself."

"Only if you do the same when I'm done."

Sal nodded.

"I've worked for the Nassau County Police department for thirteen years, ever since I got out of college. I have a degree in Criminal Justice. I made Detective I, working homicide cases, after three years. I made Detective II four years ago. I worked on cases when Jim Hines ran the homicide Detectives and learned a ton. I was still a Detective I when I worked the Purity Murders with Hines. It was like getting a PHD in solving a series of homicides. Your turn."

"Hold on, I want to know about you the person, not just you the cop. Like, are you in a committed relationship?"

"Getting a little personal. You answer first."

"Okay. I was married from the time I was twenty-three until two years ago. No kids. My ex-wife moved to Texas with her new husband. Nothing serious since."

"When I was in my twenties, I'd say I was in a committed relationship. Nothing since either. I've been busy with work since I helped on the Purity case."

"Would you like to go to dinner Friday night?"

Karen didn't respond instantly, although she wanted to. She held her tongue for a few seconds. "Yes."

"Great."

Tina was at a loss as to what her next move would be, when the doorbell rang. Marcy stood in the doorway holding a box and had a suitcase at her feet. Stunned, Tina mumbled "Come in." Tina, still in her comfortable clothes, wore a pair of men's boxers and a loose-fitting tank top. Marcy decked out in her travel clothes, wore tight fitting jeans, a colorful silk top, and slip on tennis shoes.

"Tina looked Marcy up and down and said, "Well."

"Well, what."

"Well, what the fuck are you doing here."

"As usual, right to the point. I have been doing a lot of thinking about what you said on the phone, and I have been thinking about the work I do and about our employer. Shit, we are in the murder business. And finally, I think about you and our relationship. The company has kept us apart for too long. I want our relationship back; I've missed you."

Tina again looked Marcy up and down, and said, "I can't, not yet anyway. I just experienced a major loss."

"Do you want to talk about it?"

"I hope I can trust you."

"I have taken a major risk just coming here. Your call."

Tina needed to talk to someone about Kathryn and decided to take a chance. "It's a long story."

After Tina finished crying, she invited Marcy to put her belongings in a guest bedroom, and after discovering that she hadn't eaten, took to the kitchen to make bacon and eggs. As Marcy sat at the table, Tina asked, "What exactly are you thinking? What do you want to happen? Are you planning to help me find the Instigator?"

"You are full of questions. I am thinking it is time to change careers. I have plenty of money, so it is time to retire. I want to get back in your good graces and finally I want to help you find your Instigator. The means to do it is in the box, four untraceable phones and a road map to communicating on the dark web."

"You don't have to worry about getting back into my good graces," said Tina, smiling and flipping a piece of bacon. "You never left. I was young and stupid, and just getting out of an abusive marriage. I planned to retire as soon as this job is over, but our company will not be happy with that decision. We need a foolproof plan to survive. We must launder our money, create new identities, and disappear without a trace. I have the resources to create new identities, the rest we will solve. But first I have to settle a score with the Instigator. Since I can't get his information from our company, the only connection I can use is that he is obsessed with killing Phil Messina and Jim Hines."

"I assume you have searched for something Phil and Jim were involved in that would be a reason for murder."

Tina told Marcy about how Phil and Jim investigated a series of murders that led them to some product tampering in the Purity Pharmaceutical Company. She explained that Purity was a joint venture between two multinational companies and that the tampering negatively impacted employees at all three companies. The three companies fired or demoted over a hundred employees, anyone of which might want Phil and Jim dead. Finding the Instigator is the proverbial needle in the haystack.

Marcy now understood why Tina had a score to settle with the Instigator. Tina told her she accepted responsibility for Kathryn's death. But she also believed the Instigator put Kathryn's life in jeopardy as a result of his obsession with killing Phil and Jim. And Marcy agreed.

Marcy hugged Tina and cried with her.

"I have good news. I found a replacement for Robert's money and for the bank, so we can fund the acquisition without fear of getting scammed." The Director called the Senator as soon as he confirmed the funding. "A friend agreed to take the risk and put up the money we need to close the deal."

"Great, but what does he want in return? Does he want to be an active member?"

"That's the best part of the deal. He wants to be a silent investor, and he wants a legally binding agreement to that effect. He's willing to risk his money on us finding a treasure."

"Sounds good. When can we approach the Mill owners with an offer?"

"In no less than three weeks. The State Police still have them on hold until they find all of Robert's contacts and communication."

"But they're not going to find anything. Are they?"

"I should have said, 'Until they throw in the towel.'"

Chapter 43

Jim had only been home from the hospital for a day, but he felt fine, so he agreed to an interview. Karen, Mike, and Phil arrived at Jim's house at nine in the morning, a full hour before Jim's scheduled interview with the State Police. Jim wanted to make sure he was up to date with all the details of the investigation before the interview. He felt comfortable with the details of the shootout in the Mill, even with his belief that two women were the shooters. He was less certain about Dorian's role in the whole drama, but he felt sure that Dorian was working with the shooters, and his goal was to get the group to the right place at the right time. The group finished Jim's update at five minutes to ten.

Sal Belardi arrived promptly at ten, accompanied by the CSP commander and the state Attorney General. After making introductions, Captain Belardi said, "Commander Hines, tell us about the shootout. Please."

"It's Jim from here on." Jim presented a detailed description of the events that led up to the shootout.

The Connecticut Attorney General replied, "Your description fits the forensic findings. The forensics team found only one bullet fired from your weapon and that you fired your weapon twice. They also found a bullet from an unknown weapon that did not match the one that hit you. They concluded that three weapons were involved. My only question for you, Jim, is: how sure are you that the assassins were women?"

"I'm ninety percent sure. The one I hit seemed well-trained, fast and accurate. The one that shot me was truly exceptional. Whoever she was, she knew exactly what she was doing, and I'm sure this isn't her first rodeo."

The Attorney General asked, "Do you have a theory of the case?"

"I don't like theories, I like facts. If I were to advance a theory of the case, I'd tie it to the sale of the Mill. A group of investors see value in the Mill, and plenty of value at that. Money and greed are typically motives to commit a crime, and it usually involves big money for a perp to risk murder. Hiring professionals is expensive, but well worth it because they're hard to find, and they make it difficult to identify the instigators. I think Davidson was killed because of his involvement in the Mill. I also believe Dorian might be the weak link. He was acting funny on the day of the shootout, and I think he knew it was a setup."

"Is there something of value in the Mill that makes it worth hiring a pro?"

"I don't think so, but Mike does. That's an unknown."

The three Connecticut State employees stood to leave when the State Police Commander said, "Jim, I'm truly sorry. If we had solved Martineau's murder in a timely fashion, your near-death experience would never have happened, and your move to Connecticut would have been much more pleasant."

Jim simply replied, "Thanks."

Sal and Karen's dinner date took place at a restaurant called "85 Main," which was coincidentally located at 85 Main Street in Cargill Falls. Most seats in the restaurant had a view of the falls. The two ordered drinks, perused the menu, decided on appetizers and entrees, and were ready to order when their drinks arrived. They quietly nursed their drinks for a few minutes before Sal spoke.

"What did you think of my superiors?"

"Typical bosses. Cold and reserved, especially the Attorney General. Actually, your Commander was courteous and treated Jim with respect. I guess only the Attorney General was an ass."

"I didn't think anything the AG said was bad."

"It wasn't what he said. It was his pompous, arrogant attitude. Typical politician."

Sal shrugged. "My boss told me to share everything with you. He said we can solve this case if we work together. So, I'm asking you and your team to agree to share all. Let's get these murders solved."

Karen nodded. "I'll make it happen."

"Great. Now, I want to compliment you on your dress. It looks fabulous on you. Dare I say, it's quite sexy."

Karen had spent a long time getting ready for their date, and she chose a clingy, red, low-cut cocktail dress finished with pearl earrings and a matching necklace. She asked, "Is it too much?"

"All I can say is that I bet everyone in the restaurant wants to know – 'how did that geeky accountant get a date with that supermodel?' And I bet the men at the bar want to know how to get rid of me."

Karen blushed – a bright red blush – and said, "I'm a cop, and when I'm not on duty, I usually still dress like a cop. When you asked me out, I decided to try not to look like a cop. I guess I succeeded." She toyed with the dress's straps. "I look like a whore."

"I assume it's some deeply rooted ancestral Catholic guilt making you think that way. You just look your best, and your best is head and shoulders above other women your age. Me? I obviously decided not to look good."

A still bright red Karen replied, "I think you're very handsome and very masculine, and I like you just the way you are. I wouldn't change a thing."

"When we first met, I would have said the same thing about you, but seeing you in that dress changed things."

Karen looked down into her lap and went quiet. Just as Sal started to apologize, assuming that he'd insulted her, Karen smiled and said, "Got you." They laughed.

They discovered that they had a lot in common. Both grew up in traditional Italian families, were raised strict Catholics, attended public schools, and, of course, both joined their respective police departments. The evening flew by.

Karen had walked to the restaurant, and Sal insisted on driving her to Messina's. They said goodbye on the sidewalk, then enjoyed a long kiss.

Chapter 44

As Marcy and Tina stood in the living room and looked out over the Ogunquit shore, the majestic display of the Atlantic Ocean's power seemed to fade into the background. The storm off Maine's coastline had unleashed towering waves, crashing against the rocks with awe-inspiring force. However, the magnificent spectacle failed to capture their attention as their minds grappled with the pressing issue at hand: finding the elusive Instigator.

The intensity of the storm mirrored the tumult of their thoughts. The Instigator, the puppet master behind the scenes, remained shrouded in mystery. Marcy and Tina understood the urgency of unmasking this figure, whose orchestrations had created significant consequences. The need to identify the Instigator became their primary focus, overshadowing the natural beauty unfolding before them.

As the waves roared and the ocean sprayed against the rugged shoreline, Marcy and Tina exchanged determined glances. The stormy backdrop only fueled their resolve to unravel the layers of secrecy surrounding the Instigator's identity. Tina needed to avenge Kathryn and would not rest until he was dead.

Marcy said, "Nothing I think of works. I think we need to brainstorm, bounce some ideas off each other, and talk them through until we have a solid plan. Are you willing to give it a try?"

Tina's determination was starting to crack. "I'm beginning to think there's no way to identify the Instigator. Our company has devised a foolproof system that even employees can't crack. But I'm willing to work all day today to find an answer. Hell, look at the weather. It's not an enjoyable day for a walk on the beach. Well, Miss Corporate Exec, how do we go about brainstorming? What are the rules?"

"There are no bad ideas. We talk through every idea until we agree that it won't work. When we think we have an idea that will work we keep trying to prove it'll fail."

Tina nodded. "We have at most three weeks before the company gets suspicious and decides to kill us. We have to find a way to get Jim or Phil to cooperate, then we have to get them to see the Instigator and give us a name. That means arranging for them to be in the same place at the same time. To maximize the time available to us, we need to placate the company. We have assets, thanks to you: untraceable phones and a dark web email system. Hopefully, we can discover a way to use them. Let's put our brains in gear and find answers to the questions."

The living room in Tina's house became silent as Marcy and Tina, brains in gear, searched for answers. Time passed slowly, but neither woman noticed. Finally, Tina said, "I can't come up with an answer. No matter what plan I come up with, I can't get it to work out. There's always an obstacle that I can't overcome."

Marcy did not answer Tina immediately. After several minutes she responded, "I've been having the same problem. Nothing works. But I just had one thought: what if we answered each question individually? Let's try to figure out how we would go about getting Jim and Phil to cooperate. If we like the answer, we'll move to another question. What do you think?"

"I like your idea. Let's give it a try."

What followed was a spirited discussion and eventually a consensus. Tina asked Marcy to put their agreement into words.

"Okay. We get Jim and Phil to cooperate by convincing them you're the real deal, the assassin, and explaining that their lives are in danger. We email them from the dark web with details of the murders only the killer would know and the information you found about the aftermath of the Purity Pharma conspiracies. Then we tell them about the kill contract on their lives, likely instigated by someone hurt in the aftermath. Finally, we provide instructions on how to email us from the dark web and assure them it's untraceable."

"Once we have their attention, we need to get them to the same place at the same time. Any thoughts?"

"No, but we'll find a way. We just need to think. I do have some thoughts on how to delay the company from finding out what we're up to and terminating us."

"I'm all ears."

"You have to be a 'good girl.' Don't give the company any reason to think you're pursuing the Instigator's identity. Don't call them, and if they call you, be good. Don't ask about the Instigator. I, on the other hand, will call my boss to let him know I'm a little bored and want to get some work done while I'm on vacation. That should give me cover for signing on to the company computer system. I'll snoop a little and see if I can find something that will help us."

"You're taking a big risk and putting yourself in danger."

Marcy grinned. "I know my way around the company system. I won't get caught."

"Great. Let's keep thinking of a way to answer the questions and solve our problems so we can get on with our lives. You haven't tried to talk me out of wanting to kill the Instigator. Why?"

"Because I know you loved Kathryn."

Tina's eyes filled with tears. "I know why I loved you all those years ago. Thank you for caring about me."

As Jim Hines, still nursing the effects of a gunshot wound and subsequent surgery, mustered the strength to sit up in bed, he glanced at the cane leaning against his dresser. A tangible reminder of his recent ordeal, the cane symbolized both his physical struggle and the lingering aftermath of the dangerous decision he had made.

Today, Phil and Mike had planned to keep him company, ostensibly to discuss matters related to the Mill. However, Jim anticipated that the conversation might veer into a tiresome lament about their perceived failure to protect him. He felt a need to remind them that he was a grown man who had made a conscious decision, absolving them of any blame.

With a sense of determination, Jim contemplated the upcoming day. His thoughts focused on the unexpected visit of Karen and Sal, who had invited themselves to review his thoughts on the shootout. Jim couldn't help but notice that Karen and Sal had seemed inseparable lately, prompting him to wonder if Karen had found a special someone.

Jim had been a vocal advocate for Karen's promotion to Lieutenant and his eventual replacement as Commander of Homicide. Despite his fervent lobbying, the higher-ups considered her too young and inexperienced. Jim vehemently disagreed, recognizing Karen's exceptional intelligence and admirable character traits. In his eyes, she surpassed every other detective in the homicide division, regardless of race or gender.

Jim had been more than just a colleague to Karen; he had taken on the role of mentor. Together, they tackled challenging cases, and Jim marveled at how quickly Karen absorbed the nuances of homicide investigation. Their professional relationship was a source of pride for Jim, and he continued to support her ascent in the department, eager to see her recognized for her skills and dedication. As Jim faced the day ahead, he couldn't escape the complexities of his personal and professional relationships.

Jim secured the cane and slowly and painfully made his way to the living room. He was about halfway to his chair when Mary Ann shrieked, "What the hell are you doing, you dumb bastard? Jim, you're supposed to stay in bed!"

"Mary Ann, for God's sake, I'm not going to be an invalid when four of our friends visit! I'm fine. Now I just need to get to my chair. Don't forget that I walk to the bathroom six times a night. A slow jaunt to the living room won't kill me."

Mary Ann scoffed, "Just make sure to pay your life insurance. We're going to have six visitors. Tess and Rose are coming."

Jim made it to his chair, albeit a little winded and very sore. He would rest for a while before everyone arrived.

Half an hour later, the first wave arrived. Tess and Rose tumbled in and said cheerily, "Hi, how are you?" Before joining Mary Ann, Phil and Mike sat in the living room with Jim.

Jim put his foot down immediately. "I don't want to hear any of your bullshit apologies. I'm fine, I'm not going to die any time soon. So, let's just act normal."

Phil smiled at Jim and said, "You've become a crotchety old man since you were shot. And you used to be nice."

Mike chimed in, "Amen to that."

"God, you guys are aggravating. Did you know that Karen's coming with Sal to pick my brain again?"

"If we want to buy the Mill and solve the murders, we need a plan. But, for the life of me, I don't know how to proceed," Mike said.

"I have some ideas, but let's wait for Phil's Paesanos. They should be here any minute," Jim replied.

"Will you get angry if I ask if you're in a lot of pain? Because the look on your face says you are hurting," Mike asked.

"Yes, I'm in pain, because I won't take painkillers that are addictive. And no, I won't get angry."

Karen and Sal knocked, then opened the door. After everyone said hello, they got down to the business at hand.

Jim said, "I told you last time that I believe Dorian is in this up to his ears. He's the key to cracking this case wide open. My years in homicide tell me that his mannerisms, his answers to questions, and his attempts at manipulating us during the search all point to his involvement."

Sal added, "We pressed him, and he lawyered up. And not just any lawyer: with one of the best criminal lawyers in the state. Also, one of the most expensive. So, we're at a standstill."

"Manipulate him! Tell him you have evidence. Tell him you have a witness or two. Squeeze him," Jim barked.

"Look, he doesn't have the money to pay his lawyer, so someone else must be paying. We're looking into it, but no luck so far. His lawyer advised us that he'll demand a warrant every time we want to interview Dorian. To make matters worse, his lawyer is a friend of the Governor," Sal replied.

"The Governor may be the weak link. He's a politician, and politicians care about votes. Wait, he's not term-limited, is he?"

Sal's reply killed any hope that Dorian would crack. "Yes."

"Then subtle pressure on Dorian, his friends, and his family might help. You could pressure the owners of the Mill. It's not much, but it might help," Jim added.

Finding the killer seemed hopeless, but the group was resilient and adjourned the meeting to have lunch. Mary Ann organized the effort and served a great meal.

Chapter 45

As Tina contemplated their precarious situation, Marcy continued her exploration of the company's internal computer system. The faint hum of the laptop's fan provided a steady background noise as Tina's mind raced with thoughts of impending danger.

Time seemed to stretch endlessly; each passing moment was weighed down by the anticipation of an unknown threat. Tina's meticulous nature, honed by years of experience in her unconventional profession, had always dictated the necessity of planning for every conceivable outcome. Survival and freedom depended on staying steps ahead, and this philosophy had become ingrained in her.

She stole glances at Marcy, who remained focused on the laptop screen. Tina couldn't help but admire Marcy's dedication to the task at hand. Trust was a rare commodity in the world they navigated, and Tina found solace in the fact that Marcy was an ally in this dangerous game.

As Tina wrestled with her concerns about the inevitable arrival of the company's assassin, she couldn't help but replay various scenarios in her mind. The dance between predator and prey was a delicate one, and Tina had become an expert choreographer in this deadly ballet. Her eyes darted around the room, assessing potential exits and makeshift weapons, a habit born out of necessity. The room felt both confining and liberating, a paradox of safety and vulnerability. In the midst of her internal strategizing, Tina couldn't shake the nagging fear that time was running out.

Marcy closed her laptop, ran her fingers through her hair and said, "I'm done for today. I'm not making much progress, but I plan to continue tomorrow. I found a folder in each of our assassin's files, but so far, I haven't been able to open it. I think it might be important, so I'll try again. Did you enjoy your day of rest?"

"No. I'm unsettled and not particularly happy with our plan. I'm worried that we're going to run out of time. I want us to get our new identities situated before the company starts searching for us. I need to work on gaining Jim and Phil's cooperation while you try to find information on the company computer. Do you think it could cause any problems to start this early?"

"It might, but I think you're right. We don't have a lot of time to accomplish all we have on our plate. I'd hate it if the company killed us before we start our new life."

"Very funny. I'll compose an email to Jim and Phil."

After writing a number of drafts, Tina finally believed her email was ready for Marcy to review.

TO: Jim Hines & Phil Messina

Subject: That contract HIT on you both!

It is critical that you read and understand this email. Your lives and the lives of your family depend on it.

I am the paid assassin that killed Bob Martineau in the Mill and Larry Davidson and his girlfriend in the Thompson Extra Mart. I shot Jim after he shot and killed my partner.

I used a Glock 9mm to kill Martineau. I entered the Mill through an unlocked door on the west side. I proceeded down a long hallway that was under active renovation at the time, then up two flights of stairs and down a short hallway to Martineau's office. I found the office door closed and not locked. Martineau was working on a table behind his desk, his back toward me. I shot him in the back of the head, picked up the shell casing, and left the way I entered.

My partner and I followed Larry Davidson from the Elks lodge, where he played Pitch, to the Extra Mart, even though we knew where he was going and that he planned to meet his girlfriend. We parked on the street and walked into the store, pretended to shop, and listened to Larry's conversation with his girlfriend. We learned that her relief was running late, giving us plenty of time and one less person to kill. We tried to make it look like a robbery by amateurs. Instead of one between the eyes, we made a few off-target shots. However, we made a rookie mistake and picked up the shell casings.

Our attempt to kill you both – and Mike, by the way – went wrong from the beginning. You were early and my partner and I were late. We had problems with her assault vest, and you split up when you should have stayed together. Jim, I heard you told the State Police that the shooters were women, and you are correct. My partner, my lover, is dead. Good shot, Jim. She was looking left down the hallway as you walked in from her right, drew your gun, and shot her in the chest. Her vest stopped the bullet so there was no blood, but her aorta ruptured on our way home. After you shot Kathryn – that was her name – I demonstrated my skill and shot you. You surprised me by getting a shot off.

If we work together and identify the one person that put up the money, I can stop it. The instigator asked for an impossible hit, which led to Kathryn's death. Whoever it is, I want him gone. I researched you both and learned about your adventure at Purity Pharma. What you did hurt many employees, and they are the only people who would want to kill you both. I suspect that the instigator is linked to Purity.

I hope I have proved I am the hired assassin because believing in me will save your lives and maybe the lives of your wives. It will not matter to the assassin if you are alone or in a crowd. He will shoot you and not care if collateral damage happens.

Please do not waste time judging me. You have no idea what my life is like and why I made the choices I made.

You do not have much time, so act fast. Talk it over with Mike and your wives, no one else. If you choose life, reply to this email. This email is from the dark web and is untraceable. If you decide to work with me, I will send you an untraceable phone

programmed to connect to my phone and only my phone.

"Is it ready to send out," asked Tina, "Or do you think I should modify it?"

"No change. Send it as it is and do it now. I'm anxious to see if they respond."

"Sent. Now we can relax."

Tina sat on the sofa and Marcy put an arm around her.

Dorian called the Instigator because the State Police were pushing him and pushing him hard. They were on untraceable phones.

"Look, Dorian, I got you the best criminal lawyer in the state. He feels you're in no danger. They don't have a single piece of evidence that ties you to the killing, to Robert, or to me. They're going to lean on you because you're a suspect, and that's just what they do. Again, your lawyer believes that you're in no danger."

"I'm still worried. But there's nothing I can do about it now. It's too late," groaned Dorian.

"Welcome to the club. We're all in the same boat."

"What can you tell me about Robert's suicide? Was it because the Police were closing in?"

"No way. His wife passed, and he couldn't handle life without her. They had been a couple since they were children. Now stop worrying."

After Dorian hung up, the Director decided that Dorian was unraveling and may become a problem. He was nervous and might need some of Tina's special attention. He made himself a note.

Chapter 46

Phil spent the night tossing and turning. His mind was a jumble of thoughts, all of which made little sense. He did not sleep much, and at five A.M., tired as he was, he got out of bed. Phil made himself a cup of coffee and listened to the local news and weather. After a few minutes, bored and drowsy, he decided to check his email. The email from Tina shocked the exhaustion from his mind and body.

Phil read and reread the email four times. Each time he read the email; he was not quite sure what she meant. "Your lives and the lives of your family depend on it." *What the hell?* "I am the paid assassin that killed Bob Martineau in the Mill and Larry Davidson and his girlfriend in the Extra Mart. I shot Jim after he shot and killed my partner." *She knows details only the assassin would know. She wants Jim and me to work with her to save our lives. I don't know how to respond or what to make of this email. I need to call Jim. I need his experience and expertise. Jim killed her partner.*

Phil decided not to interrupt Jim's sleep. He needed the rest. The best way to handle the situation would be to meet with Mike and Jim in the morning and figure out what to do. Phil decided to make the calls after eight.

As Tina relaxed in the tranquility of the Maine coast, the echoes of the recent storm having faded into the distance, she found herself in a rare moment of total rest. With meticulous precision, she had orchestrated every detail of their new identities and life arrangements, leaving herself with a rare sense of completion.

The weight of her wealth settled upon her shoulders as she reflected on the extensive financial arrangements she had put into place. Though she had always been financially comfortable, the extent of her resources now revealed themselves in ways she had never fully comprehended. As she pondered the affluence at her disposal, Tina couldn't help but marvel at the magnitude of her prosperity.

In a gesture of generosity and symbolic significance, Tina resolved that she would donate her waterfront home and property in Ogunquit to Maine's organization dedicated to aiding abused and battered women. The decision carried a personal resonance for Tina, a silent acknowledgment of her own past struggles and the journey she had undertaken to reclaim her life.

The act of giving back felt like a fitting tribute to Kathryn's memory and a small step toward righting the injustices of the world. Tina's heart swelled with a sense of purpose as she envisioned the positive impact her contribution could have on the lives of those in need.

As she gazed out at the endless expanse of ocean before her, Tina felt a renewed sense of determination. The path ahead would be fraught with challenges and uncertainties, but she would face it with unwavering resolve. Soon she would avenge Kathryn's death and begin a clean future with Marcy.

Marcy interrupted Tina's brief hiatus. "Tina, I got into the assassin folders and was able to open most files they contained. Come with me. I'm ready to get into your personal folder and I want you there to stop me from seeing anything you want to keep private."

"You can see it all, and anything that's not in my file I'll share with you. I expect you'll do the same."

"Definitely. Now let's see if we can find something that will help us identify the Instigator."

Marcy sat at her laptop, pressed a couple of keys, and suddenly they were looking at the icon of a manilla folder labeled "Tina." Marcy double-clicked on the icon and five subfolders appeared. Marcy double-clicked on the folder labeled "CLIENTS." Three headshots appeared. The pictures had nicknames: The Caretaker, The Director, and The State Senator. "Do you know these guys?" Marcy asked.

"No, but I'll bet if we search the internet, we can find out who they are."

"Or we can wait for Phil or Jim to reply to see if they know them."

"I'd rather we identify them. I have some thoughts on how we should proceed without involving Phil or Jim."

Marcy downloaded the pictures to her computer, then sent them to Tina.

Tina said, "Thanks. Let's identify these guys, then I'll let you in on my plan."

Phil arranged for Mike and Jim to meet him at Jim's house. He also arranged for Mary Ann to have an early lunch with Rose, Tess, and Noelle. Mike and Phil settled into the comfortable living room furniture and watched as Jim tried, and failed, to get comfortable.

"I'm still in pain and can't get into a position that alleviates my discomfort. So, let's start," Jim groused.

"Mike, the strange and threatening email that Jim and I received mentioned you. We assumed it was okay to let you read it. For now, we're not showing it to anyone else. That includes our wives, Karen, and Noelle. And we're certainly not going to say anything to the State Police. Here's a printout for you to read." Phil handed Mike a copy, handed one to Jim, and kept one for himself.

Mike said, as he started reading, "I'm not sure if I should thank you or not."

Mike read the email twice. Phil and Jim also took the time to read it.

"What do you think?" Jim asked.

Mike, still trying to process what he had just read, replied, "Jim, your instincts were right. The shooters were women and you killed one. She explains the lack of blood at the scene. She obviously knows the details, some of which we had only theorized. And she claims there's a contract in force on your lives and ties it to the situation at Purity Pharma. And she says she can stop it. Wow."

"To save our lives and the lives of our families, all we have to do is work with a hired killer," Jim said sarcastically.

"Did a lot of people lose their jobs in the aftermath of Purity?" asked Mike.

"Yes. People lost jobs and money, and some lost their freedom. There was so much corruption that it took a long time to sort it all out," Phil responded.

"We understand the email. I believe her and I agree that our lives are in danger. Now what do we do?" Jim asked.

The men discussed their options and settled on a simple action.

Jim took charge. "We've discussed our predicament six ways to Sunday and keep coming to the same action: reply to the email and agree to work with her to identify the person that wants Phil and me dead. Then, we sit back and see what she does."

Phil and Mike nodded in agreement.

Working independently, it took Tina and Marcy less than an hour to put names on the faces and gather personal and professional information on all three.

- **Robert Sullivan:** Presented a Letter of Intent to the Mill owners and recently committed suicide after his wife died. They had been together since childhood.
- **Richard Thall:** Connecticut State Senator representing Litchfield County, believed to be extremely corrupt.

- **John Christensen:** Former McKensie Company executive fired five years ago because he did a lousy job working on the structure of the Purity Pharma joint venture. Spent time in prison because he was involved in the Relieve® conspiracy. Besides his job, he lost his family, an enormous amount of money, and his pension.

"Christensen is responsible for Kathryn's death, and I'm going to kill him. We don't need Jim or Phil to identify him. I know enough about him to set up the kill. The company won't look for us for several weeks, so we have time. We can kill Christensen, get out of New England, and start a new life. We'll give the boys the pictures and let them figure the rest out. Sullivan is dead, Christensen will be dead, and Thall can rot in prison."

Marcy asked, "If they respond to our email and want to work with us, what do we do?"

"We could leave them hanging for a few days, and during that time, we can plan and execute Christensen's murder. We know he lives in a high-end apartment in Worcester. I've looked at maps of the area and zoomed in on the apartment complex. There's a large public park close by that might come in handy. We'll finalize our disposal of the house and covertly ship what we decide to keep to our new home. Next, we'll assume our different identities and devise a plan to kill Christensen. Then we'll set sail to our new life with our new and final identities as two extremely prosperous sisters. The last thing we'll do is email the boys the pictures you found in my folder."

Chapter 47

The morning in Worcester was glorious, the birds were chirping, and the sunrise was beautiful. Marcy and Tina could not have picked a nicer day to begin their surveillance of John Christensen. They had rented a small house in a working-class neighborhood of Worcester to serve as their home base while they planned Christensen's murder.

Tina said, "This is the boring part of a kill: surveillance, working to come up with a plan that not only works but ensures we succeed and aren't caught, or suspected. I've done this too many times. This has to be the last one."

"I'm depending on your expertise. I no longer want to be involved in killing people. When I think about my life and my work, I become nauseated, literally sick. I can't do it anymore. This has to be the last for both of us. I don't know how I did it for so long."

"I understand. We were fools," Tina replied.

The two women quieted as they waited for Christensen to head to his job. They determined that the apartment building had only one entrance in the front and a utility entrance in the rear. It also served as an emergency exit for tenants. Both women saw Christensen when he exited at ten minutes before seven. He walked through the parking area and turned right onto the sidewalk.

"He's heading to Union Station. I assume he rides the train to work. We'll check on him over the next two days to make sure he routinely takes the train. Let's drive to the Union Train Station to see which train he takes."

In the station, they watched as Christensen presented his commuter pass and boarded the seven-thirteen train, number five-o-eight. Tina said, "We'll check again tomorrow. For now, we'll memorize the morning schedules to Boston and determine the best way to commit a murder on the five-o-eight train to Boston."

After returning to their rental home Marcy delved into the intricacies of commuter train schedules to Boston. Tina immersed herself in a different kind of research, exploring the lethal potential of various drugs and their effects on the human body. Her intent was clear: to administer a fatal injection to Christensen, maximizing his suffering while ensuring his silence.

With methodical focus, Tina studied the nuances of drug administration, delving into dosage levels and physiological responses. Every detail mattered as she meticulously planned the execution of her revenge.

After a day spent absorbed in their respective tasks, Tina and Marcy decided to indulge in a well-deserved respite. They treated themselves to an upscale Italian dinner at Via, nestled in the heart of Worcester's vibrant Italian neighborhood on Shrewsbury Street.

As they savored each delectable bite, the weight of their mission momentarily lifted, replaced by the simple pleasures of tasty food and good companionship. Amidst the chatter of fellow diners and the aromatic swirl of Italian spices, Tina and Marcy found a fleeting sense of normalcy, a brief reprieve from the darkness that shadowed their every move.

Despite the looming task ahead, they allowed themselves this moment of peace, a reminder that amidst the chaos of their lives, there remained pockets of joy and solace. And as they shared laughter and conversation over plates of pasta and glasses of wine, Tina couldn't help but feel a glimmer of hope amidst the uncertainty, knowing that she had Marcy by her side, a steadfast ally in the tumultuous journey that lay ahead.

The reply to the first email appeared on Tina's cell during dessert. Tina smiled at Marcy and said, "They replied to our email. Let's enjoy dessert and deal with their reply while we have our Frangelico."

Tina opened the email while waiting for their after dinner drink.

TO: Originator

From: Jim Hines & Phil Messina

Subject: That contract HIT on you both!

We are convinced that you are the assassin. You know details only someone who was at the scene would know.

We need more information on your assertion that we are the targets of a contract hit because we solved the conspiracies and murders that resulted in Purity Pharma's business issues and the impact on employees.

Jim shot your partner after she leveled her gun at him. Self-Defense!

Marcy said "Not a bad response. They want to work with us but are reluctant."

"I believe you're right. We'll string them along until we see how we fare with Christensen. I'll reply."

Reply to: Jim Hines & Phil Messina

Subject: That contract HIT on you both!

You made the right decision, a life-saving decision. I have received added information and need to verify it before I involve you both.

You are right in highlighting the fact that Jim acted in self-defense. If I did not believe that he would be dead.

It will take me a couple of days to make sure the info I have received is accurate. I will contact you.

"That should give us the time we need to finish off Christensen and vanish. I'll then send them the pics you found and give them an opportunity to investigate and piece together the murders. They'll find two of the three perps dead and put the State Senator in prison. A job well done."

Marcy and Tina finished their Frangelico and headed home. Tomorrow's adventure would start early.

Chapter 48

As the sun rose over Worcester, Marcy and Tina were already in their SUV, parked outside John Christensen's apartment building. They had been watching his place since six-fifteen, hoping to catch him leaving for work. Tina was browsing the web on her phone, looking for a quick-acting sedative that she could use to knock out Christensen before she gave him a lethal dose of fentanyl. Marcy was keeping an eye on the building's entrance, waiting for their target to leave for work. At six-forty-eight, Christensen came out of the door and walked towards Union Station.

Marcy parked near Union Station where she and Tina got into position to observe the target. "He's very consistent, same time every day. We'll watch him to see if he gets on the same train as yesterday," Tina said.

They observed Christensen present his commuter pass and board the seven thirteen train, number five-o-eight to Boston. They trailed him to the platform and saw him board. "Let's go to the Miss Worcester Diner and have a large breakfast, then head home and formulate a detailed plan. I think we might need a dry run tomorrow," Tina added.

After eating, they adjourned to the little house they had rented and got to work. Marcy analyzed commuter train schedules between Worcester and Boston in order to determine the best times to kill Christensen and return to

Worcester. Tina worked on the actual killing: how to kill someone on a crowded train and go undetected. Marcy viewed her assignment as simple and fairly quick. She expected to have time to browse the company computer to see if anyone was concerned about her or Tina. Tina, on the other hand, was looking for injectable drugs that would do the job unnoticed. She had a drug supplier on retainer. At noon, both had completed their research and were ready to discuss the plan after lunch.

Marcy went first. "I had time after I finished the plan, so I looked around the company computer to see if there was any interest in us. I viewed emails and reports and, good news, found nothing related to either of us. We're not people of interest. As for the timeline: we know he normally takes the seven-thirteen out of Union Station, which gets crowded closer to Framingham at seven-fifty-four. You board the train at the same time as Christensen and sit next to him. I'll sit several seats behind you. As we approach the Framingham stop, I will get into the aisle as if I am getting off and, on your signal, I will fall into you and cause some confusion. You execute the kill and we both leave. Christensen's body gets to Boston at eight-thirty-three."

Marcy stopped talking and turned both palms up.

Tina replied, "Sounds good. How do we get home?"

"There are trains every five to eight minutes going to Worcester. We can easily take our time, not look rushed, and be on our way to Worcester before his body gets to Boston."

"I like it. We'll do a dry run tomorrow. We'll sit in the same car but stay several rows behind Christensen and carefully observe every aspect of the train ride to check for holes in the plan. Now, for the execution of the person responsible for Kathryn's death: I've decided the best way to kill Christensen is lethal injection. I've settled on Midazolam for the first injection. I plan to inject it into his thigh. Midazolam acts quickly and produces relaxation, sedation, anticonvulsant, and amnesic effects. I'll increase the normal dose. He may die without ever becoming conscious. Midazolam interacts with other drugs, including opioids, alcohol, marijuana, antihistamines, antidepressants, anticonvulsants, or even grapefruit juice. The interactions increase the risk of dying, which, of course, is our goal. To make sure he doesn't live, I'll administer an overdose of fentanyl, which should finish the job. I will preload two AUTOJECTORS for speed and ease. It will take no more than ten seconds for the two injections. What do you think?"

"Not my strong suit, but the plan should work. I know Murphy's law states 'Anything that can go wrong will.' What's the backup plan?"

"Security is nonexistent before boarding. We can easily carry a Barretta onto the train; I have two. Our backup plan is to shoot our way off the train and run. It's not the best plan, but until we have another, it's the best we have."

"Wow. So, our plan has to work, or we're dead. So, let's make sure it works."

"You're going to help even though it's dangerous?"

"Absolutely."

"Dry run tomorrow, then the real thing the day after. Our escape from this dirty business is close."

Mike, Phil and Jim were on a three-way call. Jim said, "I think we should tell Karen and Sal about the emails. I want them on our side if the shit hits the proverbial fan. And I'm concerned, she might be manipulating us, though I can't figure out how or why."

Phil replied, "I tend to agree, but I think we should wait a day. I don't want to do anything that might put us in harm's way."

Mike said, "I agree. Let's be patient."

"Okay, but my cop senses are tingling. I like being in control. I don't like being told what to do and what not to do by a killer for hire."

Tina and Marcy arrived at Union Station at six-thirty and waited impatiently in the Grand Concourse for John Christensen to show up. At four minutes to seven Christensen arrived, and after showing his commuter pass, walked to the platform and waited for his regular train. Tina and Marcy followed and stood close to, but behind, Christensen. The platform was not busy, and when Christensen boarded the train, they were easily able to get into the same car and get seats a couple of rows behind him.

Tina could have just as easily sat in the aisle seat next to him.

Tina studied the schedule as the train worked its way to Framingham. She whispered to Marcy, "Let's get off in West Natick. We can see which stop is better for our mission. They both give us time, and after West Natick, there are no stops until Boston."

The number of commuters boarding at Framingham station almost filled the train, and the commuters boarding at West Natick station completed the job. Framingham station and West Natick station were six minutes apart, and after West Natick, the next stop was Boston Landing in twenty minutes.

Tina and Marcy detrained at West Natick, took an Uber to the Natick Mall, and killed an hour before boarding the nine-thirty-seven to Worcester. After arriving home, they discussed the plan and decided that the only change to their plan was to kill the target as the train approached West Natick, not Framingham. Too many commuters got on in Framingham.

They spent the rest of the day on details, clothing, make up, and hair color for both women. Tina made certain the auto-injectors were ready and that the Barettas worked properly. At six, they enjoyed a great meal that Marcy had prepared, and by eight, they had the house wiped down and the SUV ready for the trip to their new home.

Chapter 49

Marcy lay in bed, awake since four A.M., thinking about what was about to unfold. If all went as planned, she would be directly involved in a murder for the first time in her life. And tomorrow, she would start a new life with Tina. If Murphy's law interfered, she would be in prison or dead. Tina, on the other hand, lay in bed visualizing every step, every detail of the plan, and executing it to perfection. She always approached her job visualizing success, and it had always worked. When she heard Marcy stir, she got up. They had an hour and a half before they had to arrive at Union Station, which was plenty of time to get everything ready.

They were sitting in an area of the Grand Concourse away from the crowd. Tina thought Marcy looked worried, maybe even afraid. "Marcy, are you worried about today? Do you think it's going to go wrong?"

"I think I'm just nervous because it's the first time for me. I don't want to screw up and get you hurt or killed."

"I don't want that to happen either, but if I've learned one thing in all these years, it's that if you're prepared and have a good plan, it all works out. Even if we have to adlib, we're ready. Trust me, this will be easy."

"Okay."

"I've been thinking about timing, and to be safe, I need to begin the injections two minutes before we get to West

Natick, and Christensen will be dead before the train stops. So, start down the aisle two and a half minutes before the station. I'll signal you."

"Will do."

"It's time. Let's start walking toward the platform and look for Christensen."

Shortly after getting to the platform for the five-o-eight, they saw Christensen and followed as he walked to his train. Tina walked behind him, and Marcy trailed behind her. As they waited on the platform, Tina and Marcy stood behind Christensen. When he boarded, he took a window seat and Tina took the aisle seat next to him. As she sat, he looked at this obviously poor and unattractive woman with distain. Marcy saw the look from him and had two thoughts: *the effort Tina put into her look was worth it*, and *the asshole deserves to die*.

As the train trundled along toward West Natick, Christensen leaned toward the window with his eyes closed. Tina took advantage of his inattentiveness to ensure that she had the syringe with the sedative in her grasp and ready to use. She visualized injecting the sedative into his thigh muscle, then reran the visualization several times before she felt confident of her success. She then visualized returning the syringe to her bag and quickly removing the syringe loaded with fentanyl. The decisive step would be injecting Christensen, then returning the syringe to her bag. She reran the visualization several more times, then relaxed, confident in the success of the kill.

Two minutes and thirty seconds before reaching West Natick Marcy stood and moved into the aisle. As the train continued to slow, Tina signaled her, and Marcy moved toward the exit. When she was next to Tina, the train lurched to a stop, and Marcy used the movement to fall over Tina and place her right-hand on Christensen's shoulder to get her balance. Tina used the commotion to inject the sedative into his thigh.

At first Christensen seemed unaware. Then, he looked into Tina's eyes and said, "What the fuck did you do to me?"

Marcy acted as if his comment was directed toward her, yelled in response, "Oh God, I'm sorry, I didn't mean to fall on you. Are you hurt? I hope not. Oh my God, I am so clumsy. Sorry, I'm so sorry."

While Marcy was apologizing, the sedative began to work. A few seconds later, Tina injected the fentanyl with her left hand concealed beneath a well-placed handbag. Christensen's days on this earth ended at 19,129.

Tina said, "This is my stop. He's fine."

The other commuters were too engrossed in their lives and their devices to care enough to get involved. Marcy exited first, followed by Tina. They went in separate directions at first; Marcy followed a short walking tour of West Natick, while Tina sat on a bench in the park near the train station and listened to a Boston all-news radio station.

Tina stood on the west side of the platform, waiting to board train number five-o-nine to Worcester. Marcy arrived a few minutes later and stood a distance away from Tina. They planned to be on the same train, but in different cars.

The tingle in Jim's cop senses raged as he sat around the house. Something was not right. He wanted to involve Karen, so he decided to push Mike and Phil again. A quick phone call to Mike revealed that he was busy, but he agreed that she should know. On his second call, Jim expected that he'd talk to Phil and Karen jointly since she was staying at Phil's place. Phil agreed that it was time to let Karen know about the email, and he told Jim that for the past few days, she had been staying with Sal. Jim texted Karen to alert her to receive a call at ten.

Tina and Marcy met in the Union Station parking garage. Marcy drove the first leg of the first trip of their new life together. Tina listened intently to a report on the Boston news station. It seemed that workers had found a commuter, identity withheld until notification of next of kin, dead on the five-o-eight train. The body had no signs of trauma, and for now, it appeared that he had died of natural causes.

Tina smiled at Marcy and said, "The news is perfect. While you're driving, I'm gathering all the documents we used as identification for the mission. The documents for our new identities are perfect and ready to use. I have to dispose of the old identities and send the boys an email. Are you okay driving for a while?"

"No problem."

Karen and Sal were deep in discussion trying to figure out a way to solve the murders and Jim's shooting, but they needed a key to unlock the mystery. Karen's phone beeped, alerting her that she had received a text. After reading it, she said, "Jim and Phil want to talk at ten. Apparently, they have some info to share. Do you want to listen in?"

"If it's alright with them."

"I am going to let them know you should be involved."

"Do you want me involved because we're sleeping together, or because I can help?"

"Fuck you."

"Okay, but do you have time?"

"Funny."

At exactly ten, Karen's cell chimed, and she said, "Hello, Jim."

Jim responded, "Phil's here. Is Sal there?"

Karen, a little surprised by the question, replied, "Yes."

"Let him listen. Is he there?"

"I'm here," said Sal.

"You got there fast. One might think you're a couple and are living together," Jim joked.

"Cut the shit, Jim," groaned Karen, "I'm not your teenage daughter."

"Yeah, but I love you like a daughter."

"Jesus, you'll make me cry."

"Let's get down to business. Phil and I received an email from the woman that has committed all the murders and shot me. She said there's a contract on Phil's and my life, and it might include our families."

Sal jumped in. "Jesus Christ, you're kidding."

Phil said, "It's from the dark web, and it's untraceable. If she finds out that we don't follow her exact instructions, she'll turn on us. I don't know what that means, but I don't think I'll like it."

Jim said, "I'll send you the email, then we'll have to meet later to discuss what to do."

Chapter 50

Tina cut the documents that she and Marcy had used while they were in Massachusetts into little pieces. Confetti. She disposed of it in the trash at four different rest areas along the New Jersey Turnpike. She then made certain their documents for their new life were in the right places: wallets, purses, and auto glove box. Tina and Marcy were now sisters in their late forties with an enormous amount of money. There was one last thing on her to-do list.

"Marcy, are you tired of driving?"

"No. We've taken breaks. I'll drive until we find a hotel for tonight."

"I'll send the boys an email tonight. I need my laptop to get into the dark web. I'm going to close my eyes for a minute."

Tina slept until Marcy exited for route 896 in Delaware and found a good hotel for the night. After dinner, Tina sat down at her laptop and composed an email to Jim and Phil.

TO: Jim Hines & Phil Messina

Subject: That contract HIT on you both!

I have attached pictures of the three men that contracted with my handlers to kill the CEO of the Mill in Cargill Falls. They also ordered the hit on Larry

Davidson. And most important to you: these men wanted me to kill Jim and Phil, and Mike if necessary.

I found these pictures by hacking into my handler's computer. I took an extremely dangerous step to acquire this information for you. In fact, I put my life at risk. The only identities I found for the men are "The Caretaker," "The Director," and "The State Senator." One of the three wants you both dead, and he made your murders mandatory in his contract, or he would not pay. You can save your lives by putting all three in prison or killing them. Involve anyone you need in the investigation to identify and find them. State Police, anyone. It does not matter to me.

This email is the last thing I will reveal before I vanish. If you decide to search for me, you will only be frustrated. Just like I didn't leave any clues at my kills, I myself will disappear without a clue. So don't waste your time on me. Find the guy that wants you dead.

"What now? And what are you going to do with the laptop?" Marcy asked.

"Now we'll enjoy the night before we head south tomorrow. I plan to hold on to the laptop for a year. I won't turn it on unless I want to retrieve the information that might save us if the company finds us. After that, I'll destroy it."

After reviewing the email correspondence and exchanging their views, Karen and Sal felt prepared for the meeting. The Hines residence on Grove Street welcomed the Messinas, the Robertsons, Karen and Sal, and Noelle. Jim wanted to share the emails with the whole team. Phil invited the Putnam brothers, but they could not make it. Phil would update them. The reactions of those who saw the emails for the first time ranged from shock to anger, or both.

Jim called the meeting to order and said, "Look, we're sorry we didn't share the emails sooner, but we didn't understand the source, nor the woman who wrote them. We thought it would be dangerous, but we feel it's better if everyone is aware of the threat."

Just then, Phil's laptop beeped. Phil looked at the email he had received and said, "Hold on, this is from her. I should read it out loud, it's important."

After a minute, Phil read the entire email aloud. Silence filled the room while he left for a moment to print copies of the pictures for everyone. No one knew exactly what to make of what they had just heard.

Tess said, "The Caretaker was on the news recently. He's dead, committed suicide. If I remember correctly, his name was Robert Sullivan."

Mary Ann said, "I remember that he was the caregiver for his gravely injured wife. They said that was probably the reason he committed suicide."

Sal said, "I recognize the Senator. His name is Richard Thall, and he's extremely corrupt."

Phil said, "I recognize The Director. His name is John Christensen. He worked for McKenzie and was responsible for creating the financial structure of the Joint Venture with Saga Pharmaceuticals. He was also responsible for due diligence. McKenzie fired him as a result of what Jim, and I uncovered. He was part of the conspiracy and lost everything: his job, his family and his pension. I guess he blames us, Jim."

"Phil, most criminals blame other people for their crimes. Now, let's decide on how we should approach this situation. I will start since I already have an opinion. We should turn it over to the State Police to investigate," Jim said.

"I agree," said Sal. "The police have powers you don't have, such as the power to charge a crime and arrest the criminal. I'll stay involved and keep this group informed."

Rose added, "I can't believe that we know who orchestrated the murders, that the information came from the murderer – a hitwoman, no less – and that we're finally safe. When we walked in here, there was a contract on Jim and Phil. Now, we're safe. Thank the Lord."

"When The Director and The Senator are behind bars, we'll be safe. For now, we're safer than we were thirty minutes ago, and that's great," Jim responded.

Sal interjected, "I'm going to talk to my boss and the Attorney General and get the investigation started. I suspect I'll play a role in the investigation."

Mike said, "Let's celebrate. The hitwoman solved the murders for us, and it's time to work on a deal with the Mill owners and find the treasure. I couldn't be happier."

Jim laughed. "You're premature. We need to wait for Sal's people to tell us it's over. Then we can get back to business."

For the rest of the afternoon, the Old Mill Investigators enjoyed food and drink. The relaxed atmosphere contributed to a happy mood and convivial conversation. Sal, anxious to start, only stayed for a little while.

At midnight, when Sal finally came to bed, Karen was awake and interested in learning what he had accomplished.

"I talked to the AG, my commander, and to my surprise, the Governor. I also worked out a plan with the Major Crimes unit. They'll start the investigation first thing tomorrow by questioning Thall. I also talked with Jim. My cop senses are tingling because the emails didn't implicate Dorian, and I'm sure he's part of this. Jim wholeheartedly agrees. We'll talk more tomorrow morning. I'm beat."

Chapter 51

The Cargill Falls murders had haunted the state for over a year, and now the Major Crimes taskforce was determined to unravel them once and for all. They gathered in the conference room of the State Police headquarters in Hartford, early in the morning, to divide their roles and responsibilities. The taskforce had three units, each focusing on one of the suspects: the Caretaker, the Director, and the Senator. They had to find out how and why these men had committed such heinous crimes, and what their connections were. The Governor wanted a clear and conclusive report with no loose ends. The unit assigned to the Caretaker would dig deep into Robert Sullivan's background and psychology, trying to understand his motives and methods. The same would apply to the Director. The Senator, on the other hand, was a familiar name to the State Police brass, and they suspected that his motive was simple greed. The unit in charge of him had the best interrogators in the state, and they had the authority to use any means necessary to get the truth.

The unit tasked with understanding the Caretaker and determining what motivated him consisted of five officers, three computer specialists and two detectives. The three computer specialists would gather all the online information available, and the detectives would interview family, friends, and acquaintances.

The unit tasked with finding and interrogating John Christensen also had the authority to use any means necessary to get the truth. The Police suspected that Christensen was the ringleader because of his history with Messina and Commander Hines. They believed that he would be the key to the case.

The unit tasked with interrogating Senator Thall looked forward to seeing him sweat. They decided to establish their power over him by serving the warrant they had obtained and arresting him in public. Senator Thall had championed the "defund-the-police" movement in Connecticut, and it was payback time. However, before the interrogation, they wanted to try to find more incriminating evidence on Thall's involvement in the murders.

The general background noise of conversation stopped abruptly when one of the computer specialists yelled, "He's dead!" The taskforce members crowded around the computer as the specialist explained that a cleaning crew had discovered Christensen's body on a Boston commuter train at the end of the line. "The cause of death will be unknown until the medical examiner conducts an autopsy," the computer specialist added. "The medical examiner has a backlog, and since there are no signs of foul play, Christensen is not a priority."

The head of the Major Crimes taskforce, Commander Nealis, said, "I'll contact Boston PD and try to have the autopsy expedited. We have to know the cause of death to do our work. Two of the three suspects the killer gave us are dead, and we need to find out what in the hell is going on."

Sal and Karen stopped by to see how Jim was healing and to give him an update on the taskforce. "Commander Hines, how are you, sir?" Sal said.

"Look, you're sleeping with Karen, who I consider my daughter. So, knock off the commander stuff and call me Jim. I'm better but have a long way to go."

"Okay, from now on its Jim."

Karen interrupted, "I feel like you're my father at work. And I really like Sal, and I might even be in love with him. Do I have your approval, Dad?"

"My God. I have another goombah in my life. Just kidding, Sal. Yes, of course you have my approval. He's a cop. What more can I ask for?"

Karen decided to explain what she was sure seemed like a ridiculous exchange to Sal. "A few years ago, Jim thought he insulted me and Phil by referring to an Italian scumbag as a goombah. He over-apologized and Phil and I never let him forget it."

"I stopped thinking when you said you might be in love with me."

"Good, stop thinking. Let's get down to business."

Sal smiled and started his explanation. "The taskforce is operating. The computer guys are all over the internet and looking around the dark web. The detectives are in the field conducting interviews. We're making progress. You know Christensen is dead?"

"Yes, I know. Did they get the autopsy moved up?"

"It's the day after tomorrow."

Jim smiled and said, "Thank you Sal I appreciate your effort. Now, Phil wants to get everyone together so we'll all get the same information and can start planning an offer to the Mill owners. When do you think the taskforce will allow the negotiations to begin?"

"I'd think in about two weeks. Do you still believe that the 'item of value' in the Mill is a hoax?"

"Yes, but Mike still thinks it's there."

"And you still think Dorian is dirty?"

"I do. I believe that he's involved and that he set up the tour in the Mill in a way that would get the three of us killed. I hope the taskforce will look closely at Mr. Dorian Gregson."

Sal nodded. "He's definitely on Commander Nealis's radar."

Chapter 52

Commander Nealis called the taskforce to order. The three units were back in the conference room at the Hartford headquarters. "It's been three days since the last time we were all together. I want to hear that we've made progress. Anyone?"

Detective Weller, assigned to the Caretaker unit, stood up. "I struck gold. I interviewed Robert Sullivan's neighbors. A Mrs. Spelman knew Sullivan; in fact, she referred to herself as a close friend of both Sullivans. She would take care of Amanda when Sullivan was unavailable. He started having meetings at night a little over a year ago and Spelman would stay with Amanda. On one occasion, after asking Spelman to take care of his wife, Sullivan decided that she was too ill and canceled his request. He then held the meeting at his house. On the night the meeting was at Sullivan's house, Spelman took a walk. She noticed a pricey-looking car with an unusual license plate parked in front of the house. The Connecticut vanity plate read 'CT SNTR.'"

Nealis responded, "That's Thall's car. Is she a creditable witness?"

"Absolutely. She has all her marbles and I already have a signed affidavit. We now have corroboration. We got him."

"Weller, get out of here and arrest State Senator Thall. And make a scene. Embarrass the man. Now get out of here."

The remainder of the meeting was much less exciting. Christensen's upcoming autopsy was the only highlight.

Detective Weller and his partner learned that Senator Thall was enjoying lunch at The Capital Grille, which was arguably the best restaurant in Connecticut. The detectives spotted Thall and walked to his table, where a half-eaten large, medium-rare Filet Mignon sat in front of him.

Weller said calmly, "Senator Thall, if you do as I say, no one will notice. Stand up and put your hands behind...."

Thall cut off Weller mid-sentence. "Do you know who I am, you asshole? I am State Senator Thall, and I am going to finish my...."

Weller cut off Thall mid-sentence and, loud enough for most of the diners to hear, exclaimed, "Richard Thall, you are under arrest for the murders of Robert Martineau, Larry Davidson, and Mae Lamphere, as well as the attempted murder of retired police commander James Hines." Weller then jerked Thall to his feet and, as the Senator struggled against his grip, said, "Resist and I will break your arm. Put your hands behind your back and allow me to cuff you. I'm going to walk you to a car and take you to police headquarters."

"I want a lawyer," cried Thall.

"You can call your lawyer when we get to headquarters. Let's go."

The ride to police headquarters only took ten minutes. Thall called his lawyer, then a uniformed officer placed him in an interrogation room and handcuffed him to the table. He sat there alone for almost three hours before his lawyer entered.

"Where the fuck were you? I called you almost three hours ago!"

"It seems they lost track of you. You must have really pissed them off."

"Let's do this. I want to go home."

After a short while, Weller entered the interrogation room and nodded to the lawyer. A crowd gathered to watch through the two-way mirror.

Thall spoke first. "I didn't murder anyone. I don't know what in the hell you're talking about."

Weller responded, "I just have a few questions, and if you're truthful, we'll be out of here in a heartbeat. Are you ready?"

"Yes," Thall replied angrily.

"Do you know John Christensen?"

Thall looked startled, but replied, "No. Why do you think I do?"

"I'll ask the questions. Okay, you don't know Christensen. Do you know Robert Sullivan?"

"Again, no."

"Have you ever been to Robert Sullivan's house?"

"I said I don't know him. Why would I go to his house?"

Thall's lawyer jumped in. "I don't like your tone, detective. This interview is over. Senator let's go. Uncuff him."

"This interview is not over. Again, have you ever been to Robert Sullivan's house?"

Thall's lawyer responded, "Are you prepared to arrest Senator Thall?"

"Yes."

"Do you have a warrant?"

"Yes. Are you prepared to go to jail, Thall, or do you want to answer my questions? And answer them honestly?"

The lawyer scowled. "I want to talk to my client in private. Turn off the microphones. And I want to see the warrant."

Weller said, "Sure."

Once Weller was out of earshot, Thall's lawyer turned to him and accused him, "You're lying. Weller knows it and you know it. What did you do? They have an arrest warrant for you accusing you of three murders and an attempted murder. You need to be straight with me. It's the only way I can defend you. Tell me everything."

Thall told his lawyer everything.

"Don't say another word. You're going to jail tonight. I'll see if I can have you arraigned tomorrow and get you released on bail. You have to be quiet. Not a word, understand?"

"I don't want to go to jail," hissed Thall.

"That ship has sailed. I'll do everything I can to get you the best deal I can. But understand, they know more than they're telling us. What in the hell were you thinking? I'm going to call Weller, and again, don't say a word."

Weller walked into the interrogation room and said, "Well?"

Thall's lawyer responded, "My client will not answer another question."

"In that case, Senator Thall, I am arresting you for the murders of Robert Martineau, Larry Davidson, and Mae Lamphere and the attempted murder of retired police commander James Hines. Your arraignment will be tomorrow."

With that said, Weller cuffed Thall's hands behind his back and walked him to a holding cell to await arraignment.

Sal and Karen watched through the two-way mirror from outside of the room. Both smiled as Weller cuffed Senator Thall. Sal said, "The team investigating John Christensen procured a warrant to search his apartment. They're going in first thing tomorrow, and I hope they find evidence of the murders. The team assigned to Sullivan has come up empty so far. We have Thall's cell phone in the vicinity of Sullivan's house, and when the state prosecutor presents that, in addition to the other evidence, the judge won't give him bail. Thall will rot in jail."

Senator Thall's arraignment took place at nine A.M. on the following morning and, as Sal predicted, the judge denied bail. Of course, Thall's lawyer said that he would appeal. But realistically, he had no chance of winning.

The arraignment concluded at the same time the team searching Christensen's apartment was able to open his small safe. The team found what they believed to be meticulously organized documentation of the murders. The taskforce would analyze every detail contained in the documents and give the Governor a report sufficient to declare the case closed. The state prosecutors would corroborate the documents and use them to prosecute Thall.

Chapter 53

Before the Connecticut television stations and newspapers were able to report the story, and even before any of the national media had the story, Phil Messina provided the details to Harry O. Prior to putting the story on air, he contacted his sources in Hartford and confirmed the story. They also told Harry O that some of the details of the story were still under review, and that he was the only news guy to have it. That was enough for Harry O to run with the story.

WINY, your local community radio station, is breaking the news that the state has solved the murders and shootings that have plagued the Quiet Corner over the last year. No other news organization has reported this news. So, get ready to hear 'who done it,' and how they did it.

The people responsible – the perpetrators, if you will – are Robert Sullivan from Massachusetts, John Christensen (also from Massachusetts,) and Connecticut State Senator Richard Thall. Also responsible is the as-yet unknown hired killer. That is correct, the three men hired a killer, and one of them is in the Connecticut State Government. They also provided information to the killer to assist in committing the murders.

The investigation broke wide open when an unknown informant provided some information on the identities of the perps, and that motivated state police officials to organize a taskforce that ultimately identified them. Robert Sullivan died by his own hand before the informant identified him, and John Christensen died from a lethal injection. His murderer is unknown. The taskforce investigated every aspect of Sullivan's and Christensen's lives and found records of their involvement in the murders. A detailed review of the records also led to Senator Thall. The police arrested Thall, the judge denied bail, and State Senator Richard Thall is currently housed in the Brooklyn Correction Facility.

I realize that there are gaps in the details of the story, and I will work hard to fill them in. The good news is that the people who orchestrated the murders in the Quiet Corner are either dead or in prison. Even though the police have not caught the hired killer, they believe that we are not in any danger.

The breaking news delivered by Harry O brought relief to the Old Mill Investors assembled at the Hines residence. The tension that had hung over them since their recent offer to purchase the Mill dissipated as they learned that the State Police had finally resolved the murders, and that the perps were either dead or in prison. The newscast concluded and cheers erupted among the investors. They were no longer worried about their own safety.

However, three members remained cautious: Jim, Karen, and Sal. Their police experience had taught them to be vigilant. They suspected that Dorian might still be involved in the murders and could pose a threat to their next attempt to acquire the Mill. As negotiations to purchase stock in the Mill progressed, they would stay alert, ready to act if necessary.

Mike, smiling from ear to ear, said, "Now we can get about the important task of becoming wealthy. Once the Mill owners accept our offer, I'll find the treasure, no doubt in my mind. I've always wanted to have more money than I can spend, and I want to leave a pile of money for my son and his wife and for my granddaughters. I can't wait to start."

"Our competition no longer exists," Phil said. "We'll talk to the Mill owners and revisit our offer. Hopefully, we can reach a quick agreement on the structure of the deal. Then, Mike, you can have access to the Mill without having to dodge bullets," Phil said.

Elijah and Nathan Putnam decided that it was the right time to make an important announcement to the group. Nathan said, "Elijah and I have been discussing our involvement with the group. We find our involvement in this group both stimulating and rewarding, and we appreciate the honesty and the sincerity that is present in every member of your group. We've decided to fund all the money needed to close the deal with the Mill owners. You won't have to liquidate any assets or take any risk with your future. After Mike finds the treasure and we start amassing cash, we ask that you make us whole. For example, if we buy stock in the Mill for four million dollars, my brother and I will put up the entire four million. Then, as we liquidate the treasure, we get twenty five percent until we get our four million back. Once we're even, we're done, no more payments and no equity in the Mill. All we ask is that we get visitation privileges."

Phil said, "You're going to risk four million dollars with no chance to make a profit. That's not a good business deal on your part. Why?"

Elijah shrugged. "We're old men and have more than enough money to last us the rest of our lives. And it makes us happy to give you the opportunity to become wealthy beyond your wildest dreams. To us, that is priceless."

Mike said, "Fantastic! Now let's party."

Mary Ann had plenty of food and drink and the old Mill Investors celebrated the abundance of good news that the day had brought.

Mary Ann managed to pull Rose, Tess, and Noelle aside for an impromptu meeting. "I have an idea. Let's throw a party for Karen and Sal to celebrate their relationship."

"Great idea," Rose replied, "Let's make it an Italian-themed night."

Tess said, "Figures you would come up with an Italian theme, Rose. How about an Irish theme?"

Rose laughed and said, "The whole menu for the evening would consist of corned beef and cabbage and Irish whiskey."

"Now, now," said Noelle, "Sal and Karen are both very Italian, so let's go Italian. It'll be a blast." The women hugged and set up a series of meetings to plan an Italian night at Mary Ann's.

While the ladies were discussing Italian night, Jim, Karen, and Sal were discussing Dorian. Jim said, "We need to keep our eyes open all the time, but I feel like if there's another pissed-off person that wants Phil and me dead, it will happen in conjunction with Mike looking for the treasure."

"Right. We need to have a security plan in place for the treasure hunt," Sal added.

Italian Night

Noelle volunteered to host the other women for wine and snacks and to plan Italian Night. Beyond being a way to celebrate Karen and Sal, it was a good excuse to enjoy a night of good Italian food and drink. Gathered around the living room were Rose, Tess, and Mary Ann in addition to Noelle. With wine poured, snacks tasted, and the chit-chat done, the party planners got down to business.

Mary Ann said, "I want to have it at my house. Jim's still a little gimpy, and he'll be more comfortable if he needs a bathroom."

Everyone agreed. Mary Ann added, "I think we should start with the menu. That's the most work. Rose, any thoughts on food for the party?"

"Just because I'm Italian doesn't mean I have the menu planned."

Tess said, "Yes it does."

Rose smiled. Tess had already forgiven her for the snarky comment she made about Irish food. "I'd start with antipasto: assorted sliced deli meats like salami, spicy capocollo, prosciutto, mortadella, Italian cheeses cut into irregular chunks, maybe a good Parmigiano-Reggiano, marinated olives, peppers, focaccia bread. Next, I'd have Italian wedding soup."

Noelle said, "They're not getting married."

"Despite its name, it has nothing to do with actual weddings. The term wedding soup refers to the marriage of flavors and ingredients in this soup. In addition to small meatballs, it contains vegetable broth, tomato-basil soup, carrots, celery, escarole, parsley, and a hard-boiled egg."

Tess responded, "I'm getting full, Rose. Is there more?"

"A lot more. When we finish the soup course, we can relax, then move on to the main course. I suggest we prepare three dishes: sugo alla Bolognese, conchiglie ripieni, and sugo e Polpette. Those are better known as pasta with Bolognese Sauce, stuffed shells, and sauce and meatballs. We can keep the main dishes warm while we socialize, then eat when we're ready. The same applies to dessert, tiramisu. It serves right from the refrigerator."

Noelle asked, "Is 'sugo' Italian for sauce? And what are the ingredients in Bolognese sauce?"

"Yes, both Phil's family and my family called sauce 'sugo.' The Bolognese ingredients start with cubed pancetta sauteed with several different vegetables, olive oil, herbs, and grated cheese. Then you add ground beef and veal. I have recipes for every course."

The women discussed the preparation required for each course and selected the dish or dishes that they would prepare. Mary Ann volunteered to do all the cooking, but everyone else wanted to prepare at least one dish. The next topic was decorations, and the theme was obviously Italian.

Rose offered, "I have a lot of decorations we can use, and in fact, we won't have to buy any. I have a dozen thirteen-inch-tall Italian flags, napkins with lemons printed on them, a runner for the table, and other stuff. I have enough to decorate Mary Ann's house. Next on the agenda is beer, whiskey, and wine to have with our antipasto. I suggest imported Italian beer and wine, and Irish whiskey."

Tess asked, "Why Irish whiskey at Italian Night?"

Rose responded, "Phil, Mike and Jim drink Jameson or Proper Twelve and say it's the best. Next are the after-dinner drinks. I suggest Frangelico, Amaretto, and Limoncello, all imported. Okay: the last thing is music. I think it'll be fun to play the Italian singers from the forties and fifties."

"I don't know who you're talking about," Noelle said.

"Louie Prima, Frank Sinatra, Dean Martin and a few others. I have all the music we'll need," Rose answered.

The four women talked through all the details required to prepare for the big night, then relaxed with wine and talked some more.

Mary Ann, excited when she arrived home, told Jim about the food, the drink, and the decorations for Italian Night at the Hines residence.

Jim's reaction to the plan was predictable. "I get enough Italian bullshit from Karen and Phil during the day! And now for a whole night, I have to live it in my home?"

Mary Ann gave Jim "the look" and said, "Grow up, Jim. You're talking like a ten-year-old. Lighten up and enjoy the party. I'm going to bed, and you're not welcome."

"God damn it."

The women started decorating two hours before the party. The house definitely looked and felt Italian, with flags and other items decorating every room on the first floor. The four women were pleased with their work and chatted about how wonderful the house looked. Jim, on the other hand, looked miserable.

The Putnam brothers were the first guests to arrive and looked awestruck as they took in the scene before them. Nathen said, "I am not sure if I am in Italy or the United Nations. And Louie Prima singing – my God, I haven't heard him in ages. I am impressed. Jim why do you seem so gloomy?"

"God damn it, why do you Anglo-Saxons like Italian music?"

Nathen let the comment pass as other guests arrived. Soon everyone was talking, drinking, and picking at the antipasto board.

Mary Ann announced, "Corso di Zuppa!" When a few guests seemed confused, Mary Ann said, "Soup's on."

Jim grimaced and said to Mary Ann, "When did you learn Italian?"

She gave Jim the look again and said, "Lighten up and have fun, or shut up."

The wedding soup was a hit with all, and a couple of people asked Sal and Karen if they had set a wedding date.

Mary Ann announced, "Primo Corso."

Jim was having fun and being nice to the others even though Mary Ann continued to speak Italian. So, she whispered, "You're welcome tonight."

Jim's smile widened.

The entrees were a success, some people going for seconds and Nathan going for thirds. Jim had two full plates and said he loved the pasta Bolognese because it was "al dente." It was the first time in his life he had used that term. Mary Ann was pleasantly shocked.

When they all had their fill, they sat around the table and sipped on the after-dinner drinks. Every so often someone would get up and have some dessert, which now included cannoli that the Putnam brothers had brought.

The get-together was advertised as a celebration for Sal and Karen, but it was really because the danger had passed.

Chapter 54

Phil and Mike acknowledged Janet Howell with a nod as she entered the conference room attached to her office in the Mill. Janet said, "I'm terribly sorry that I'm late. I had to resolve an issue with the renovation, and I'm the only one who could authorize the change. It took a while, but it's settled, and now no one will interrupt us."

"Great. Other than dealing with the Mill renovation, how have you been?" Phil asked.

"I have everything under control, except the finances. So, I'm anxious to hear your new offer."

Mike said, "I'm positive I'll find something hidden in the foundation walls, and I'm sure that that 'something' will have value. I can't wait to start looking around."

"Mike is an eternal optimist. But he's exceptionally good at what he does, and if there is a treasure in the Mill, he'll find it."

Mike chimed in, "I certainly will."

"Our offer is slightly different, and I hope you'll see it as superior. Our last offer was that if Mike found anything of value in the Mill, we'd pay down your liabilities in an amount equal to your LLC's equity in the Mill. Let's assume, for example, that the Mill appraised at $23 million, and your liabilities were $18 million. Your equity would equal $5 million. If Mike is successful, we would apply $5 million to the debt on the Mill in exchange for fifty-percent ownership in the Mill. When the transaction is complete and we fund $5 million to reduce the debt on the Mill, we will collectively only owe $13 million. The equity in the Mill would equal $10 million. We would share equity and debt equally. Anything of value that Mike finds we, would also share equally."

"That's the way I remember your last offer. What has changed?" Janet asked.

"Two investors in our LLC want to fund the full amount of our stock purchase to a maximum of ten million dollars. Phil had obtained the maximum amount the Putnam brothers would invest when he attended a meeting with the brothers and their lawyer. They'll structure it as an interest-free loan and will receive twenty-five percent of our distribution as we liquidate the treasure until they get their money back. They don't want interest or any stock in the Mill. It's all financed by our half of the Mill. No financial effect on you or your partners."

"The Putnam brothers must really like you guys. That's very generous of them."

"I'm sure they want their generosity kept quiet."

"Fine. I assume you still want to explore, and you're no longer concerned about an assassin putting a bullet in you."

Mike said, "I have an idea of where Isaac Putnam hid the treasure, but I still need to look around. Now that the police have done their job and the bad guys are dead or in jail, I'm not worried."

"The only person I trust to keep my interests in mind while leading the tour is Dorian. Any issues?"

Phil and Mike looked at each other, obviously concerned, but said, "No problem."

Janet said, "Phil, write up a formal Letter of Intent and I'll run it past my lawyer. It should take about two weeks."

Janet told Dorian about the offer and asked if he would guide Phil Messina and Mike Robertson again as they explored the Mill. As the only living human that knew the precise location of the treasure, Dorian was in the proverbial catbird seat, and he intended to keep it that way.

As soon as he arrived home, Dorian found the untraceable phone he could use to call the Boss. Not long after the State Police had cracked the case, all of Dorian's contacts were either dead or in jail. Dorian did not know anyone wealthy enough to buy the Mill, and therefore, he knew that his knowledge would no longer be valuable. If he was going to be rich, he would have to devise a new plan. Then he received a call that changed everything. The caller knew about the treasure and claimed to have enough money to purchase the Mill. He offered Dorian a hundred thousand dollars immediately and ten percent of the treasure. Dorian negotiated and the "Boss" increased the percentage of the treasure to twenty.

Dorian never met the Boss. Instead, the Boss gave him detailed instructions to find a briefcase full of cash hidden in the linear park. Dorian followed the directions and found the briefcase. He received the keys in the mail, opened the case, and stared at one hundred thousand dollars in twenties.

The Boss answered on the second ring. "Yes, Dorian?"

"Things are starting to happen. Messina's LLC made a new offer on the Mill, and Janet accepted. She's waiting for her lawyer to sign off. In about two weeks Phil and Mike are going to start exploring the Mill, and I'm the guide."

"Excellent. Are you still the only one who knows where the treasure is?"

"Yes. And I won't take them anywhere near it."

"I must make some arrangements. Call me when you know the time and date or if things change. Thanks."

The Boss immediately called the company that had managed Tina. "Have you found the traitors yet?"

"No, but we are still looking. What do you need?"

"I need two hitmen in about two weeks at two locations in Cargill Falls. I assume I still get a discount because of your screw-up on the last contract. I'm betting she killed my friend before she disappeared."

"We think that she and her girlfriend killed him. You will receive the discount as agreed. Rest assured that we will find them."

"Further instructions to follow." The Boss disconnected.

"Phil and Mike will tour the Mill as soon as the Putnam Group accepts our Letter of Intent to purchase the Mill. I estimate a week or two. We need to be ready," Jim said to the police officers gathered around his kitchen table.

Commander Nealis said, "I agree, and it's up to us to protect Phil and Mike. We need a failsafe plan."

Karen responded, "Since Dorian is involved, they might hide another killer in the Mill. They may also hire a second killer to take Jim out."

Sal said, "We'll have to have people in the Mill and at your house, Jim. And Mary Ann can't be home. Jim, get your shotgun, rifle, and Glock oiled in case we miss the killer."

Jim smiled. "Think through the situation and come up with a potential plan. Let's meet in two days, discuss the plans, and decide on the best way to beat the killers."

The Treasure Hunt

Twenty years after killing Major Beck, Isaac Putnam returned to Virginia. Armed with the maps he had taken from the major's body and information he had acquired on Beck over the last three years, he was ready for the treasure hunt. The most significant pieces of intelligence, to Isaac Putnam's mind, came from the drunken ramblings of soldiers in the 43rd Battalion Virginia Cavalry. His paid informants had reported back to him, and he had paid well for tidbits of information and rumors about Beck's treasure.

Isaac intended to focus on a two-square-mile area of the Virginia forest, near the town of Woodstock, and look for the abandoned wolf den. Hopefully, a new tenant would not have moved in. He told his wife that he would be hunting for six to eight weeks. He carefully packed and readied everything he needed for the long train ride: clothing, food, guns and ammunition. Putnam calculated that it would take close to a week to get into the forest.

During his third week in the Virginia forest, Putnam was becoming frustrated. There were many pine trees in the woods, but he saw none that fit the description written on the map: "Two large, isolated pines, similar in size, spaced about 30 feet apart." Then, while wandering, he entered a clearing and at once saw the pines. He immediately recognized them as Beck's. He stood between the pines and, facing south, walked thirty paces and came face to face with the opening to a wolf den. Judging by the smell, a new occupant had taken up residence. He retrieved his rifle and checked it. Secure in the knowledge that his rifle was ready, he looped a rope around his chest and walked to the den opening. Fear coursed through Isaac's body. *Did I survive the war only to die in a wolf den in the state of Virginia, my body never found?* he wondered. Isaac slowly crawled into the den. He heard the wolf moving and coming closer, as if to see whoever was dumb enough to enter his home. Isaac readied for the confrontation, knowing that he would have only one shot. He saw the wolf, heard it snarl, and fired in the same instant. The wolf died a second after Isaac's bullet entered its right eye.

Isaac tied the wolf's hind legs together and used the lead of the rope to pull the dead wolf out of the den, then went back in to see if the legend was true or false. He again crawled through the narrow opening, which turned left after about ten feet, widened out, and revealed a large hollow.

Darkness was fast approaching, so Isaac Putnam decided that discretion was the better part of valor and set up camp for the night. He would find out what the cavern contained in the morning.

Chapter 55

Janet Howell was meeting with the lawyer representing the Mill to review the 'Old Mill Investors' Letter of Intent. The lawyer seemed to worry about the minutiae and did not grasp the monetary crisis facing the Mill owners. They were at risk of defaulting.

"I think you don't understand the big picture. You're raising issues with the offer that are meaningless and only hurt the Mill. We need to accept the offer to have a chance to survive. I'm going to heed my own counsel and sign the Letter of Intent," Janet said.

"My job is to make you aware of the legal pitfalls that are in the Letter of Intent. I am protecting the Mill."

"Legal concerns be damned. I'm signing and will get the ball rolling before it's too late to save the Mill."

"Since you insist on signing the LOI, I will have to send a letter detailing my concerns to all the owners."

"Have your letter in their hands by ten tomorrow morning or don't bother writing it. I'll wait until then."

Janet could not believe the lawyer's gall. He worked for the Mill owners and represented them, did he not? She would decide how to proceed, not the lawyer. Dorian would conduct the tour in three days.

Jim looked from Karen, to Sal, then to Commander Nealis. He said, "Okay. Let me hear the plan. We have two days to implement it."

Sal said, "We're putting motion-sensing cameras around the perimeter of the mill and on your house. They're top-of-the-line and extremely sensitive. And we'll have enough so if one fails, we still won't miss anyone going into the Mill. We're concentrating on a couple of key entry points. Karen and I will be in the area minutes away. Our thought is that any assassin would get into position before the tour starts. Jim, do you have any questions on the Mill?"

"Besides you and Karen, how many other officers do you have in and around the Mill?"

"None. We have two positioned in fairly close proximity. We don't want any visible security; it might scare the assassin away. Karen and I will have the element of surprise on our side."

"Don't forget Dorian. He might give the hitter extra firepower."

"We plan to arm Phil and Mike, which also gives us extra firepower."

"The plan is risky, but I guess that's good. I worry that Mike or Phil might shoot themselves in the foot or, worse, shoot each other. You know, I assume, that neither man has ever shot anyone."

"I think they'll handle whatever situation presents itself. Don't forget that Phil saved your life with a crystal replica of the Capitol dome. Securing your house, on the other hand, is more complicated. The best starting point for an assassin to get to your house is the cemetery. It's easy to exit the cemetery and get into the wooded area behind your house. Once in the wooded area, it's easy to get into a position to use a high-powered rifle. Or he might sneak up to your back door and gain entrance by picking your lock. And then it's you and the sharpshooter against the hitter."

"Do you have State Police snipers, or do you have to use the military?"

"We have three trained sniper teams. We're going to use motion sensing cameras in the wooded area and in the cemetery, in addition to the two sniper teams in the wooded area. We've already picked out the spots for the teams. If we see anyone carrying a gun or rifle, even if it's in a case, we're going to shoot to kill. If we see a person and it seems like they're not carrying, we'll ask them to stop. If they don't stop, we'll shoot to kill. Our last line of defense is the officer assigned as your bodyguard, who is a sharpshooter. And of course, there is you. I've heard you're a decent shot."

"The plan is solid. A lot of things can go wrong. But it should work."

"Do you know how to use a gun? The bigger question is: can you shoot at somebody? I don't think I can," Mike said to Phil.

"I don't know. I guess if my life depended on it, I would probably squeeze the trigger. At least we've had a couple of days of practice and will have two more days to hone our skills."

Mike and Phil were at the Sportsman Club in Thompson. The State had confiscated the entire club until the day after Mike and Phil had finished exploring the Mill.

Mike said, "The bad guys are dead or in jail. But Sal and Karen think Dorian is also a bad guy and might have something planned. I personally don't think so, but it's good to be prepared."

"Too bad you can't shoot as well as you bowl. You can hit the pocket, sixty feet away, twelve times in a row with a bowling ball. But you miss the target every time from thirty feet away."

"Fuck you, white boy. Just keep shooting."

Chapter 56

One hour before the scheduled tour, Sal and Karen were in position in an unmarked car overlooking the Mill. Sal's laptop was open, and they were looking at the feed from the cameras installed in and around the Mill. During the night before, the State Police techies, with the assistance of Janet Howell, had installed tiny cameras in the basement corridors of the Mill. Unlike the cameras placed outside of the Mill, the cameras in the corridors were not motion-sensing. The feeds from the cameras monitoring the perimeter were blank.

"I hope our efforts are a waste of time, and that Mike, Phil and Jim are not in any danger. I really hope that all of our preparation was for nothing," Sal said.

"Me too. I'm still concerned about Dorian."

Fifteen minutes later, one of the motion sensing cameras activated. The camera was located on a path in the woods near the river. A tall, thin man dressed all in black was slowly making his way toward the Mill. They did not see a gun, but his movements were suspicious.

Karen said, "I'll call Nealis and tell him we have suspicious activity."

Commander Nealis, who was in charge of the overall operation, was in the command center, a van stocked with the latest high-tech equipment. The van, parked in downtown Cargill Falls, had fast access to both locations. Nealis acknowledged Karen's call.

The next camera set up along the path sensed motion. The man in black was advancing toward the Mill. Meanwhile, Nealis reported activity in the cemetery. Another man, dressed head to toe in black and carrying a metal case, was walking toward the wooded area behind Commander Hines's house.

The cemetery man entered the wooded area and stealthily moved toward the house. His mission was now obvious to the police. The spotter from sniper team one yelled "Freeze!" The assassin quickly turned and ran toward sniper team two, weaving through the trees. A sniper fired. The bullet struck the assassin in the shoulder and spun him to the ground, and the case flew wildly out of his reach. The impact of the bullet seemed to render him unconscious, and he groaned and lay on the ground, unmoving. Sniper team one moved cautiously toward the assassin, hoping to take him alive.

As the sniper team neared the assassin, he screamed as if he was in pain and clutched his chest. He unexpectedly raised his right arm, which contained a pistol, and got off a wild shot just as a red hole appeared on his forehead and blood poured out. Ending his days on earth at 10,037.

As the events were taking place in the wooded area near the cemetery, activity was accelerating at the Mill. The assassin's journey had progressed, and he was close to the Mill. Karen alerted Nealis and also Mike and Phil. The killer approached an outside door that opened into a basement corridor: a door that, in theory, Mill employees always kept locked. Karen and Sal watched as the killer casually walked up to the door, opened it, and walked into the Mill. Fortunately, the corridor cameras followed the killer to his hiding place. Mike and Phil's tour would start in three minutes.

With a drawing of the basement corridors opened on his lap, Sal said, "I'll go in the same door as the assassin. I can see where he's hiding, and I'll watch his movements on my phone. You'll enter the basement at door C, follow the corridor, intercept Mike and Phil, and protect them from Dorian. I'll deal with the paid assassin."

"Sounds like a plan. I'll use my phone to follow the action. I'll take care of Dorian. I'm fairly certain that he unlocked the door for the assassin. Take care of yourself."

"That goes for you too."

Sal quickly made his way to the door, keeping an eye on the assassin via his phone. He opened the door as little as possible and squeezed into the corridor. The killer was in the same hiding place, holding his pistol, ready for the kill. Sal moved slowly down the corridor, keeping one eye on the killer as he did.

Karen moved quickly down the hallway until she got to the perpendicular corridor occupied by the killer. She knew he would see her if she walked past. Karen decided to hide behind stored building materials and wait for the tour to arrive. She planned to stop them before they got to the intersection, where the killer could get a good shot.

The killer squatted behind a stack of lumber, gun out, waiting. Since he had focused his attention away from Sal and toward the intersecting corridor, Sal walked almost upright, giving him the advantage of a better view for the upcoming confrontation.

Karen heard voices and knew that the tour was close. When the three men came into view, she began to move into the hallway, her gun drawn ready to shoot Dorian if need be.

Sal pointed his gun at the killer's head and yelled, "Drop the gun, now!" The killer turned toward Sal, the movement as fast and smooth as he had ever seen, but Sal squeezed the trigger before the assassin finished the turn. Sal's aim was perfect, and the bullet hit right above the bridge of the killer's nose, ending his days on earth at 9,385.

The shout and the gun shot occurred just as Karen started to move into the corridor, and all three men reached for their guns. Dorian looked at Mike and started raising his arm. When Karen had fully entered the corridor, Dorian choked and turned his gun towards her. His expression looked like the face of a trapped rat. Not wanting to be an easy target, Karen kept moving, lowered her shoulder, and executed a roll. She ended up on her feet and put two bullets in Dorian's chest and one in his head, ending his days on earth at 18,724.

Realizing that a number of citizens would have heard the gunshots, Jim called Harry O. Jim described the events in general and Harry O readied an announcement.

"According to a confidential source, two shootouts have just taken place: one at the Cargill Falls Mill and another near the cemetery on Grove Street.

"The Mill owners were conducting a tour of the Mill for two potential investors. Apparently, a paid assassin targeted the investors, according to the Connecticut State Police. The shootout resulted in the death of the paid assassin and a Mill employee, Dorian Gregson. Connecticut State Police are in charge of the ongoing investigation.

"At about the same time, a second shooting occurred near the cemetery on Grove Street. A man visiting the cemetery appeared to have a concealed weapon when the police confronted him. He started to run, and an officer shot him. He later died. The State Police are also investigating this shooting.

"The State Police believe there is no longer a danger to the public. WINY will stay on top of the story.

"Harry O reporting."

Chapter 57

Commander Nealis appropriated a conference room in the Troop D barracks in Danielson, then assembled the participants in the shootings. Since three people had died, Nealis needed the incidents well-documented. When the participants settled down and the chatter slowed, Nealis stood up.

"We're here today to produce a detailed after-action report. Three people are dead, and two shootouts happened this morning at two locations in Cargill Falls. Private Sparling will send contributors a transcript of their comments for editing. Questions?"

Nealis waited, and when no one responded, he continued.

"On my order, the Connecticut State Police, in anticipation of attacks on a guided tour of the Mill and on Jim Hines at his home, employed defensive tactics at both locations. Cameras and police officers were set up both outside and inside of the locations and strategically positioned to protect the citizens at the locations. Next, the head of the sniper teams, Sergeant LaCasse."

"We positioned two sniper teams in the wooded area behind the Hines home on Grove Street. We observed a man dressed all in black advancing through the cemetery toward the area. Team-1 ordered him to stop, and instead, he ran toward team two. A team-2 sniper, hoping to take him alive, shot the assailant in the shoulder. The bullet spun him around and knocked him to the ground. He pretended to surrender, then pulled a pistol and the sniper executed a head shot."

Nealis asked, "Questions? Okay. Next is Sal Belardi."

"I was outside the Mill in a car with Nassau County Detective Parisi. When a camera activated, Parisi notified Commander Nealis and the men on the guided tour. Our man entered an exterior door that is normally locked, and we decided to enter the Mill by different doors. I dealt with the assassin and Parisi dealt with the tour guide, Dorian Gregson. We suspected that Gregson hired the assassins. Detective Parisi, your turn."

"I wanted to prevent the investors and the tour guide from crossing the corridor where the assassin had placed himself. If they did, they would be sitting ducks. I had just gotten into position when the tour approached the assassin's position. Just then, Sal shouted, and Gregson pulled out a pistol and began to turn it on Mike Robertson. I exited my position, and when Gregson turned his gun toward me, I fired three times."

Nealis asked, "Anyone else? Yes, Mr. Messina."

"Just that Mike and I asked Gregson if he was concerned because of the shootout last time. He said no. I asked if he had a gun on him, and he said no, absolutely not."

Nealis said, "We'll attempt to identify the assassins and their employer, and we'll dig deep into Gregson. Our information on Gregson, so far, is that he couldn't possibly afford to pay for a professional. Judging by their strategies, abilities, and equipment, the assassins were professional. We're out of here. Thanks for coming."

Janet Howell asked Phil to stop by the Mill. She had been upset by the shooting and wanted to restart the search for the treasure. She decided to give Mike unhindered access to the Mill until he found something or gave up. When she saw Phil pause in her doorway, she invited him in.

"Hi Janet, a real mess the other day. How are you doing?"

"I'll admit it shook me to my core, but it also forced me to come to my senses. Mike is welcome to search the Mill as often as he wants and for as long as he wants. We'll stay out of his way."

"I know Mike well. He'll want to search in the evenings. And he's a grinder, he won't give up easily."

"I'm good with that. When will you start?"

"The sooner the better. We'll be here tonight."

The Boss growled into the phone, "What the hell happened? I paid top dollar for a contract kill and you failed."

"Two of our best men are dead and the Connecticut State Police are looking into their lives in hope of finding their employer. That causes us real concern. I don't think they will connect them to us, but we are ceasing operations in Connecticut for a few weeks."

"You lost two assassins, and I lost my inside man and a guy who possessed knowledge critical to me. And I just learned that Messina and Robertson are going back into the Mill to look. Shit."

"Sorry, but there's nothing we can do."

The call disconnected and the Boss considered his plight. *I wanted the treasure, but I can live incredibly well without it. I really just want Phil Messina and Jim Hines dead, and I'll add Robertson to that list. I'll be patient for a few weeks, no rush. Then they die.*

Beck's Booty

Armed with his rifle and trusty Bowie knife that he had had since his Union Army days, Isaac reentered the den, ready to defend himself against any remaining threats. He made his way carefully to the narrow opening, followed the passage to the left, and proceeded for about ten feet to a large hollow or cavern. The cavern contained seventeen wooden boxes with their lids latched shut. Isaac pried open one crate and found a treasure in gold, silver, and jewelry. He opened two more crates and found more gold, silver and jewelry. One of the crates also contained bearer bonds. Though excited by the discovery, he paused and took a breath. He needed a plan that would keep the treasure secure and untouched until his return. Isaac decided to draw a detailed map, to bury the wolf deep, to cover the opening, and to leave the area looking as natural as possible. He would then return to Connecticut and find a place to hide the treasure until he figured out the best way to deal with the discovery.

Isaac Putnam hoped to use a large amount of the treasure to make the lives of the Mill workers and their children better. He also planned to invest in the existing businesses in northeast Connecticut and in promising new ventures. He knew that would ensure plenty of job opportunities in the Mills and for the local craftsmen.

The first item on his agenda was the creation of a room to store the seventeen crates of treasure. After wandering around in the Mill basement for several days, he came up with a workable plan: not perfect, but workable. He saw that in two places, the foundation walls formed rectangles that protruded outward. One protrusion was four feet wide and three feet deep. The second was also four feet wide, but it was ten feet deep. The protrusions were thirty-three feet apart. Isaac hired an independent contractor to close off the protrusions with two four-foot-long stone and cement walls. Centered on each wall was an opening three feet by six inches wide, capped with a lintel. When the contractor completed his work, Isaac installed a heavy door equipped with a heavy-duty lock in each opening. The doors were set inside the foundation twelve inches. The large rectangle would hold fifteen crates and the small rectangle would hold two chests.

Next, Isaac rented a parlor car and bought a boxcar. Both would sit on the railroad siding next to his Mill for three days, then a train would haul them to a siding he had rented in Woodstock, Virginia. He needed three days to get all his equipment loaded and to install four heavy-duty locks on the boxcar doors. Isaac also used the time to stock the parlor car with his creature comforts. The trip to Virginia was comfortable.

The trip lasted two days, and the engineer uncoupled Putnam's cars on the siding and chocked the wheels. The engineer stopped by Putnam's parlor car to make sure his VIP passenger was satisfied with the trip.

Isaac replied, "One hundred percent satisfied, and thank you. I will let you know when I am ready to return. It will be at least two or three days."

The next morning, Isaac rented a buckboard wagon for its ease in handling rough terrain, and two strong horses for his trip to the wolf den and the treasure. His first journey to the wolf den took an hour. He loaded eight of the seventeen crates and rested for the afternoon. Dragging the crates out of the wolf den and loading them onto the buckboard was draining, and he wanted it to be close to dark when he would arrive back at Woodstock. Having rested, Putnam covered the crates with a blanket and set out for Woodstock. In the waning twilight, he loaded the treasure into the boxcar and locked all four locks. Even with the treasure safely stored in the boxcar and locked up tight close to his bed, he still slept with one eye open.

The next day was exactly the same. Isaac loaded the remaining nine crates into the box car. He had also bought two small, lockable chests as part of his plan, and after moving some of the gold, silver, and precious stones into them, he locked the boxcar. He had already arranged to begin the return trip to Cargill Falls to begin at seven in the morning.

Isaac was the only one to know about the treasure so far, and he intended to keep it that way. He would offload the crates and chests at night when no one was around and move them into the rooms he had prepared in the Mill. Then, he would cover the doors with stone and cement so they would blend into the rest of the foundation. He would not reveal the treasure until he was sure he could have it appraised, sold, and the money distributed in a way that fit his plans for the people of Cargill Falls. He stored the seventeen crates in the large room and the two chests in the small room.

After all the work was complete, Isaac Putnam decided to take two days off to enjoy his family. He was sure no one had seen him, and he was positive that the treasure was safe. He rested for the first day and then spent an active second day with his children. Isaac thoroughly enjoyed the time he spent with his wife, who was the love of his life, and his precious children. That night, while he lay in bed, he felt a strange pain and his usually active mind went blank. An aneurysm in Isaac Putnam's brain ruptured and he died instantly, ending his days on earth at 16,195.

Chapter 58

Finding where Isaac might have hidden the treasure was much easier when looking at a drawing than when he was ensconced in the basement. A lesser man might have given up, but Mike was determined to find the treasure. He knew that it existed. The fact that the drawings did not match the foundation sure complicated the search. After several nights of using the foundation drawings for guidance, tonight he decided just to walk along the foundation wall and look for an anomaly. Mike hoped that something about the foundation would trigger an idea.

After about two hours of walking, Mike's mind was beginning to wander. Suddenly, he stopped. He had seen an irregularity, but at first, it had not registered. Mike slowly retraced his steps until he found the inconsistency: what appeared to be fresh cement filling a half-inch hole. He got excited, then realized that he could think of dozens of reasons for the fresh cement, only one of which was that he had found the treasure.

Mike opted to hold off on doing anything until the next day. He marked the spot so he could find it again. He needed tools to do the job and decided to see what the Mill had before leaving. He remembered seeing Gregson's toolbox stored on a shelf.

Mike found Gregson's toolbox and easily pried open the lid. The toolbox contained everything he needed, including a small camera on a flexible cable. The camera would fit through a half-inch hole in a wall and display what was on the other side. Mike grinned, thinking, *that bastard, Gregson, found the treasure and was involved in the conspiracy to kill off the competition. He knew exactly what he was doing.* He called Phil and told him what he had found, and they worked out a plan.

Phil called Janet the next morning, told her where Mike wanted to work, and asked her to get all of the Mill employees out of the area by two o'clock. He also asked her to meet him and Mike in the basement. Phil explained, "It's too soon to get excited, but Mike found something he thinks is worth pursuing."

Janet said she would make it happen.

Mike met Phil near an exterior door that was close to where he wanted to work. He had Gregson's toolbox with him, which he had taken home beforehand to more thoroughly examine its tools. He asked Phil to carry the toolbox, reached into the bed of his truck, and pulled out a jackhammer. Phil just shook his head. Janet was waiting and she was excited.

Mike said, "The plan's simple. I'm going to drill a half-inch hole through the foundation wall, feed the camera through the hole, and see if the treasure is on the other side. Ironically, Gregson's toolbox contained all the best tools for this project." He got the tools ready and started drilling a quarter-inch pilot hole. The drilling was purposely slow so as not to overheat the drill bit and damage it. Suddenly, the bit moved through the wall faster and required less pressure. Mike knew that it had entered a softer material, maybe wood.

When he was certain that the drill bit had passed through the wall, Mike backed it out and examined it. There was definitely wood behind the stone and cement. He inserted the half-inch bit into the drill and started broadening his pilot hole. He explained, "This wall isn't an outside wall, but it should be. There's no light behind it. Let's get the camera set up. Phil, did you download the app?"

"Yes, Mike."

"Good boy."

It took around fifteen minutes to set up the camera and link it to the app. It worked on the first try. Mike fed the camera through the hole, and when it was on the other side, Phil used the app to turn on the light and the video. All three simultaneously gasped when two wooden boxes materialized. The boxes looked just like treasure chests from old movies.

Phil asked slowly, "Mike… what do you do now?"

"Jackhammer."

"How can you jackhammer a wall? Aren't jackhammers normally used on a horizontal surface, like a floor or a road?"

"Easy. I'm going to flip the Mill on its side."

"You're a real ass."

"You two go have something to eat. I need a couple of hours. Be back at five."

When Janet and Phil returned, they found medium-sized stones neatly lined up along one corridor wall. Mike had even swept up residual dust and small chips of concrete into a small pile. Mike, covered in sweat and chalky with concrete dust, stood in front of the now-exposed wooded door. He had a big smile on his face.

"Standing before you is the door to our future, an old wooden door, with two half-inch holes drilled through it. I drilled through the same hole as Gregson. Someone discovered the hiding place before Gregson, probably Larry Davidson, that's the only explanation for the second hole. I'm ready to open the door and see if a treasure awaits," Mike said as he pulled the door open.

Phil and Janet preceded him into the room. Mike opened a chest and all three looked on in awe. The chest contained household items made of gold and silver, rings of all sizes adorned with diamonds and other jewels, and cups filled with precious and semi-precious gemstones. Diamonds, rubies, sapphires, and emeralds sparkled under their flashlights.

Mike opened the second chest and, in addition to items like those in the first chest, immediately noticed a modern-looking envelope. Janet asked Phil to open it, and inside was a letter neatly folded in thirds. Phil unfolded it.

Cargill Falls – The Mill Conspiracy

TO: Whoever finds this letter,

My name is Larry Davidson. While working on renovations, I stumbled upon this treasure stored behind the foundation wall. I did not tell the Mill owners, but rather decided to enrich myself. I told Robert Sullivan, my friend and mentor and a man I trusted, about the discovery.

Unbeknownst to me, Robert had severe financial problems: medical bills for his wife were piling up and his business was failing. Robert convinced me we should purchase the Mill. Greed fogged my thinking.

Robert recruited two investors and we made an offer on the Mill. Despite our offer being above the appraised value, the Mill owners rejected it. Robert and the other investors hatched a plan to kill Bob Martineau. I tried and failed to talk them out of it.

The group hired an assassin, a woman named Tina, and she was successful. That is when Robert began seeing me as a liability. He felt that I was weak and worried and that I might go to the police. I became worried for my safety, wrote this document, and reconcealed the treasure. If

I am no longer alive, then Robert and his investors have executed me.

Before making the offer to purchase the Mill, I got to know the investors. John Christensen and I talked a lot about our past lives. About five years ago, the federal government arrested John and charged him with manipulating procedures for the production of a prescription drug. He accepted a plea bargain and went to jail. A good friend and an associate of his oversaw the conspiracy and also went to jail. They were cellmates in prison. I think his name is Bob Cohen.

Phil stopped reading. *Bob Cohen? Unbelievable.* He gathered himself and continued.

The other investor was Richard Thall, a Connecticut State Senator. He is a real dick and only cared about money and himself. We never got close.

Larry Davidson

No one knew what to say, the implications of the letter were many. How did it affect the deal, how did it affect the State

Police investigation, and how did it affect the attempts on Phil and Jim's lives?

Mike broke the ice, "Isn't Bob Cohen old-piss-the-pants?"

Phil answered, "Yes, he is. We need to get this letter to Parisi. She will get the Police involved. We also must get it to Jim. Janet, I want to scan this letter and email it."

"I have everything you need in my office. Mike, will you secure the door?"

Mike nodded.

Janet continued, "I will keep everyone away from this area."

Emails sent and treasure secured, they huddled in Janet's office and contemplated the future.

Chapter 59

An extremely busy two weeks had passed since Phil had circulated the letter from Larry Davidson. Karen Parisi invited the Old Mill Investors and the Mill owners to a meeting. She wanted to get them up to speed on the investigation.

"The news is good," Karen said. "The content of the letter from Larry Davidson changed the direction of our investigation. Before the letter, we focused on identifying the people responsible for the attack. After, we focused on Bob Cohen and his relationship with John Christensen. We executed search warrants on Christensen's apartment and office again and found enough evidence to get similar warrants for Cohen. Cohen kept detailed records. he obviously saw himself as a businessman, not a criminal, and the documents and records he kept literally proved the case for us. As we speak, State Police officers are serving Cohen with an arrest warrant at his place of business. The state's attorney will ask the judge to remand Cohen to prison until he's tried. The evidence proves that Cohen's goal was to kill Jim and Phil because they uncovered his covert operation at Purity Pharma, and they humiliated him by referring to him as old piss-the-pants. He paid for the last two assassins: one to kill Phil and Mike as they toured the Mill – Mike was collateral – and one to kill Jim at home. Our guys are now safe. We can all breathe a sigh of relief. Anything else?"

"Yes," said Janet Howell. "As of an hour ago, the Old Mill Investors are officially fifty-percent owners of the Mill. Phil and I are working on getting the treasure appraised. And finally, Mike, why the grin?"

"You folks know that I thought there was more treasure in the Mill, and that I've looked for it every night for the past two weeks. Last night, I drilled a hole and pushed the camera through. Well, I made an MP4 file so you can see for yourself."

Mike fumbled with his laptop for a minute or two while connecting it to the television – not because he did not know what he was doing, but because he wanted to build suspense. He hit "play." The TV screen stayed blank for a long fifteen seconds, and then a large wooden box appeared on the screen, then another. The camera moved, and a room filled with large wooden boxes materialized. Altogether, the room held seventeen boxes, each of which was larger than the first two Mike had found. The room grew quiet.

Mike whispered, "There's treasure in them there boxes."

In unison the audience said, "Phenomenal!"

Epilog

Despite his meticulous planning and financial wealth, Cohen's strategies to avoid arrest were futile. The Connecticut State Police swiftly swooped in and executed his arrest warrant. His story unfolded as an instructional narrative, illustrating the futility of attempting to outmaneuver legal consequences when the evidence is overwhelming. Immediately after his arrest, Bob Cohen hired the best lawyer he could find and ordered him to get him released on bail. Cohen had planned for the possibility of his arrest and had an escape plan in place, including new identities for his family and enough money in an offshore account to provide an extremely comfortable life. Unfortunately, his arrest happened without warning and the judge at his arraignment denied him bail.

Cohen's lawyer looked at the evidence the authorities had amassed against him and advised him that he would not get bail. He explained that he would try to get Cohen the best deal possible, but that he should expect to be an old man when he got out of prison. Cohen fired that lawyer and two others before accepting the fact that he was going to prison for a long time. He took a plea deal that kept him in prison for a minimum of twenty-five years. The moment Cohen signed the deal, his wife emptied the offshore account and filed for divorce.

Cargill Falls – The Mill Conspiracy

For his participation in the same murder-for-hire scheme, former Connecticut State Senator Richard Thall was serving a minimum of twenty-five years in the same prison.

Tina and Marcy's journey from New England to Naples, Florida, was a story of transformation and intrigue. Leaving behind a dark past where Tina was a hired assassin with a long string of murders and Marcy an executive in an organization that managed such lethal services, they embraced their new identities. In the sunny climes of Florida, they became affluent sisters in search of a peaceful abode. Their stay at the Ritz-Carlton Hotel in a suite overlooking the Gulf of Mexico served as a base for a relaxed search for the perfect home, a stark contrast to their former lives.

Tina and Marcy, who had since adopted the names Beverly and Elizabeth Gould, strategically planned their house-hunting schedule in Naples. They dedicated their mornings to the search, ensuring that they had their afternoons free to unwind by the hotel pool or on sun-kissed beaches. As evenings rolled in, they indulged in culinary delights offered by the hotel's dining options or explored the gastronomic scene along Naples' renowned Fifth Avenue. Their diligent search bore fruit in three weeks when they found their ideal home, and after a further two months, they completed their move, turning a new page in their Floridian adventure.

The Gould sisters' journey is a testament to their dedication to changing their lives. Over the next two months, they meticulously selected each piece of furniture, art, and accessories to ensure that their Gulf-front mansion on Gorden Drive reflected their exquisite tastes. Despite the demanding task, they balanced their time to savor the luxuries of their new home, enjoying leisurely moments by the pool and rejuvenating walks along the beach. With the mansion finally echoing their vision of perfection, they were ready to immerse themselves in the vibrant social scene of Naples, Florida, a community known for its affluence and cultural richness. Their story is one of change: not just of a residence into a home, but also of the sisters themselves, as they transitioned into active members of their new community.

It took over a year and a half to appraise and auction the Civil War treasure that Mike Robertson had found hidden in the Mill. Mike was a true believer and the only one to doggedly search for the treasure. The auction, scheduled to start in two months from his discovery, would last for weeks. The Mill owners decided on Christie's to manage the auction. The choice of Christie's, a renowned British auction house, underscored the importance of the event, promising a well-managed and high-profile sale that could attract collectors and history enthusiasts from around the globe. Before the auction, Christie's estimated that the auction would yield the Mill owners over a billion dollars before taxes and fees.

The Mill owners understood that the lengthy appraisal reflected the significance and complexity of the treasure, and they wanted to ensure that the historical and monetary value of each item was accurate. They also understood the necessity of returning treasures to their origin states and families, if need be. Regardless, they would soon have a large fortune to manage, a fortune that would transform their futures.

The Mill owners also understood that they would need an agreement in place detailing how they would spend and distribute the money. The owners appointed a committee of three, Phil Messina, Janet Howell, and Jim Hines, to develop a financial plan for the money and to have it approved by all the stockholders before the auction. They held their first committee meeting in a small conference room in the Mill, overwhelmed with the task before them.

"How in the hell are we going to get everyone to agree on how to spend that much money?" Janet said.

Jim responded, "We have to agree to a plan first, and we have only one month to do it. Phil, will you get us started and propose a plan for the money, so we can see if we're thinking the same, or if we're at least in the ballpark?"

Phil projected his computer screen to the large flat screen TV and said, "I've prepared a preliminary plan for us to consider. I'd like you to reserve any objections until I've presented the entire plan. Questions at any time. Okay?"

Both Janet and Jim nodded.

"We can't be sure of how much the auction will net us, so I'll talk in general. As of the moment, we have $15.8 million in debt on our balance sheet. We'll pay the debt in full first-thing. We have a solid cost estimate for the remaining renovations, so I suggest we earmark that amount plus twenty-five percent. I feel like both of those options are easy. Now it gets difficult. Are you both okay so far?"

Again, both Janet and Jim nodded.

"Now for the tough decisions. I propose that we use the rest of the money from the auction for two things: one, for distribution to the stockholders; and two, to set up a charity. How does that sound?"

Janet asked, "What will the charity do? Who will benefit?"

Phil replied, "I'll get to that. First of all, the money we set aside for a charity is tax-exempt."

Again, both Janet and Jim nodded.

"I suggest that we distribute fifty percent of the money from the auction to the stockholders and fifty percent to the charity. We can adjust the percentages based on the final amount the auction brings in. We have two choices of how to distribute the money to the stockholders: we can either do it based on the amount of stock held, which is the legal choice, or based on a formula that considers only people."

Janet replied, "I've thought about how we might accomplish it, and I think that the fairest way is to consider people, not stock ownership. I believe that because even though Isaac Putnam hid the treasure in our building, we would never have found it without your team. I'm sure the rest of my team will agree."

Jim said, "Alright, let's get to the details. No matter what we finally decide, everyone will be wealthy beyond their wildest dreams."

The committee finalized the plan and presented it to the stockholders and after a civil discussion, they accepted the plan. The stockholders tasked Phil with setting up the charity with the State and Federal governments. They chose Southern New England Uplift (SNEU) as the name of the charity, and the stockholders wanted themselves installed as the Board of Directors.

After the Christie's auction, which was quite successful, the stockholders commenced their new lives as affluent members of the community.

Mary Ann Hines used the money that she and Jim had received to open a restaurant in Cargill Falls. She hired a great chef who created a fabulous menu, and the working conditions she created ensured that customers interacted with a happy, well-paid and well-trained staff. Jim, on the other hand, took a part-time consulting job with the Connecticut State Police. He mainly consulted on homicide cases.

Mike and Tess Robertson decided to invest in and manage commercial properties in the tri-state area. Together, they built a large and thriving company that provided secure, well-paying jobs for their sizable workforce.

Noelle loved genealogy and was able to assist more people and charge less. She became extremely busy and loved every minute of her new life.

After marrying Sal Belardi, Karen Parisi resigned from the Nassau County Police Department, much to the Department's displeasure. She moved to Cargill Falls and decided that she would not return to work until her and Sal's future children were older. Sal transferred to State Police Troop D barracks in Danielson as Commander.

Rose Messina became CEO of Southern New England Uplift (SNEU), a charity whose mission was to assist hard-working but struggling families with food, clothing, and shelter issues. SNEU also provided training programs to families to help them improve their lives. Rose even implemented a program to identify high school students who had the grades and test scores to get into top universities but lacked the resources. To help those students to fit in and not feel inferior, SNEU would also cover books, clothing, and transportation.

Phil chose a more solitary life's work. He loved his ancestors obviously because they were his family, but also because they had the courage to move to America and start a new life which enabled him to live the American dream. He realized the strength of character it took to uproot your life and start over in a new country.

Phil decided that he would try his hand at writing a murder mystery, but only after he had created a family tree and documented his family's history.

An author! That sounds like a fantastic plan! As an author I will have creative freedom and independence. I can work at my own

pace, explore my ideas, and share my stories with others. Plus, I won't have to deal with the stress of corporate management.
  Phenomenal!

R. F. Mineo

R. F. Mineo, an author with a penchant for crafting thrilling mysteries, has been inspired by encouragement from friends and family. This support, amplified by the critical acclaim of his debut novel "Fatal Conspiracies," propelled him to embark on a new literary venture with "Cargill Falls." A novel that intertwines the past and present in a captivating mystery.

Rich's business career has spanned over three decades, including a prominent role at a large corporation in the Medical Diagnostic and Pharmaceutical business units. What's more, Rich has been the Managing Partner of a small investment banking firm and operated an antiques business. Rich was born in Scranton, Pennsylvania, and graduated from Penn State University.

Rich served as head of the State of Connecticut Fundraiser for the Special Olympics. His other philanthropy includes volunteering at a nearby hospital and the local YMCA. When he's not writing, Rich enjoys spending time with his two adult children, four grandchildren, and his wife of 58 years, Wanda.

Rich's work has taken him up and down the Eastern Seaboard, and he has lived in an array of towns, such as Oyster Bay, NY, and Newark, DE. Today, Rich and Wanda Mineo reside in Woodstock, CT.